©lack

MW00365931

GOBLIN SLAYER
SIDE STORY II
DAI KATANA
The Singing Death ②

©lack

Legend has it that the former hero, a Platinum-ranked adventurer, faced such a creature all alone… The very attempt would merit being counted among the brave.

"We were coming to get you! Come on—let's go adventuring!"

Suddenly, someone calls her name. Female Bishop stops, taken aback by the friendly exclamation. She looks as if she's seen a ghost.

©lack

CONTENTS

DAI KATANA

The Singing Death

GOBLIN SLAYER

SIDE STORY II

DAI KATANA

The Singing Death

2

KUMO KAGYU

ILLUSTRATION BY lack

YEN ON
New York

GOBLIN SLAYER
SIDE STORY II
DAI KATANA
The Singing Death

KUMO KAGYU **2** ILLUSTRATION BY lack

Translation by Kevin Steinbach ✦ Cover art by lack

This book is a work of fiction. Names, characters, places, and incidents are the product of the author's imagination or are used fictitiously. Any resemblance to actual events, locales, or persons, living or dead, is coincidental.

GOBLIN SLAYER GAIDEN 2: DAI KATANA <CHU -Volume 2->
Copyright © 2020 Kumo Kagyu
Illustrations copyright © 2020 lack
All rights reserved.
Original Japanese edition published in 2020 by SB Creative Corp.
This English edition is published by arrangement with SB Creative Corp., Tokyo, in care of Tuttle-Mori Agency, Inc., Tokyo.

English translation © 2021 by Yen Press, LLC

Yen On
150 West 30th Street, 19th Floor, New York, NY 10001

Visit us at yenpress.com • facebook.com/yenpress • twitter.com/yenpress
yenpress.tumblr.com • instagram.com/yenpress

First Yen On Edition: June 2021

Yen On is an imprint of Yen Press, LLC.
The Yen On name and logo are trademarks of Yen Press, LLC.

The publisher is not responsible for websites (or their content) that are not owned by the publisher.

Library of Congress Cataloging-in-Publication Data
Names: Kagyū, Kumo, author. | lack (Illustrator), illustrator.
Title: Goblin Slayer side story II: dai katana / Kumo Kagyu ; illustration by lack.
Other titles: Goblin Slayer gaiden 2: tsubanari no daikatana. English
Description: First Yen On edition. | New York : Yen On, 2020-
Identifiers: LCCN 2020043585 | ISBN 9781975318239 (v. 1 ; trade paperback) |
ISBN 9781975333539 (v. 2 ; trade paperback)
Subjects: LCSH: Goblins—Fiction. | GSAFD: Fantasy fiction.
Classification: LCC PL872.5.A367 G5313 2020 | DDC 895.63/6—dc23
LC record available at https://lccn.loc.gov/2020043585

ISBNs: 978-1-9753-3353-9 (paperback)
978-1-9753-3353-5 (ebook)

1 3 5 7 9 10 8 6 4 2

LSC-C

Printed in the United States of America

GOBLIN SLAYER
SIDE STORY II
DAI KATANA
The Singing Death

2

Characters

You Are the Hero	Blessed Hardwood Spear	Sword Maiden Lily

YOU
G-SAM
HUMAN MALE

At the entrance to the Dungeon of the Dead in the northern reaches of the Four-Cornered World, there is a fortress city. A human adventurer has just arrived there. He is a warrior who has mastered the ways of the sword.

FEMALE WARRIOR
N-FIG
HUMAN FEMALE

A girl you meet in the fortress city. An "old hand," she's already been down in the dungeon. A human warrior who wields a spear.

FEMALE BISHOP
G-BIS
HUMAN FEMALE

A girl you meet at the tavern in the fortress city. She lost her eyes on a previous adventure. She can identify items by the power of the Supreme God.

DAIKATANA
The Singing Death

COUSIN
G-MAG
HUMAN FEMALE

Your older cousin, who accompanied you to the fortress city. She's a kind woman who looks after you like a sister would, but sometimes you think she's not all there. A human wizard, she supports you from the back row.

HALF-ELF SCOUT
N-THI
HALF-ELF MALE

An adventurer you met on your way to the fortress city. As entertaining as he is keen-eyed, he serves as your party's scout.

MYRMIDON MONK
G-PRI
MYRMIDON MALE

An adventurer you met in the fortress city. An old hand in the dungeon, he serves as your party's strategist. He is a myrmidon or "Bugman Monk" who serves the Trade God.

Those who knew how it began were no more.

Perhaps some unfortunate farmer moved a stone that should have stayed put. Maybe some foolish child undid a seal in a shrine somewhere. It may have even been a fiery stone shooting across the heavens.

Whatever the cause, it was not so very long ago that the Death began stalking the continent.

Disease traveled on the wind, consuming all the people it encountered; the dead rose, the trees withered, the air grew foul and the water rancid.

The King of Time issued a proclamation: "Find the source of this Death and seal it away."

Thus heroes arose all over the continent, and so they, too, were swallowed one by one by the Death, leaving nothing but their corpses.

The only exception was a single party, which left these words alone:

"The maw of the Death lies in the northernmost reaches."

None left knew who discovered this. For those adventurers, too, were spirited away by the Death.

The Dungeon of the Dead.

The entrance to this vast abyss yawned like the jaws of the Reaper, and people gathered at the foot of it, until finally a fortress city was born.

In this city, adventurers sought companions, challenged the dungeon, battled, found loot…and sometimes died.

These days of glory went on, and on, and on, repeating over and over.

Riches and monsters welled up without end—as did the incessant hack and slash.

Life was spilled like so much water as adventurers drowned in their own dreams until the fire disappeared from their eyes.

Sooner or later, all that remained, glowing like an ember, were the ashen days of adventuring, which went hand in hand with the Death…

Critical Hit of the Tiger

"Heyo! Sounds like it's going swimmingly for you." It happens one morning when you've started getting used to exploring the second floor. You sit down at your table in the tavern to await your companions, only to have someone else sit down nimbly across from you. "I heard you finished off those newbie hunters?"

You didn't see this coming. The shadow under the hood shifts. You can detect a grin on the face that watches you: someone who looks like a mischievous young girl. The curves of her body are almost statuesque.

Mm. You nod, putting the pieces together. It's that informant.

Keeping one ear on the hubbub of the busy tavern full of adventurers, you thank her. Not for praising you, of course. For the information she gave you.

"Aw, don't mention it. I'd be lying if I said I didn't think I'd get something out of it."

Hmm. You don't pry further but fiddle with the drinking cup in front of you. It's just lemon water. You won't eat until your party members get up. You're fairly certain you'll all go into the dungeon today, but it would be best to check with them first.

"So where's the crew?"

You left them in the stables. You didn't think they could keep up with you, with your need to train and practice day and night. Still, you feel a touch of disquiet at the girl's approbation. The tavern is full of adventurers with money on their minds; there's no special need to flatter you in particular. Perhaps it's simply that those who do good in this world expecting no reward are…unusual, let us say.

You know that, and you feel a bit bad, dragging your party members along on your own damn foolish, idealistic crusade. It's perfectly natural not to wish to do something that isn't going to get you anything in this life. You don't recall hearing any rumors about your party for being so special or anything.

But that leaves the question of where this informant got wind of you…

"Oh, just around town, you know?" she says, as if this should be perfectly obvious. "People trade rumors like how you talk about the weather—just a way of saying hello. And people like to talk about parties that are making a name for themselves." She waves a hand to summon a waitress and orders a lemon water.

You watch the server go, rabbit ears flapping, ample bosom bouncing, round butt shaking along with her tail, and you think:

Most likely sources of info about us would be the old armorer or the nun at the Trade God's temple.

They were the only ones you told after you came back from the newbie hunters' den. The dead have no need for equipment. Sell it off, make a little money the living can use. You don't have any qualms about that. And anyway, a modest donation was necessary to have the rank tags you retrieved properly buried.

The armorer or the nun, then… And considering the nun's personality, you're pretty sure it was her.

A few coins in the palm and she'd likely tell anybody anything.

When you mention your suspicion, the informant only says, "Ah, who knows?" and cackles. "Anyway, I'm glad things are going so well for you. But remember, if you let your guard down, you'll die. Occupational hazard for you."

You purse your lips. Pretty nasty thing to say—even if she's exactly right. But you don't voice your objection.

Come to this tavern regularly for even a few days and the observation becomes inescapable. A party of adventurers who had been sitting around a table the day before last weren't there yesterday. And today, a different party with brand-new equipment fills the seats. You have no way of knowing how long they can resist the Death.

That's something you don't even know about your own party.

"Point is, don't turn your back." The girl seems able to read your mind—and she giggles. "After the second floor comes the third floor, and after that comes the fourth. Long road ahead. Can't have you dying." You nod as she sips her lemon water. Yes, you agree. Can't have that.

After all, you can slash your way to the second floor now—and soon the third. And that isn't entirely unknown territory; others have gone before you. If you want to see how far your blade can take you, you'll have to challenge that third floor.

"Though, t'be fair," the girl says, snapping you out of your reverie, "I guess they still haven't found the stairs down to the fourth floor."

You look up, and across from you is a half-drunk lemon water. One of the waitresses must have neglected to clean it up, you conclude, and reseat yourself in your chair. Suddenly, you notice the murmur around you rising like a tide, and you feel like you're smack in the center of activity here in the tavern. You figure your party members should show up anytime now…

"My pardon—would you mind if we shared this table with you?"

The voice is unexpected but clear and strong, exuding such refinement as to give you a twinge of jealousy. You turn to discover the handsome young man in his diamond armor and equipment. Beside him is a silver-haired young woman so small she almost looks like a shadow.

A rhea? you wonder for a second, but no, she must be human. She seems so slight, though. A scout, perhaps.

You reply that as they can see, you're by yourself and don't mind at all. The man nods and sits facing you. The young woman brings a chair over from a nearby table and sits with her legs dangling. Maybe she means to indicate that she's not here to eavesdrop.

You ask if they're partied together, to which the Knight of Diamonds

replies, "We're associates. She comes from the orphanage, but I must say...she's saved my skin many a time."

You remember that the knight is supposedly the third son of a poor noble house, but you can't help noticing the quality of his equipment. You say so, trying to keep the conversation going, to which he replies, "Oh, hardly," and smiles almost shyly. "What matters is the quality of what's inside the equipment." After a pause, he adds, "...I've been hoping to get a chance to speak to you properly."

You guessed that much. But you don't say so and instead ask him what you can do for him.

"You needn't be so modest. It was you who defeated those notorious rogues, was it not?"

You respond with a noncommittal shrug. There are many adventurers in this town. It might have been you, or it might not.

"Perhaps, but in this particular tavern, not so many with the ability and resolve to challenge the third floor of the dungeon." The Knight of Diamonds sweeps the adventurers seated throughout the building with a keen gaze. They sit around tables pawing through treasure, drinking wine, celebrating, and making no effort to hide their joy. It's a lively place, friendly in its own way, but also purposeless—the Knight of Diamonds lets his eyes drop. "To challenge adversity by one's own volition, to confront it and win out—I believe your party and mine are perhaps the only ones here to do all that."

You don't quite like the undertone of his remark and only shake your head and question whether that is, in fact, the case. Adventurers want to know what's in it for them—you're no different in that regard. To risk one's life for money, to save the world, to walk the path of the sword—all motives have their value.

There is no hierarchy in alignment. Ultimately, it's merely a question of whether you live or whether you die.

"...You have a most interesting way of looking at things," the Knight of Diamonds remarks. Then he *hmm*s, nods, and changes the subject. "Rumor has it there's a real up-and-coming party out there."

Probably so. You suspect no other town has such high turnover of adventurers. Then again, other cities have Guilds; everything is different out there. Here, whatever you've "contributed to society" has no meaning. The depth to which you've descended and the money you've earned tell all: Your skills are the only things that matter. Rank and trust don't come into it; this is the place to see what you can win by your own strength. In the dungeon, that's all there is.

"From what I hear, they're led by someone who wields a fine saber much like yours."

Hoh. You rest your hand on the hilt of the sword at your hip almost without realizing it. This is interesting indeed. You'd like to meet this person sometime, if you have the chance.

"If destiny is on your side, and if you both survive, then I have trouble imagining you won't meet."

That seems reasonable. You smile and agree with the Knight of Diamonds. You observe, however, that he's fully armed and armored despite the early hour, so you ask if he's going exploring.

"That's right," he confirms. At his hip, he bears not only a straight sword but a dagger as well. He didn't have that before. "Oh, this…? Mm, let's say I was caught napping last time, and I think this might prove useful in a fight."

Draw, stab—allowing for a reverse grip, the two actions could be done in a single motion. You make a sound of admiration, then remark that it seems no one has discovered the stairs down to the fourth floor yet.

"You have quick ears, sir." The Knight of Diamonds doesn't try to hide anything but confirms that the rumor is true. As for who you heard this information from…well, it probably doesn't matter that much.

You'll pray for his success in battle. You tell him so, and he grins like a sleeping lion. "Any prayers would be most heartening."

Then…

"Urgh, sorry, didn't mean for it to get so late. It's just with that slime yesterday… I still feel kind of…ugh…*slimy*…" Belated footsteps are accompanied by a sleepy voice. You don't have to look to know it's Female Warrior approaching your table.

You can tell she's getting closer, but then she's suddenly interrupted. The small girl with the silver hair asks you very seriously: "Slime?"

Yes, slime.

"Huh." After a second's silence, the girl says, "Pardon me." She looks away, and a series of noticeable tremors begin to run through her body. The Knight of Diamonds likewise wears an inscrutable expression. You shrug. It's just a fact—nothing you can do to change it.

You take great pleasure in imagining the expression that must be on Female Warrior's face at that moment.

§

"Ha-ha-ha-ha-ha-ha-ha-ha-ha! Well, slimes do seem to like her!" Half-Elf Scout's cheerful laughter echoes around the gloomy darkness with its faint wire frame. You maintain your silence, trying very hard not to look in Female Warrior's direction where she's stretched out on the ground.

You're in the dungeon. You might be resting, but you absolutely must not let your guard down.

"She's on the front row. Sometimes there's not much she can do... At least, that's what I think," your cousin observes. You don't disagree that it's not entirely Female Warrior's fault. She and you, along with Myrmidon Monk, bear the onus of forming the front row of your party's formation. Any of you has a one in three chance of being the first thing an enemy attacks—it's just a matter of luck.

"Anyway, the slimes in this dungeon aren't especially dangerous," says Myrmidon Monk with a disgruntled clack of his mandibles. He seems surprisingly adept at avoiding that one in three chance. He flicks his curved saber to get the goo off it, then slowly replaces it in its scabbard. His tone carries an undercurrent of significance, as one might expect from a disciple of the Trade God, deity of the wind, bearer of words.

You've heard that there are different varieties of slime. Some are intelligent, and some can even use magic.

"We're just lucky they don't have acid or poison or the ability to swallow us in a single gulp."

True enough. Cold comfort, but it's also true the gooey enemies who appear on the first floor aren't very powerful.

As you ponder these things, your cousin slips over to Female War-rior to check on her. "Are you doing all right?"

"……Yeah," Female Warrior mumbles, nodding with the earnestness of a disappointed child. She squeezes out the slime-soaked clothes from over her armor, wipes her face, then slowly gets to her feet. Then she smiles with a calmness and clarity that puts you in mind of a quiet sea before a storm. "I'll have to make you pay for laughing at me—later."

"Uh…oops," Half-Elf Scout says, wiping the grin off his face.

You silently repeat a Lightning-Deflection spell once or twice and start thinking fast. Your party managed to decimate the slimes even though they took you by surprise. You're not sure if that's a good omen or a bad one. You look down the corridor, the path leading deeper into the first floor, with which you're already quite familiar. The dark abyss that confronts you beyond the white wire frame bears an odor of death you can never quite get used to.

"Uh, um," Female Bishop says, tugging on your sleeve. You ask her what's the matter, and she unrolls the sheepskin parchment contain-ing your map, leaning close to it. "Today, we're…challenging the third floor, right?"

Indeed. You nod without much enthusiasm but reiterate that such is your plan. Not that you were feeling hurried because of that chat with the Knight of Diamonds, though. You're fairly sure. At least, that's what you keep telling yourself.

Exploration of the second floor has proceeded apace, and you think it's time to put your skills to the test. To find out whether you and your sword can stand on the front lines in this Dungeon of the Dead…

"I just want to double-check our path…," Female Bishop says. "We want to take the shortest route, right?"

"It sucks having to work our way down the stairs every single time…," Female Warrior comments, turning sullen again. You give a wry smile and tell Female Bishop yes, that's what you want.

"Understood, sir." Her slim face relaxes into a smile, and she gives a serious nod at this responsibility.

The dungeon is a big place. You can't imagine how anyone gets by down here without a map. Some people joke about it being the deepest dungeon in the world, but to you, it's no laughing matter.

Maybe it's the constant, complete focus demanded by exploration and combat, but your sense of time is fuzzy down here. You enter in the morning and emerge at night. Once in a while, a party thinks they've been down there just a day, when it's actually been several. More often, though, battling for days on end produces a lapse in concentration and results in the party's demise. If you go a few days without seeing a given group in the tavern, chances are good you'll never see them again.

Not that anyone goes out of their way to discuss that fact.

"The whole thing is rotten through and through, no question," Half-Elf Scout says grimly when you share your thoughts. "Just trudging through these hallways, everything looking the same; you start to get sort of hypnotized."

"It would be so great if we could just pop in and out. You know, like with a Gate spell!" Your *second* cousin claps her hands as if extremely pleased with her own idea. And it's an excellent idea. Or it would be, if Gate wasn't a lost spell!

"Besides, even Gate isn't all-powerful," Myrmidon Monk notes, opening his jaws with a sort of imperious *click*. "A person trips a Gate trap, or screws up the inscription on their scroll, and there's a good chance…"

"?" Your cousin gives him a questioning look.

"…Well, let's just say the walls are full of 'em."

Your *second* cousin's face suddenly contorts with terror. She steps back several paces, trembling, and glances at the stone wall over her shoulder. Female Warrior, watching with an amused smile, claps a hand on your scout's shoulder and says seriously, "Big responsibility."

"…Don't scare me like that, lady."

You tell him not to worry. *You*, after all, keep a safe distance while he's opening treasure chests.

"Aw, Cap…" Half-Elf Scout groans, but then he bursts out laughing. It wouldn't be possible to joke about this if he didn't know you were always right there for him while he was picking locks.

"…I think there might be something in that darkness," Female Bishop says suddenly as she runs her fingers along the lines of ink on the map.

Female Warrior cocks her head, then brushes some hair out of her face. "What do you mean, *something?*"

"I'm not sure, myself… Something similar to a Gate circle, perhaps."

"Eek!" Your *second* cousin yelps, but you ignore her, crossing your arms and letting out a breath. You presume that by *that darkness*, Female Bishop means the zone of blackness in the corner of the first floor.

Even in the gloom here in the underground, you can see a short distance ahead. The wire frame rising out of the darkness proves it. But there's one place where you can't see anything at all, not even your hand in front of your face. You pass the yawning opening each time you travel from the first to the second floor and back. If the entrance to the dungeon is the maw of a monster, that must be a path to the abyss itself…

"Ah, that place…," Female Warrior remarks, sounding sad about it. "I've heard people have tried to go in there."

"And let me guess. None of them ever came home," Myrmidon Monk says, and Female Warrior nods.

So many of the adventurers in this town are interested in nothing but money; they want nothing to do with adventures that won't yield a profit. If some foolhardy folk go into the darkness and never come back, well, then…

"…I told you: Whoever set this place up is rotten to the core." Half-Elf Scout spits. You agree completely.

"C-come on, let's keep going! Safety first, remember!" your *second* cousin says, still looking thoroughly terrified. You agree completely with her, too.

You nod, patting Female Bishop on the shoulder. Time to go. Long road ahead.

"Oh, right." She nods, quickly rolling the map up, and stands. "Let's go!"

Good enthusiasm. Heartening to hear.

§

Several rooms and battles later, you arrive at a long rope ladder leading downward. This is the second floor—though in the dungeon, with its almost unchanging scenery, it's all too easy to lose track of where you are. There's only the encompassing gloom and the faint wire frame passageway.

Female Bishop, feeling her way along corridors of ink on the map, gives the instructions. "We've found the ladder to the third floor before, so I don't anticipate too much trouble with getting lost…"

You'll let her lead the way. You say as much, then you check your katana and help your companions double-check their gear before you continue down the hall. Thankfully, you haven't yet run into any wandering monsters. You can't avoid encounters with the guardians of the various chambers, but you've been able to keep combat to a minimum, and that's a good sign.

"When going into a new area, you have to conserve your spells as much as possible," your cousin (responsible for your party's resource management) says from the back row, as if admonishing a child about his allowance. "You never know what might happen, so you have to be careful!"

Female Warrior chuckles from beside you as she watches you try to brush off your cousin's advice. "You can use some magic, too, can't you? Color me jealous."

It's not that impressive. You shrug, glance over your shoulder, and then lower your voice. You don't want your cousin to overhear this part, because you know it would go to her head—but you tell Female Warrior that *she's* the better caster.

"Hmm?" Female Warrior is grinning about something; you ignore her and turn the corner. You've never gotten comfortable with the way you can't see what's ahead, even after your eyes have adjusted to the dark. The only sounds to speak of in the empty halls are your own footsteps and the noise of your armor. There aren't even any odors, so that your senses almost feel paralyzed.

You had to learn how to relax yourself, so that you wouldn't be constantly at 100 percent focus. You can't let down your guard, but it would be worse if your attention snapped at a crucial moment. That's why you allow your party members to banter—and even sometimes deign to take part yourself.

"You used Magic Missile in a battle recently. How many times can

you do that?" Myrmidon Monk asks, and you reply that the answer
is not that many. Two or three times, maybe, but you're a swordsman
and still inexperienced. You don't necessarily have the wherewithal to
unleash a magic spell while also fighting in melee combat.

"I guess that means when we get back up top, you'll have to study
up on your magic, too, O brave leader," Female Bishop says with a
laugh. She gives a ringing shake of the sword and scales to indicate the
direction to go. "I bought a new spell book the other day... I think it
could be very helpful, you know?"

You reply that yes, you do know. You mean two things by that.
Female Bishop doesn't seem to remember what you're talking about.

That's right: You know that between adventures, she and your
cousin study magic intensely. All the more so, whether they realize
it or not, since you survived that battle on the second floor. You don't
talk to your cousin about those girls, and she doesn't ask. You think
maybe that's for the best. Instead, for now, you just give a tired smile
and look to your scout for help.

"Nah, Cap, knowledge is power!" he says. Uh-oh. "Lots of people
in this world, they can't read or write or do numbers. You learn a
bit; you get a whole different taste of life!" He crosses his arms like
a lecturing professor, and there's really nothing you can say back. You
grumble that you would rather work on your swordsmanship, and
Female Warrior pipes up pointedly, "Hey, I think your little brother is
saying something."

You immediately correct her: You're cousins.

"Don't worry, Big Sis will help you with your magical studies!"

Stupid *second* cousin.

"...I don't much care either way," Myrmidon Monk says with a
deliberate clack of his mandibles, then lets out a breath. "But are we
heading on or turning back? Make up your mind."

Before you know it, you find yourself standing in front of one of the
big, thick chamber doors. You ask Female Bishop if this is the place,
and she responds "Yes" with a small nod, clutching the sword and
scales. "I'm given to understand goblins don't appear on the second
floor... I can manage."

You look around again at those beside you and those behind

you—your party members—making sure they have all their gear. Everything looks good.

"Hey, can I kick it down this time?"

No, you tell Female Warrior, you're going to keep that little job for yourself—and then you smash the door down with a kick.

—!

Waiting for you as you all pile into the room are rotting humanoid monsters!

"Zombies!" shouts someone who recognizes them. Decaying adventurers, perhaps, called back from the depths of hell—in any event, decomposing corpses that press toward you. The reek of rotting flesh and organs that now belong to the dungeon: the odor of the Death. The smell mingles with the miasma, working its way into your nose, causing your stomach to spasm.

"U-urgh..." Female Warrior frowns but doesn't back down, while Myrmidon Monk bounds into the front row. "Undead ought to be weak to Dispel! *O my god of the wind that comes and goes—*"

"I'll coordinate with you! *Sword-prince, by your blade—*"

Female Bishop joins Myrmidon Monk in creating complicated sigils with her hands, one after another.

"*—send home these souls!*"

"*—cut away the curse that binds these!*"

They thrust out their palms as they intone these incantations, and a pure, holy wind fills the chamber. As soon as it brushes across the rotting flesh, the stuff begins to drop away.

But that's all.

Some of the creatures have nothing left to hold their bones together and collapse into piles of dust, but some don't. The undead shuffle closer, lesioned filaments wriggling from their decaying bodies. The way they move is uncanny—not like humans, but like dolls being helped along by children.

They thrust out their arms, moving in a sort of forward stumble far removed from proper walking, and the sight is terrible. The stench of the Death overpowers Female Bishop, who cries out, "These aren't...! These might not be undead at all...!"

"Who cares? Looks like if you destroy their bodies, they stop moving…!" Myrmidon Monk says. That's the important point. You smile slyly at his succinct appraisal, then draw your beloved blade.

You glance at Female Warrior out of the corner of your eye to find she has a smile on her own face, her spear at the ready. You want to know if the back row is all right. You seek confirmation without ever taking your eyes off the enemy. Half-Elf Scout responds with a vigorous shout: "Just leave this row to me, Cap!"

"If things get tight, I'll use my magic, but if it comes to that…"

You nod wordlessly at your cousin's voice. If that's what it takes, then you aren't ready for the third level yet. You'll have to give it up for today.

"They might come charging. Try not to get bit, okay?" Female Warrior says half-jokingly, watching the monsters approach step by shuffling step. You wonder if they have the smarts to worry about proper distancing. You weren't sure they'd be willing to get within reach of your blade, but it turns out you needn't have worried. One of them shambles right into range.

You bring your sword up in a sweep from below, carving off the creature's right arm.

"BRAAAAAAAAINNNNNN?!?!"

Bodily fluids splatter. You flick your wrist over, bringing the blade down on the left arm in a slash from above. When the zombie stumbles, you give it a solid kick in the torso.

"I'll take that!" Female Warrior leaps in, bringing her spear down in a single blinding strike. The creature's flesh gives way with a revolting cacophony of rending skin, cracking bones, and dissolving organs. Female Warrior steps neatly away from the stuff that spatters on the floor, showing her experience with this kind of thing. Maybe it's all those slimes she's done in…

"BRAINNNNNN! BRAAAAAAAIN!!"

The silly thought seems to distract you—just as you could have feared it might. One of the corpses grabs you from one side, sinking its teeth into your arm.

There is no pain. You give a click of your tongue, and with a sort of shake of your arm, you slam the creature against the dungeon wall. There's a sickening sound as brains blossom across the wall.

"Is that you, leader?!" Female Bishop cries from behind you. You give a wave, indicating it's no big deal.

The headless corpse in front of you is a more significant problem. It slides to the ground, but only for a second. Then, twitching spasmodically, with no head at all, it gets up again! Rotting goo pumps from the stump of its neck, the bizarre wormlike things wriggling.

"Don't think of them as living creatures! These are just inert *things*!!" Myrmidon Monk slashes the leg from another corpse with his curved scimitar as he shouts.

Yes, that's right. You register the truth of his words as you drive your blade into the headless zombie's chest. You can hear the bones and then the spine crack, and this time the corpse goes down for good. You give it a few more blows for good measure, making sure the body has returned to dust. That makes two of them.

These things take a bit of work. You shake your sword to get the blood and organ meat off it, then compose your breathing and make for the next enemy.

"Ain't a single one of 'em got any kind of weapon. Dunno if that makes us lucky or not," Half-Elf Scout observes from the back row. It means less trouble but also less profit. You grin: He's right.

But you aren't going to let your attention wander again.

You close the distance with a smooth slide of your feet, bringing your sword down on the shoulders of another zombie—twice. The collarbone cracks under the impact; you're turning even as its arms fall to the floor.

"Hiiiyah!" As you spin, Female Warrior swiftly takes your place, driving her spear into the monster. For sheer, single-strike power, her spear is probably the most potent weapon in your party. People tend to think of spears as being mostly for stabbing or sweeping, but you can add to their force by leaning into a blow.

"BBBBBBRAAIN...?!" The zombie Female Warrior slams into turns back to dust—that's a third one down.

Female Warrior spins in an unbroken motion, delivering a strike with the butt of her spear to the corpse at your feet. "Phew... Blast it all, I'm going to be out of breath by the time this is over...," she complains, brushing hair off her sweaty forehead.

You apologize to her for making her do all the work. The constant downward sweeps are not particularly efficient.

All you really have to do is physically prevent the zombies from moving, but to really finish them off, you have to actively destroy them. Which means Female Warrior's fighting prowess is the key here, but...

"Our leader and I could go around finishing them off one by one, eh?" Myrmidon Monk clacks, his scimitar still working.

"True enough," Female Warrior says with some concern as she combos the zombie your monk has just brought down. She crushes its face in with the heel of her metal boot, then smiles broadly. "You want to handle the last two, then?"

You glare at Myrmidon Monk. "This just got interesting," he remarks blandly.

You let out a sharp breath, then turn to the zombies shambling toward you. Unfortunately for you, they show no sign of retreating. Do they not care about what happened to their companions, or are they only interested in the living?

"It certainly appears we won't need any magic or miracles besides Dispel," Female Bishop says.

"Yep. Kinda sorry I didn't get to do anything, though...," your cousin adds.

Even as they speak, you make a sidelong swipe across the midriff of one zombie. Sheesh—they might conserve their spells, but your physical endurance has a limit, too.

How deep can this dungeon go? And how many corpses will you have to make to get there?

Everything you see, everything you have to do, makes you think how twisted the Dungeon Master around here seems...

By the time you finally stop to catch your breath, there's a substantial pile of zombie bits on the floor.

§

"Everything okay?" Female Warrior, seated firmly on the floor and smelling faintly of sweat, looks in your direction. You reply that you're unharmed and continue digging the zombie teeth out of your gauntlet with a dagger.

Once your group was sure that the room was clear, you decided to take a brief rest before heading down to the third floor. The circle you drew with pure water will keep you safe, if only briefly.

Female Bishop kneels before the pile of zombie bones in the corner, praying for their repose. Myrmidon Monk, meanwhile, is working with Half-Elf Scout to check the treasure chest—the various gods must be keeping busy.

Across from where you and Female Warrior sit, your cousin is rifling through her items. Well, as long as she doesn't do anything rash, you're happy to let your *second* cousin do as she pleases.

"Wasn't asking about you—I meant your glove," Female Warrior says with a giggle, resting her chin on her knee and peering at you.

You say that your glove is unharmed, too, as you pry loose the last of the teeth. Three or four of them scatter across the ground, clicking noisily. All rotted, disgusting. You brush them away with a grumble and thank Female Warrior for her hard work.

"You can say that again. I wish you wouldn't make me do *all* the heavy lifting."

Hey, you'll pay her back by taking some slimes off her hands next time.

"Hmph," she replies, pouting, and jabs you in the side with her elbow. She finds a place your armor doesn't cover and manages to leave you a bit short of breath.

"Hey, don't bully the poor girl," your *second* cousin chides. You object that you're the one being bullied.

You look over to see what she's been up to and find hard-baked goods in her hands. They aren't the things you bought as provisions before setting out; instead, you suspect...

"The third floor is coming up! We'd better make sure our stomachs are full!"

Blasted *second* cousin. You frown, take two of the cheerfully proffered treats, and toss one to Female Warrior.

"Hee-hee, thanks." She smiles and stuffs the treat into her mouth. "Oh, delicious!" she exclaims. You nod, then take a bite of the bread, now knowing it's safe to eat. It has a crunch to it, hard-baked as it is to help it stay fresh for days. The same objective has led to the use of a copious amount of sugar in the recipe, and all you can taste is sweetness.

It's more than a bit of an indulgence, but each of your party members is free to use their personal share of the money as they see fit. You don't intend to criticize your cousin's choices; indeed, it would be something of an indulgent excess itself to do so. Instead, you chew silently, and your *second* cousin puffs out her abundant chest with immense satisfaction.

"Aw, can't leave you to test the stuff for poison, Captain," Half-Elf Scout says, coming back with a bag full of loot from the treasure chest, a crooked smile on his face. He grabs one of the treats. Your cousin shoots you a glare, but what else is new? She tends to be careless, leading her to make a lot of mistakes—you can't help worrying if anyone will ever want her for a bride.

"Well, I never! Your big sister doesn't screw up at cooking that often!"

That often, eh? Silly *second* cousin.

"I think they taste great, myself. Those are harsh words for a little brother." Female Warrior laughs out loud, then looks to Female Bishop with a *Don't you think?* expression.

"She went out of her way to make them for us; I think the least we could do is be grateful."

Yes; for once, your cousin didn't oversleep, giving her time to bake these treats...but it took her so long that you left late. But then, they are pretty tasty... Hrmm. Maybe the pros win out over the cons.

"Which ones don't have any mint or ginger in them? I mean, I'll eat any of them, but...," Myrmidon Monk ventures.

"These ones, I think!"

She *thinks*. Stupid *second* cousin.

Myrmidon Monk brings one of the treats to his mandibles, attempting to look nonchalant, so you avoid any follow-up. Instead, you bring up the subject of the battle you just fought, provoking a further smile from Female Warrior. You ask her what it is, but she says, "Aw, nothing really," squinting like a cat.

You don't press the matter, turning instead to your mapper, Female Bishop, to see how things stand with the map. "Ahem, right. Umm..." She unrolls the sheepskin paper hurriedly, tracing the lines of ink with her fingers and nodding. "...The staircase should be just ahead, so getting down to the third floor shouldn't be a problem as such."

"When you start doing the mapping of the third floor, be careful where you put the staircase...or the ladder or whatever it is," Myrmidon Monk says, crunching noisily through his snack. Bits of baked bread fly from his mandibles.

"Hey," your cousin gripes, picking some crumbs off the hem of her robe. Myrmidon Monk turns his antennae and compound eyes briefly in her direction but then goes on as if nothing has happened: "The floors aren't necessarily laid out precisely above one another."

If perchance you ever get your hands on a Gate scroll, or ever get caught in a Gate trap, a slight miscalculation of your coordinates could be fatal. You could end up gods knew where and never figure out where you were again. Everything you've heard suggests you might be lucky even to wind up in a hallway at all.

"So just about at the third floor...," Half-Elf Scout muses, his arms crossed and his face drawn.

"Something the matter?" Female Warrior asks with a quizzical look, but he replies, "Nah. Just thinkin', there haven't been too many floor traps up till now, but I bet we won't be so lucky downstairs."

"I agree..." Female Bishop nods. Noting locations where you encounter traps on each level is also part of her job. It's not that there have been no traps on the first two floors—even that dark zone would probably qualify. But there have been few things that were genuinely deadly, nothing to worry you overmuch. Nevertheless, there's no indication that the next level will be the same.

"Might be they hope people will let down their guard after a couple of floors, and then—*bam!*" Myrmidon Monk says seriously while he picks up his crumbs as instructed by your cousin.

Half-Elf Scout seems unsure what to say for a moment, but then with palpable tension, he remarks, "Man, the Dungeon Master around here sure is twisted."

For some reason, Female Warrior is staring at you and shaking with suppressed laughter. You snort. Beside her, Female Bishop has a finger to her lips; she looks melancholy. "Maybe we should have asked one of those other adventuring groups to show us their map…"

"Eh, answer woulda been no," Half-Elf Scout says with a shrug and a shake of his head. "They risked their lives to get that information, and it's what puts food on the table for 'em. They wouldn't cough it up any sooner than they'd give us their actual cash."

You agree with him. Your own companions are one thing, but when it comes to other parties, well, they may be fellow adventurers, but they aren't your friends or buddies. You think perhaps that third son of the poor noble family might have obliged…but even then, you know it would be an awfully impolitic request. You think of it from your own perspective: You and your party have walked around this dungeon, Female Bishop carefully recording everything on your map—you certainly wouldn't give it up for free.

"Yes… That's true." You notice Female Bishop scratching her cheek as she looks at the ground, as if she's holding something back, and you decide to add a comment of your own:

'Naturally, if everyone agreed, that would be a different matter.'

"…! Yes, of course!" Female Bishop looks up and nods happily, sending ripples through her hair.

You relax when you see that. Ignoring the party's smiles (what do they have to smile about?), you shake out the arm the zombie bit. Even you realize the gesture looks staged, but it is important to make sure everything is still in good working order. Your gauntlet stopped the zombie's teeth, so you aren't hurt, and there's no numbness. The glove itself isn't even damaged.

"Still, bad luck," Female Warrior says, watching you test your hand. She reaches out with pale fingers. "Never took such a heavy hit before this."

She means the teeth marks still distinctly visible on your gauntlet. She runs her fingers over the surface of the glove, almost scratching it, then whispers in your ear, "I'd certainly hate for all of us to be destroyed down on the third floor because our leader has bad luck."

With her leaning toward you, you can feel her body heat, the softness of her limbs when she's not on her guard. You think her words, with the edge they carry, are actually a sort of joke, almost a friendly gesture toward you. Needle a person in order to relieve the tension, or say something terrible just to hear them deny it...

"Hmm...?"

Well, even so, it's not easy being the one who gets teased.

You shrug as if you've seen through her, then set about tightening the fasteners on your armor, which you loosened earlier. It's time to get going. You instruct everyone to make sure to check their armor and gear.

"Yeah, sure, we're on it." Female Warrior, stretching out lithe as a cat, quickly inspects her own armor. Female Bishop lets her fingers brush over the map one more time, then folds it up, and Half-Elf Scout likewise begins to stretch out his hands. Only Myrmidon Monk sits stone-still, making no move.

"Phew, there! Clean as a whistle." Beside him, your *second* cousin wipes sweat from her brow, smiling brilliantly as she gets to her feet. There's a pile of crumbs in her hands. Someone laughs at the sight, and then someone else joins in, drawn into the laughter. Female Bishop looks this way and that, the question mark almost visible over her head, until Female Warrior whispers in her ear. Female Bishop covers her mouth with a sound of surprise, and her cheeks soften into a smile, but Myrmidon Monk remains silent.

"......"

He finally gets heavily to his feet, his mandibles clacking; otherwise, he makes no sound as he checks over his equipment. Trying to suppress your own grin (someone has to preserve Myrmidon Monk's dignity), you give the command to move out.

The third floor is just ahead.

§

With a shout, you drive your katana toward the onrushing beast. The small, white-furred animal yelps and bounces across the dungeon floor like a ball. Just as nimbly, it kicks off the wall and bounds through space.

"RAAAAAAAAABBIT!!"

"Dangerous little bugger...aren't you?!" As you pull your sword back, Female Warrior flits past you, her spear singing out. The haft strikes the creature, which bounces along the ground again. You hear organs rupturing, and this time it doesn't get up.

You give Female Warrior your thanks ("Don't mention it!"), then walk over to inspect the corpse of this creature you've never seen before.

Things do start to get strange on the third floor.

"It looks like a...bunny," your cousin says, trotting up to you and peering at the body.

Think so? You cock your head, then remark that maybe it's something more like a capybara?

"Cappy...ba-ra?" Female Bishop repeats, apparently unfamiliar with the word, and Female Warrior chuckles.

Mm, you grunt. Then you cough and agree that yes, it does seem quite bunny-like.

The pure white fur (grimy though it is), the long ears, and the exaggerated back feet all look like those of a rabbit. But its front teeth are extraordinarily long, sharp, and deadly. Rabbits can be troublesome, yes—by eating crops in fields, not trying to murder you in a dungeon hallway. This creature is clearly a meat eater. Human meat, you surmise.

"Long, long ago, some king somewhere was exploring with one of his knights, when they were attacked by a monstrous rabbit," Myrmidon Monk clacks out, almost to himself. "They were only able to defeat it with the help of a sacred item, or so I've heard. If we aren't careful, we could end up the next meal for one of these things."

"If you say so. Didn't seem like all that to me," Half-Elf Scout comments, and you nod. It was the first thing you encountered on descending the rope ladder to the third floor, and although it got the drop on you, you managed to survive the battle. It didn't strike you as that much more powerful than you are...

"Uh, um, may I ask something...?" You're just probing the rabbit's remains with your hand when Female Bishop tugs unexpectedly on your sleeve. You ask her what's wrong, and she says, "I know it's a very important matter...and I'd like to make certain of our position. May I use the Point spell?"

Ah. You nod in understanding. She's thinking of the warning Myrmidon Monk inflicted on her upstairs. From the perspective of your continued exploration, it would be a good idea to make sure of where you are.

What does your esteemed cartographer think of that?

"Doesn't matter to me either way," he says, mandibles clacking. "Let her do what she likes."

Well, that's not very helpful. You look at the ceiling, frowning at the unchanging white lines.

Finally, unable to come to a decision, you call your cousin over.

"Never fear, Big Sister is here. What can I do for you?" your *second* cousin asks gleefully. You want to know if, as the party's resource manager, she feels it's all right to use a spell here.

"Let's see…," your cousin says, putting a thoughtful finger to her lips. "I think it should be fine."

You remark that she came to that decision awfully quickly; she brings her hands together in front of her bountiful chest and continues, "Well, we're just trying this out today. We've made the third level—now let's think about getting home, all right?"

The way she looks up at you pointedly for agreement, like an older sister scolding her younger brother, makes you cast your eyes to the ground. You seem to remember her being taller than you once—but, well, never mind.

You consider your cousin's advice for a moment, then call Half-Elf Scout over to ask him about the current take.

"Hrm? Lessee here… Not bad, not bad at all."

Treasure chests are found only in rooms, and rooms are guarded by monsters. You didn't go out of your way to go into many rooms on your way down, but you still managed to come up with some loot.

"Found a few bodies on the way and helped myself to some spare change. Oughtta cover having their tags buried." He shakes a jangling leather pouch at his hip and grins. Your cousin frowns a little at the innocent gesture, but you nod and acknowledge what he's done. Dead men don't use weapons, and they don't need cash. Nor will they complain if you relieve them of the same.

Besides, if and when you finally fall, you hope someone will bury you.

The thought crosses your mind of the body bags Female Warrior was dragging behind her the first time you met her. You realize now what a kind and decent thing she was doing.

"...Whatcha thinkin'?" Female Warrior inquires.

Nothing—it's nothing. You turn aside her sharp gaze with a smile, then conclude that it seems a good idea. Your plan is to try one room on this third floor, then go back up without pushing yourselves too far. Using up a spell here will give you a firm foundation, not to mention being helpful the next time you come here.

When you mention this, Female Bishop bows deeply and says, "Thank you very much," her face shining. "In that case, I'll do it right away. *Ego...quelta...zain.* Confirm my presence."

She intones words of true power that echo throughout the world. Words, it's said, were invented by the god of wind, and letters by the god of knowledge. Perhaps, you think, this is because words are sound, effectively wind. You feel the words Female Bishop speaks fill the chamber.

As a fighter who is nonetheless conversant with magic, you have to be familiar with how these things work. You suspect that at this moment, the world appears as a grid in Female Bishop's mind. This spell to locate one's position on it is considered to be a fairly basic one.

"...I've got it," she says, letting out an anxious breath and putting a hand to her as yet undeveloped chest. "It's true, there is a slight displacement from the floor above. If I'd started the map without realizing it..."

"Huh! That there's one convenient trick," Half-Elf Scout remarks, crossing his arms. If he, a scout, wanted to do the same thing, he would have to rely entirely on his own experience and intuition. But polished and accumulated as it is, he would have a much better chance than an inexperienced tracker like you. The fact that his magic is also better than yours... Maybe that's what they call talent.

"If we ever get lost down here, I'll be countin' on that spell!"

"Heavens...," Female Bishop says, putting an embarrassed hand to her cheek. "I can't use it more than once, and it's nothing special anyway."

"Well, once you do learn to use it more than once, I guess we won't be needing our scout anymore," Female Warrior coos, a broad smile on her face. "Hrm!" Half-Elf Scout scoffs, looking at the ceiling.

You feel your mouth ease into a smile at your friends' antics; you wipe your blade down with a special paper for that purpose and put it back in its scabbard.

"Are we moving on?" Myrmidon Monk asks, and you nod.

The scenery in front of you is all too familiar: the dark dungeon, only the faint lines of the wire frame visible through the gloom and the miasma. The place never looks any different, and yet you can assume that whatever waits for you ahead won't be the same as what you've already seen.

So start with a first step. Find a room, go inside, fight a battle, and go home. Just like the first time you challenged this dungeon—the first time you encountered the Death that lurks in these depths.

A good omen would be a nice way to start. You look at the furry white corpse and think. What position does this creature hold on this floor? You can't imagine it's the strongest thing around. But whatever it represents, your sword worked just fine on it.

That's all you need to know to inspire the courage to go on. You nod with fresh resolution, check your gear one more time, and then tell your comrades it's time to go.

You take a step forward, and the ground beneath your feet disappears.

§

"Leader!"

Yikes—a pit trap! You flail your arms as you fall, a victim of gravity. Your fingers brush against something, and you grab on as hard as you can. There's a burning pain as you scrape your palms, the muscles of your arms and shoulders complaining mightily. Still you don't let go, and the reason is simple: You don't want to die.

"H-hey, Captain, you okay?!"

"Gods… You weigh a ton…!"

You look up when you hear Half-Elf Scout and Female Warrior, and finally you realize you're holding on to the haft of a spear. Half-Elf

Scout has his arms wrapped around Female Warrior's midriff as she braces herself at the edge of the pit, trying to fish you out.

"Here, give me that. I have better grip strength."

"Yeah... Be my guest...!"

Myrmidon Monk grabs the spear, and Female Warrior lets out a breath. You swing your body upward, bracing your feet against the wall of the pit. You push against the wall as hard as you can.

"I'm going to pull now," Myrmidon Monk says. "Work your way up, one step at a time. If your hand slips, it's over for you."

You respond with a *yes-please*, and then you work your way slowly, painfully out of the hole, up along the wall. You can feel the sweat on your forehead, and your breath comes in gasps. You grit your teeth, clenching your core muscles. One step, two steps, three, four. It seems you didn't actually fall that far.

Just another way of saying that if your friends had been an instant later to help you, they wouldn't have been in time.

Thus, you return from the pit by the skin of your teeth, crawling panting onto the floor of the third level.

"Geez, you've gotta watch where you're going!" your cousin exclaims, running up to you pale as a sheet.

You're not sure watching where you were going would have made that much difference, but it remains that this came from your failure of attention. Nonetheless, you were saved, and you thank your party members for rescuing you, then take a drink from the canteen at your hip.

"Ugh, now my hands hurt...," Female Warrior complains, wiping sweat from her brow. You apologize and also thank her especially for her split-second reactions. Without her, you would have fallen for sure.

"Er... Don't mention it," she says quietly, not quite looking at you.

You take another swig from your canteen, then give your equipment a quick once-over. You hope you didn't drop anything in the pit...

"Dangerous stuff down there. Don't go falling again, Captain," Half-Elf Scout says, tossing a torch into the pit and watching it drop. It's a good choice—torches serve no purpose in the maze. Finally getting your breathing under control, you, too, look down into the dark.

At the bottom of the pit are several sharp spikes, already piercing the bones of one unlucky victim. Without your party members, you would have ended up just like this person who went before you. Even if by some tremendous chance you'd avoided being skewered, you would certainly have broken your legs and been unable to move, at which point your only option would have been to wait for starvation to claim you.

Deeply embarrassed by your own pathetic mistake, you thank all your party members yet again. If you screwed up like this ten times, you might have no choice but to kill yourself to maintain your honor.

At the same time, you're glad it was you who fell into the trap. Female Warrior, Myrmidon Monk, or Half-Elf Scout might have survived like you did, but Female Bishop and your cousin could have been in real danger.

"...So we are dealing with proper traps starting on this floor," Female Bishop says, her expression tense. With a quick motion of her hands, she makes a note of this feature on the map.

As you stand talking, the cover over the pit trap snaps shut, and it looks like an ordinary floor again. You fell through it, and yet you would never guess that there was a trapdoor here.

"Guess that's our warning—better watch our footing from now on," Myrmidon Monk says. You nod at him and turn to Half-Elf Scout for his professional opinion. His response is to the point—a different point. "First things first. We'd best move to a new place, Captain. Sometimes y'get so thrown off by a trap that you just stop...and then you fall right back into it."

That makes sense. You want to avoid that at all costs. You thank your party one more time, then instruct your scout to take point. You have Myrmidon Monk take up his former place at the back of the line.

"You sure?" Myrmidon Monk clacks, and you say the most important thing right now is to be careful of traps.

"Hee-hee. Looking forward to working with you," your cousin says to him with a grin as he lines up beside her. Female Bishop dips her head. "Y-yes, we'll be counting on you..."

Well, you trust him to keep an eye on things. And of course, your cousin can't help sticking her nose where it shouldn't be. You think it'll be fine.

"All right, Cap, we're off!"

Mm. You nod to Half-Elf Scout, who sets off at a quick clip.

Female Warrior, her spear on her back, groans and makes a show of rubbing her hand. You fall into step beside her.

"Not a lucky boy today, are you?"

You reply that you thought the omens looked good. Then you turn your eyes back on the depths of the third level.

Gods, this floor is equal parts gratifying and awful.

"...I wonder if there are slimes on this level...," Female Warrior suddenly whispers, and you find yourself grinning at this unexpected show of vulnerability.

Maybe you just need to let off steam, or maybe it's a simple tease: Either way, you say that slimes would be better than pits, and Female Warrior says, "True enough," smiling weakly.

You're all on edge because this is your first visit to the third floor. You steady your breathing, relax your shoulders, and look around again—but it's still the same unchanging black-and-white maze. Half-Elf Scout is ahead of you, his sharp eyes darting left and right as he steps gingerly on each floor tile. You ask if there's some trick to spotting traps, to which he replies, "Good question," and crosses his arms, frowning. "Y'look at every surface real close, and if anything seems the least bit off to you, y'don't take any chances."

So that's how it works.

"That's all there is to it." The rest is experience and intuition—and being used to it, he tells you. You acknowledge what a significant part pure gut instinct plays in all this.

Accepting his response, you leave Half-Elf Scout to his work, looking back instead toward the end of the line. Though you haven't been together too long, your party has already gelled. But this is the first time you've changed the makeup of your formation. You think it's going well, but...

"Goodness, is it that difficult?"

"Uh-huh. Harder than reading the old texts." Myrmidon Monk nods seriously. If it weren't for the bandage covering them, you think Female Bishop's eyes would look as round as saucers. "Reading what's about to happen in the game of Wizball? Much more difficult. Just when you think you've got it won, you take your eyes off things for a second, and it's over for you."

"I hope *he* doesn't get it into his head to start betting on games, claiming it's a way of training his intuition…"

What rude things your *second* cousin says. When you tell her as much, she replies, "Oops, you heard that?" putting a hand to her cheek and giggling. "You don't have to worry about your older sister back here. You just keep your eyes front."

Dumb *second* cousin. As the words leave your mouth in a mumble, you see that even Female Bishop is trying to restrain her laughter, her thin shoulders shaking. Yeesh. You look to Myrmidon Monk for help, but he only clacks his mandibles, his antennae pointed away from you. "Makes no difference to me."

Bah.

You give an exasperated shake of your head and look forward again.

All of this might seem like simple banter, but each of you is doing your job. Never letting your vigilance lapse, yet not worrying more than is necessary. It's all right; you have this down. Or so you keep telling yourself as you walk carefully forward.

"Captain," Half-Elf Scout says sharply. "Chamber ahead."

A great, heavy door looms before you.

It's the moment you've been waiting for.

§

You kick the door open, but to your surprise, you're greeted with a long hallway. Unlike in the average chamber, no monsters appear to be waiting for you. That's a relief, but it also takes the wind out of your sails; you relax your grip on your weapon.

Beside you, Half-Elf Scout and Female Warrior exchange lighthearted banter:

"Huh… More fool me, getting all excited," Half-Elf Scout says.

"Yeah. If I'm going to feel that nervous, I'd like to at least get a treasure chest out of it," Female Warrior replies.

"You said it!"

They might sound silly, but letting out tension is important. You don't even think of reprimanding them.

"Do we go forward? Or turn back and look somewhere else?" Myrmidon Monk asks, indicating that he doesn't care either way; you say that you're going ahead, of course. The party isn't that far from the staircase yet—not far enough to worry about getting home anyway. With your companions alongside and behind you, you proceed step by step deeper into the dungeon.

"It certainly is unsettling, being down here for the first time…," Female Bishop whispers, even as her quill scratches the paper. Conversation subsides, leaving only the sound of her writing and the party's boots tapping along the floor. Led by your scout, looking this way and that, you head into the darkness.

Some distance down the corridor, you discover a door in one wall. You raise a hand, signaling to the others to stop. The hall seems to go on—this might be a chamber.

"Want to take a look? We haven't really found anything around here yet…" You nod at your cousin's suggestion, then touch the surface of the door delicately. It's the same iron portal you've seen everywhere else in this labyrinth. So cold you can feel it through your gauntlet. Almost as cold as your blood runs when you think about what might lie on the other side of it.

You check your armor and equipment, draw your sword and check the blade and the fastenings, and otherwise prepare for battle. You tell your comrades to do the same and continue your own inspection.

"Mm, thanks," Female Warrior says, holding her hair up so you can check the back and sides of her armor, as if this is all routine to her. There's a hint of teasing in her voice, but your lives depend on this, and you all take it seriously.

You nod. All looks good. Next, you clap Half-Elf Scout on the shoulder.

"Y-yeah, hey. Think it's okay… Nothin' unusual, Cap." He seems a little startled at first, but his voice quickly returns to normal, and his head bobs up and down. You smile. He's going to be fighting in the front row, but there's no need to be quite so tense. You and the girl are there to handle offense; he just has to focus on support. It's the same thing you expect of Myrmidon Monk when he's up with you—nothing's different.

"Yeah, sure, I get it," Half-Elf Scout says. "Just, y'know, Cap... y'haven't been very lucky today. Gotta be careful."

The omens are good. That's what you say to his little remark, and then you glance toward the back row. Female Bishop and your cousin are twirling around for each other, checking each other's equipment. Next to them, Myrmidon Monk is making sure of the scimitar in its scabbard, then he looks at you and nods. If he says no problem, then you believe him. You're ready to go.

Good.

You nod, give a shout, and then, as is your wont, smite the door with a powerful kick.

Eeyowch!

There's a hollow *thud*, and you grab your foot, feeling a pain you've never felt here in the dungeon before.

"Ooh, that looked nasty." Female Warrior giggles, and you don't blame her. The door took your blow and didn't move an inch!

"Hey, are you okay?" your cousin asks, worried, but Myrmidon Monk only shakes his head in disgust. "Doesn't even need a miracle. It'll fix itself soon enough. Don't think twice about it."

It's not exactly that it's all the same to you, but still crouched over, you wave to your scout with one hand. Better let a pro take a look at this one.

"On it!"

"That... That really seemed painful...," Female Bishop says, though she's half smiling as she asks, "Would you like me to rub it?" You shake your head emphatically. Compared to being wounded in combat, this is nothing. So why does it hurt so damn much?

You finally manage to get to your feet. You've survived the dungeon's deadly traps. You are *going* to kick this door down no matter what.

"Hmm... No traps," Half-Elf Scout reports. "Regular locked door."

Son of a...

"Hang on a sec. I'll give it a try." Half-Elf Scout pulls out the toolkit he normally uses for opening treasure chests and starts working on the lock. You've heard this kit called "the seven tools," but it must be a figurative expression, because it looks like a lot more than seven to you. There's what appears to be a thin metal needle and a fine rasp, each tailored to the exact needs of a scout.

"No traps, he says," Female Warrior whispers from beside you, chuckling at your little screwup. You purse your lips and reply that there might be slimes on the other side of that door.

"Bah," Female Warrior says, frowning. Then, by way of poking further fun at you, she quips, "You really aren't on your luck today, are you?"

You cross your arms sullenly. But you don't feel tired. The omens really are good.

A short while later, there's a *click* and a scraping of metal.

This is hardly the only chamber whose door has a lock on it. Adventurers used to be very careful about checking everything thoroughly, dealing with things properly, but apparently, they got tired of it at some point. Eventually, they adopted a custom: When you're confident a door doesn't have any traps on it, you just kick it down.

So was it your inexperience that kept you from kicking this door open, or was it, say, the fit of the door itself? It must be the latter. You're sure of it.

"Um…" Female Bishop, wondering if there might be something productive she could do while you waited for Half-Elf Scout to pick the lock, unrolled the map and gave it to Myrmidon Monk. He runs a carapace-plated finger along it, then says, "Don't worry about it," with a shake of his antennae. "What do you think, leader?" He hands you the map, and you give it a quick glance. There's always a possibility of being attacked, even when you're just standing around like this, so you have to keep one eye on your surroundings. Thus, you don't look at the map very carefully, but as far as you can tell, there are no problems.

"Thank goodness…" Female Bishop puts a relieved hand to her as yet undeveloped chest when she receives approval from you both. She takes the map back and folds it up carefully—but then she makes an innocent gesture of curiosity. "I still find it very strange…"

You ask what it is she finds strange. She replies, "It's just a small thing, but… Why are all the doors closed, do you suppose? We've opened some of them many times ourselves."

"Because the master of this dungeon is rotten to the core," Myrmidon Monk says, clacking and giving a deep nod of his head. "They might be enchanted with some sort of magic that makes sure they're always locked."

"That's the Lock spell," your cousin adds quickly. She probably figures magic is her department. She sounds very confident, puffing her ample chest out. You hate to admit it, but that *second* cousin of yours is a better magic user than you or Female Bishop. And why do you hate to admit it? Because if you did, it would absolutely go to her head…

"It's a simple spell, but it shows how proficient the caster must be if it activates automatically."

Meaning you're facing a powerful magic user. You grunt thoughtfully, during which time Female Warrior calls to your cousin from beside you: "Does that mean there's a spell for opening doors, then?"

"Sure there is," your cousin replies as easily as anything. "But just like Lock, its effectiveness depends on the caster's ability…"

"Gee, 'Sis,' I guess that means when you grow up a little, you won't need a scout to open doors for you anymore," Female Warrior says, putting her hands together with a grin. "Aww…," Half-Elf Scout groans. You frown and tell him he's got nothing to worry about. After all, locks are as locks may be, but your *second* cousin will never be able to handle finding enemies and traps.

"And what exactly is that supposed to mean?" she demands.

Exactly what you said. You pretend not to know what she's upset about, and your cousin puffs out her cheeks in annoyance.

Now, that's quite enough chatter. You inquire if the door's open yet.

"…Yep, ready to go," Half-Elf Scout answers. He lets out a long breath and wipes some sweat from his brow; Female Bishop walks over to him with a canteen.

"Here," she says, offering it to him. He accepts it with a "Thanks" and takes one mouthful, then two. "Man, it really wears on a guy, not knowin' what might happen while he's working. Might be traps, might be monsters."

You shrug a little and look around at your party. You made an idiot of yourself earlier, but it won't happen again. If you screw up twice in a row, you're going to take your anger out on the master of this dungeon.

"Ready when you are," Female Warrior says breezily.

"Yep, anytime…!" Half-Elf Scout adds, holding his dagger in a reverse grip that's visibly trembling.

You tremble a little with excitement yourself. If Half-Elf Scout is ready, then so are you. You steady your breathing, pull your sword from its sheath, and take up a fighting posture, then aim another kick at the door.

Now, to arms!

You all tumble into the room like an avalanche. In the gloom of the chamber, there are four squirming forms—no, six, counting the back row.

"They've got staves!" your cousin shouts. "Look out, they're spell casters!" You squint against the darkness, trying to make out what you're really facing. Now you see it: The ones in the back wear robes and carry staves in their hands. Some kind of wizards, you suppose. But the thing that draws your attention are the men on the front row. They wear dark outfits that blend into the dim surroundings, and they have on strange masks. Their faces are white as if covered in powder, and red patterns with great, large eyes are drawn on them.

You don't get the dramatic appearance. If it weren't that their eyes and faces moved not at all, you could almost take them to be the monsters' actual faces.

"We haven't faced these enemies before—don't let your guard down for a second!" Myrmidon Monk shouts from the back row. You hear Half-Elf Scout and Female Warrior respond in the affirmative. You don't say anything at all but vigilantly grasp your katana in both hands, moving with sliding steps, checking the footing, trying to judge the distance.

Your toes bump something. A bone that goes rolling away—does it belong to a human or a monster? Down in this dungeon, there are probably more who died after losing their way and running out of strength than there are dead beasts. One wrong move and you might well become one of them. But in the dungeon, no flower blooms in a spinal column lolling in the corner of a chamber.

"........."

The masked men likewise slide forward, spreading out through the room without a sound. You suspect they're trying to make space for the spell casters in the back row. Beneath your helmet, you glance quickly left, then right. The men crouch, so low they're almost on the ground, but they move smoothly—and swiftly.

You hear a hush of blades slipping from scabbards, each of the men drawing a straight sword from the holsters on their backs. You click your tongue; you didn't even see them move. They probably slid the scabbards around toward their hips and drew them from there.

We can do this.

Without taking your eyes off the enemy forms in front of you, you tell your cousin that you'll let her manage your magical resources.

"Right!" The response comes from Female Bishop, her voice tense. Your cousin is probably concentrating, trying to find a gap in the formation through which to launch her spell, just like your enemies. Your many years together lead you to trust her with the back row; you make your breathing even and face the masked men.

Two.

Two of them come rushing at you. One each toward Female Warrior and Half-Elf Scout. Maybe they see you as their most dangerous opponent. The thought brings a crooked smile to your face. Troublesome, but you're grateful.

It means there will be that much less for your comrades to deal with.

Sweat runs from your forehead down your cheeks. You no longer even have the time to spare to glance at your friends to either side. Your vision constricts, until the enemies are all you can see. The sounds around you recede into the distance, like a ringing in your ears, and all that's left is your complete focus on your foes.

You pull your sword in, stepping back, sliding your right foot behind you so your left foot is forward. If they try to come from below, you'll block with your left, then swipe up and disengage.

The distance closes. You see what your opponents are targeting. You know the distancing. You don't think they can see your sword.

If they were coming one by one, you could dispatch the first one and then turn to the second. They aren't making things so simple. If they both come at you together—what will you do?

It'll be fine.

Cut down the first one with your first strike, then get the other one with the return stroke before his blade can reach you. Seize the initiative in a volley of blows that will last only an instant. The fractional difference in distance between you and each of your opponents: That's the path you'll take. The spot you'll aim for. You breathe evenly.

Shf, shf. You slide forward, trying to lure them in. *If I have to come to you,* you try to communicate, *I'll cut you down.*

You can't see their faces for their masks, but they seem unmoved by your provocation. They crouch lower and move backward, their behavior showing that they understand what's happening in this fight. Gods, they're making this difficult. Fine, one more step...

"—!"

Even as the thought crosses your mind, there's a dry scrape across the stone floor, and one of the men vanishes. You reflexively lash out with your sword, but the blade cuts empty air. You feel nothing under your hands.

A belated instant later, a figure springs up silently, directly in front of you.

A leap!

No sooner have you understood what happened than a red-streaked white face presses in on you.

So this is a "tiger"...

The next second, everything is a brilliant red, the floor and the ceiling seeming to switch places.

You are decapitated!

§

"—!!"

You hear Female Warrior scream, yelling your name. Your cousin, too, exclaims inarticulately when she sees you collapse. You try to answer, but no words come out of your mouth, only blood. You press

©lack

your hands to your throat, feeling the strength drain from your body with the gushing red liquid as you slide from your knees to the ground. You strain to get up, but you're drowning in your own blood.

The voices of your friends, the sounds of battle: all seem somehow far away now.

What a tremendous screwup! The thought passes lazily through your mind as you fight to open your eyes, try to see what's happening on the battlefield. Your vision is lopsided; Female Warrior moves to rush over to you, her lovely face pale.

That isn't good…

"Don't break formation, they'll get through!!" Myrmidon Monk shouts before you manage to make a sound.

"…!"

"Take this!!"

Female Warrior is biting her lip. A blow was coming to finish you for good, but a dagger deflects it in the nick of time. It's Half-Elf Scout. He's flung his knife to protect you from the ninja's attack.

He's up against the proverbial wall, though, too. It was all he could do to fling the dagger and parry the blow. His isn't a combat class to begin with. It's laudable that he was even able to block the ninja. "Stay calm! The cap's still kickin', but it's close!!" He looks absolutely desperate as he continues to defend, never taking his eyes off his own opponent. "Do we keep fightin', or do we fall back?!"

"I don't care either way!!" Your body seems to float; it must be Myrmidon Monk picking you up in his arms. He pulls you to the back row, where you see your cousin, brought back to herself by the shouts, clutching her short staff. "…! I'll take over command!" she says, with a quick glance at your wounds that seems to assure her you aren't going to die immediately.

There's no time. That's exactly why your cousin is working so hard to understand exactly what she has to do. When her lips form the words, "I'm sorry," you nod ever so slightly. "I have to prioritize controlling this situation over healing you right now!" Your cousin's judgment is quick and perceptive. "I'm going to use Dance and then Fireball! Coordinate with me, use Silence! We'll keep them from attacking!"

"R-right!"

"How about me—want me to move up? I don't mind!" Myrmidon Monk offers.

Female Warrior nods, her face grave, and Myrmidon Monk starts in, his mandibles clacking. His scimitar is already out, and he's trying to put himself in position to move anywhere at any time.

"Go for it!" your cousin calls.

"Mm!"

There is no hesitation in the exchange. Myrmidon Monk cinches a cloth around your wounded neck, then runs forward. You try hard to press on the cloth, watching it turn redder every moment, hoping to stop the blood flow.

Female Warrior, working her spear tirelessly, calls with a note of concern, "Hey! Does that mean you're leaving him alone?!"

"No time for questions; let's just do it…!" Female Bishop replies, clearly struggling to stay calm. Female Warrior looks about to object to being ordered around by a younger woman, but then she closes her mouth and clucks her tongue. "…Right, sure!"

"You heard the lady. Let's get ready, here…!"

Obviously, the party hasn't been stopping for a quick rest while they have this conversation. Each of them has been trying to play their role as best they can in a rapidly changing situation. From what you can see, your collective destiny in this battle will be determined by simple combat strength.

"You son of a…!"

The people with the tiger-like masks might be adventurers, enchanted by the miasma of the dungeon, or perhaps they're simply monsters who happen to look like men. Whichever it is, they're fearsome opponents.

With you down for the count, there's only one dedicated fighter on your party's front row. Female Warrior is working her spear as hard as she can to keep the enemies at bay, but it costs her physical stamina, and her concentration is fading. Still, she strives to face down two of the ninjas by herself, her breath coming hard, sweat forming on her brow and running through her hair. If her footing starts to grow unreliable, then this fight is over.

"Whoo, these guys're stern stuff…!"

"Less talking, more fighting!"

If Female Warrior goes down, Half-Elf Scout and Myrmidon Monk alone will have no chance of defending the party from the four enemies. Your front row will collapse, they'll easily get to your back row, and then your cousin and Female Bishop will meet a grisly demise. Even if they avoid that fate, with enough time, the enemy magicians are sure to finish their spells and unleash their magic. Perhaps your party has no chance after all…

"*Musica concilio terpsichore!* Music united with dance!"

This, though, is when the fight really begins. Your cousin intones words of true power in a clear voice.

"…?!"

"…?!?!"

She's just one move ahead of your opponents, but the ninjas' feet come up off the ground. They start trembling, like they're dancing, in time with the melodic incantation, their hands slicing through the air.

Even without her eyesight, Female Bishop doesn't miss this opportunity. *"Let the light of quietude be upon you…!!"*

She strikes forth with the sword and scales, appealing directly to the gods. A curtain of silence descends with her sacred invocation. This noiselessness, brought about by the Supreme God with his respect for Order, envelops the wizards weaving their spells on the back row. They may wave their staves, but no words come forth from their mouths.

There's still a hint of youth in Female Bishop's face, but a smile, somehow cold, comes upon it. "There, now they're deprived of their spells…!"

"You're mine!"

"…?!"

Female Warrior's voice rings out. She takes the feet out from under one of the ninjas with a sweep of her spear. He floats back through the air, and the spear follows him in a great arc, the tip plunging into his belly before he hits the ground. He folds like a chrysanthemum blossom, but when he hits the ground, it's like a cat landing from a great height.

"Tough bastard…!"

That must have damaged him. If he's alive, he can be killed.

But with his face hidden, it's hard to tell. The two ninjas try to surround Female Warrior, their movements not quite human and not quite bestial.

You knew it was going to be all about simple fighting strength. Your cousin, who until this point has been maintaining the Dance spell, waves her staff in the direction of the enemy group. Your party has prevented the enemy from attacking as best it can. Now you have to go on the offensive yourselves. A simple, immovable fact.

"*Carbunculus—!*" your cousin exclaims, and in the blink of an eye the laws of the world are overwritten. You can smell the air boiling as heat focuses at the end of your cousin's staff, and a conflagration ensues. Sure, it's easy to tell when the spell is incoming, but it's also easy to aim.

"I'll coordinate with you!" Female Bishop calls, raising the sword and scales. "*Crescunt—!*" The holy sigil shines with the light of the Supreme God, glowing with magical fire. These words of true power, capable of overwriting the very laws of the world, are acknowledged by the deity who rules over Law.

Together, the two young women call out the last of the words that will reshape the world around them. ""*Iacta!!*""

A ball of fire launches forth from each of the girls' implements. With a *whoosh*, they fly past your front row, exploding smack in the middle of the enemy formation. An explosion, heat, a burning wind against your skin: You reflexively squint your blurring eyes.

"Hoo! You girls know how to put on a show…," Half-Elf Scout remarks, rolling away from the choking black smoke that begins filling the room.

"Don't let up. We have to make sure we really got them…!" Female Warrior says, coughing gently but keeping her spear ever at the ready. There's no breeze in this confined space, yet the smoke vanishes in short order. All you smell now is the reek of charred flesh and bones.

There is no sound from beyond the screen of smoke—it parts to reveal only corpses. Corpses with singed robes and staves in their hands.

Nothing more.

"Well, now…" Myrmidon Monk clacks his mandibles and waves his antennae. Half-Elf Scout takes a quick glance in every direction.

Female Bishop continues to hold her sword and scales at the ready while your cousin adjusts her grip on her staff. Perhaps her hands are slick with sweat.

Five seconds pass, then ten—and nothing happens. The miraculous silence finally dissipates, leaving the gentle crackling of burning meat.

"Arrgh…!" Female Warrior loudly slams the butt of her spear against the stone floor in frustration at your escaped enemies.

§

"How is he…?" Female Warrior asks, her voice trembling as she trots over to you. The moment the battle was over, your friends rushed together around you, each of them breathing hard. You somehow manage to move your mouth, but no words come out; instead, Female Bishop's slim hand reaches toward your neck. She adjusts the cloth that you and Myrmidon Monk tied in such a hurry, delicately but carefully making sure it's in place, and then she gives a quick nod.

"The bleeding's stopped," she says. "It's a deep wound, but…well, this is a start."

"All right. Thank goodness…" Your cousin's grim look gives way to a breath of relief as she wipes some sweat from her brow. She's a very effusive person, but you rarely see her look quite so panicked.

You struggle to tell them to prioritize getting home, and your cousin says, "I know," and starts to smile. "Let's go back up. We'll save our spells as best we can…"

"…Why aren't you healing him?" The question is abrupt. Female Warrior stands with her hands together in front of her chest, a cold, clear smirk on her face.

Tension comes into the air. From where you're lying, you can clearly see your cousin swallow heavily. "Uh, well… That is…"

"You didn't do it earlier, either. Why not?"

Your cousin, feeling cornered by Female Warrior's pressing of the point, doesn't seem to know quite what to say. Likewise, Female

Bishop, her hand still at your throat, appears unsure where to put her sightless eyes and says nothing.

Rescue, instead, comes from a completely unexpected quarter.

"...Ain't got a real choice. Didn't know what would happen then, don't know what's gonna happen now."

"Hmm," Female Warrior says, her smile never slipping at Half-Elf Scout's interjection. "Your point being?"

"We were outnumbered in that fight." The scout's accustomed easy attitude likewise never slips. His arms are crossed, and his tone is serious, but even that seems exaggerated, like he's putting on a show. "With the cap out, we were down one. Someone to take care of him, that'd be two. The poor get poorer, y'know? ...And this is the third floor."

"..."

"Say we use up our miracles healing the captain right here. Then the next big, bad thing comes around the corner, and that's it for us."

"Oh..." You can almost see the blood drain from Female Warrior's face. It's not regret or fear so much as it is the realization of how agitated she had become—the adrenaline ebbing away.

The third floor—yes, that's where you are. Not the first floor, which you walk almost with impunity now, nor the second, where you know how things work. You have no idea what other powerful, unknown beasts might wander these halls.

"...Yeah. Yeah, sure... Of course..." Female Warrior nods as obligingly as a little girl. It seems to bring your cousin back to herself as well. She shakes her head, rippling her hair, then bows politely. "Look, I'm sorry. I should have just explained. Please..."

"No, don't worry about it... There wasn't time. Hey... I'm sorry, okay?"

"It's all right..."

The two of them look at each other uncertainly but fall silent.

Now that you think about it, you realize that since its formation, your party has been through a lot—but never something like this. The two girls aren't used to having such a sharp difference of opinion that it brings them to argue with each other.

Their stumbling apologies are interrupted by the clacking of

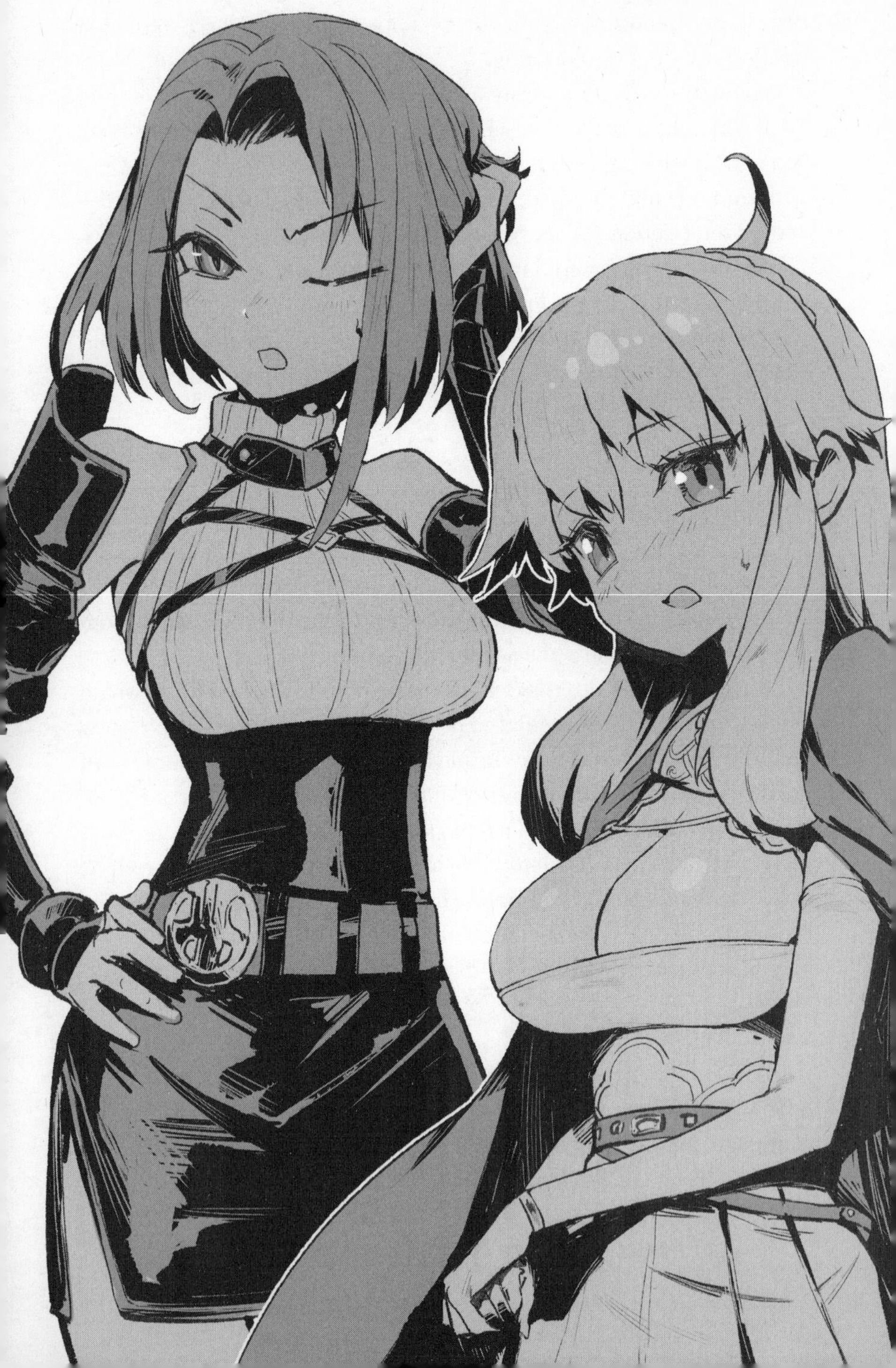

mandibles. "Break up the party and go our separate ways, apologize and make up—doesn't matter to me either way," Myrmidon Monk says. He's standing directly beside you with his arms crossed and his antennae waving in a distinctly annoyed manner. "But whichever it is, let's do it after we get this half-dead heap of human to the temple, shall we?"

"Yes, certainly," Female Bishop says, and then she smiles. "I'm sure our dear leader hates to be kept waiting, don't you think?"

Damn right, you try to say but can't; you manage a slight smile instead. It causes someone to chuckle, and at that the entire room relaxes.

You likewise feel relieved. If your screwup had caused the party to fall apart, death would have been too merciful for you.

As everyone else promptly starts preparing to withdraw, Half-Elf Scout exclaims, "Hang on a sec!" He scuttles over to the scorched wizards, producing purses from the singed robes. "Ooh, these guys were loaded. Listen to those coins jingle. We're rakin' it in!"

"Well, at least you earned something from getting yourself hurt like that," Female Warrior says with a glance at you. "Although I get the feeling we're going to spend it all fixing you back up." The gentle jab seems aimed at repairing the atmosphere.

You shrug, leaning on your katana like a walking staff to help pull yourself to your feet. The others are quickly alongside you to support you.

"Are you all right? Just tell your sister if it hurts…"

Stupid second *cousin* is what you want to say, but to be perfectly frank, it's too much trouble. You've lost too much blood. You don't feel pain so much as an overwhelming fatigue. Your eyelids feel heavy as lead.

"All right, Cap, chin up. We'll have you back up to the surface in no time. Here's hoping we don't run into any more 'friends'.…"

"This'll slow down our exploration a bit… Do you suppose this was only what they would call the appetizer?" Female Bishop asks.

"Maybe, and they say the stairs to the fourth level haven't even been found yet," your cousin replies. "We don't have to rush—let's just take it nice and easy!"

"Good advice, including for our trip home, here. We could get hit by slimes on the first level again."

"No fair, saying that… That was so awful."

As you listen to your friends chatter, you quietly swear on the Dungeon Master's hair that you'll have your revenge.

"Heh, guy's gotta be bald, I guarantee it," Half-Elf Scout quips, and things get even more relaxed among the party.

"Hey, with you out of action… I want to kick down the next door!" Female Warrior, now the party's only dedicated front-row fighter, sounds like an eager child. You give a wry smile and a nod, and she laughs out loud, a cheerful grin blossoming on her face.

You're not sure whether it's deliberate, or if she's really back to her usual self already. But the edge between her and your cousin is gone. Privately, you're deeply relieved.

Female Warrior seems to intuit how you're feeling, because she grins like a contented cat and jabs your cousin with her elbow. "Turns out he's the first one to make us go to the temple, eh?"

"You know, you're right! Somehow I always thought that would happen. I mean, it sort of had to, right?"

Female Warrior is grinning; your *second* cousin is smiling, too—curse them both.

You purse your lips, hoping to communicate: *Shut up and get me to the surface already.*

A second later, your consciousness blinks away like a cut string.

§

When you come to, a starry sky fills your vision. You felt like you were down there for ages, but it was really only about half a day. They say space feels warped inside the dungeon, and it seems to do the same to your sense of time. A cool night breeze brushes your cheeks as you raise your heavy eyelids.

The chill breeze and fresh air help you get a hold on your still fuzzy consciousness. You're already well away from the dungeon entrance, nearly at the gate to town. Somehow you didn't imagine you would live to see another starry night like this.

You could thank the gods; but if you don't, that's fine, too.

"Oh, you're back. Hee-hee, see how easy it is when we don't run into any slimes?" Female Warrior chuckles as she looks at you.

Your cousin nods: "We're out of the dungeon, and everyone's alive. I'd call that a good dive, wouldn't you?"

With your slackened muscles, honestly, even standing is hard. You'll have to let your *second* cousin's remark go this time.

Female Bishop sees how you look and says, "Let's hurry to the temple. We're not out of the woods yet…"

"Yeah, it looks like he can't even talk," Female Warrior remarks.

It's Myrmidon Monk who gives an *Okay*. Then he works his carapace-clad body under one side of you. "I'll take this side. Somebody get the other one."

"Just leave it to me!" Half-Elf Scout slips up to support the other side of your body. Then, with you leaning on your two party members, you all hurry through the streets of the fortress city toward the temple.

You attract the looks of passersby. Some of them are adventurers. At first, they appear pained to see your companions dragging your blood-soaked body. But they quickly realize that you're still breathing, and with evident relief, they make way for you.

This is the fortress city. For those who would challenge the dungeon, the Death is ever present; it cannot be escaped.

They may not be your friends or companions or anything else, but they're adventurers just like you.

It's not a short distance to the temple. It feels strange, though— surrounded by your party members, it somehow doesn't hurt so bad.

As you linger on the edge of death, the members of your party support you. They change places, then change again in a rotating array of faces and voices. If it hadn't been you who had been struck down, if it had been someone else, they would have done the same. You're sure of it. The thought brings you happiness as you struggle with your guttering consciousness.

Presently there's a banging sound, and you realize that the temple doors have opened. Your friends all but drag you to the altar, and you hear them, as if from a great distance, requesting your healing.

The last thing you remember is a brief pronouncement from the nun, who regards your prone form with a cold glance:

"Huh. So you're still alive."

§

"Hey, kiddo, remember the legend of the master archer?"

The first time your master asked that question, you were still young and had just begun learning the sword. But while your master still looks the same as back then, you are your present self as you sit before her.

Your master was a bit sex-crazed, often out chasing women, but sometimes the two of you had these little chats, as well. She reaches into her *gi*, toward her slight chest, and gives you a toothy smile. "They say he learned the art of shooting without shooting, that he could hit a bird without firing an arrow. Eventually, he threw away his bow."

You nod: You remember. You don't know how you answered when you were younger, but now, you remember the story.

"Good," your master says, the word merging with the rustling of the branches as the wind blows through her hut.

Outside, it's summer. The blue sky is warm, the clouds dizzyingly white. You smell the rush mats, the incense, the medicine, and finally the sweat on your body and your master's.

"Question." Your master exposes one shoulder as if hoping to beat the heat a little, brushing hair away from a pale neck as she leans back easily. "This master archer. You think he was all he was cracked up to be, or was it just a con all along?"

You let the question hang in the air for a moment, then reply that you think he was truly a great man. If he was a master indeed, then of course he would no longer need his bow. It would be no impediment to him to be without it.

Your master's grin widens at that answer. It's the same way she always smiles, neither happy nor mocking. "I see, I see. So that's your thinking. The real masters, the ones who really know what they're doing, don't have to worry about weapons." She stretches her arms as she speaks, hiding nothing of herself as she relaxes, and then she takes up the katana lying by her side. The pale blade sings out as she draws

it. It gleams dangerously even in the gloom of the hut, hinting at what a fine piece of work it is.

"It's anonymous." She seems to have noticed your gaze. She rests the plate lightly against her shoulder and says thoughtfully, "But us, we revere our equipment. Only natural, isn't it? If you can pick up just any old thing and be strong…" Now the sword slices silently through the air, driving directly at you. There was distance between you, separation, yet the blade ends up at your throat as though space has constricted. "Then how much stronger will you be if you put a little thought into it?"

Her smile is like a tiger bearing its fangs. Your master is capable, without twitching an eyebrow, of eating you alive or of backing off entirely.

It's no longer clear to you how you answered back then. But as for now, the present you, you form syllables of protest with your mouth. "Mm?" your master says, urging you on.

You tell her a master with a great weapon against an amateur with the same will win out every time. That much is clear. In other words, it's the skill and not the sword that tells.

"Izzat right?" your master remarks when she hears your answer and slides her sword back into its scabbard.

The instant she appears to do this, though, *poof*: The sword is resting across your knees. Startled, you pick it up, and your master spreads her arms as if to say, *Look*. She tilts her head slightly. "But there's fortune in battle, too. A master with a crappy sword versus an amateur with a masterpiece? Can't be sure how it will turn out. Why, you might be able to kill me right now."

She exposes her pale, unsunned throat and chest, giving you the innocent, inviting smile of a girl, and laughs. Her body seems so slight you can see the bones through her skin. It feels as if even with only the strength you had back then, you could break them easily. If you tore open those thin blue lines, would they gush with startling red blood?

In the distance, you hear the cicadas crying their protests against the heat. But then you feel the sweat forming on your brow, and even the cicadas stop. Too tired to go on or eaten by birds?

You swallow heavily. The sound of it seems so great. This must be what it feels like to face a real tiger.

It's not the fact that your opponent could devour you in the next instant—but that you might be able to cut her down. The possibility. That the very idea enters your heart is what's so terrifying.

Finally, you grip the hilt of the sword, hands slick with sweat, and gently set it beside you on the floor, on the side of your dominant hand. It's only proper etiquette.

There's fortune in battle. One can't know how fortune will go, meaning there is no guarantee of success in any challenge.

"Mmm. So that's it, eh?" Your master straightens up; her murmur might indicate a loss of interest or an increase. Either is possible. "You talked about skill earlier. And luck. Said gear didn't have much to do with it. That's an answer…and not an answer."

As she speaks, your master stretches out with one bare foot, reaching for a tray sitting at the edge of the floor of the hut; she grabs it with her toes—unladylike thing to do—and pulls it over to her. She takes a packet of medicine from the top of it, a full sake bottle and a bowl with no lip, and pours the bowl full of the drink.

"All right then, another question." She takes a satisfied sip of the sake, swallowing noisily. Her red tongue licks away droplets on her lips; her cheeks, more colored than before, relax into a smile. "You're a master." Her finger extends suddenly, pointing at you, then at the air beside you. "And so is your opponent. However!" She takes another mouthful, then two mouthfuls, watching you with languid eyes. "Your opponent holds the masterpiece weapon, you the piece of junk. Now, what do you do?"

You can't answer.

Couldn't then, can't now.

Even in such a situation, you would probably throw yourself into the fight. But that—that's both an answer and not an answer.

When your master sees you, lost for words, she chuckles good-naturedly, deep in her throat. "Heh, that's about right. No one can say and do the right thing all the time, every time."

Then she lets out a warm, easy breath, all four limbs spontaneously relaxing. There's no tension in any part of her, and at the same time she loosens her collar, looking up and letting the wind fill her *gi*. It's utterly mannerless, this way of relaxing, and it has none of the intimidation of moments ago. She looks just like a cat stretching out in the sun. Red-faced, you drop your eyes to the floor.

"You can have that sword," she says. She rises quickly, kicking away the empty bottle and starting off at a slow walk. Going to go "play" again, you suppose. Even as she walks right by you, you don't hear a footstep.

"We can have another little riddle game sometime. Maybe you'll know the answers; maybe you won't."

The door clatters open, then rolls shut again with a clack. You look up slowly, then gradually draw out the sword lying by your side. It gleams dangerously. But not blindingly; this is the gleam the sword will one day possess.

The blade comes out of the scabbard without a sound, and without a sound it returns. It's not just a sword.

There's a faint smell left in the room, a mildly fetid odor of sweat mixed with your master's medicine. Not wanting to relax your posture, you take a slow breath, looking studiously at the sword in your hands.

From beyond the paper that covers the sliding door, the cicadas begin crying again. So they survived, after all.

It's unbearably hot.

§

"Ah. Eyes open now, are they?"

No, no, that can't be right.

You tell yourself this despite the chilly whisper that reaches you through the dark.

You're so far yet from being enlightened, from being someone whose eyes are open.

Nowhere near true understanding.

"I meant something a bit more utilitarian."

You hear a small, dismissive snort, and finally you physically open your eyes. Even before you register what you see in front of you, you pick up the cold chill of the stone bed—no, the altar—that you're lying on. Then the wavering light of the candle reveals what's around you, and you catch your breath.

"Something wrong…?"

You're in a great hall filled with the susurrating echoes of prayer; who wouldn't be surprised to see the young lady before them, so totally devoted to her god? Especially when they registered that her skin, pale and translucent as glass, wasn't covered by a single scrap of clothing?

It's the nun you so frequently meet at the temple—but it takes you a second to realize that. Her average-sized chest looks as if it were carved from marble, the lines of her body smooth and neat and beautiful. Her composed, porcelain face has the faintest flush of pink in the firelight. You finally manage to look away when you realize she's staring daggers at you.

"…I'm apt to charge you for the look, you know."

Does that mean you can look if you pay? You chase the naughty thought out of your mind.

You bow your head in embarrassment—realizing in the process that you're buck naked, too—and she mutters, "Gods…" Then she goes on: "It's all right; I'm not angry. Frankly, your reaction was substantially less lewd than most adventurers I've encountered." You look up at a rustling of cloth to find she's pulled her habit back on.

You glance around, locating your own clothing folded neatly nearby, and promptly get dressed. The two of you sit back-to-back on the altar as you silently dress, finishing by tying your belt.

"I must admit, I'm impressed you made it back here." As she pulls her hair up from under her collar, her aroma seems to come with it. Maybe it's the incense. It's the first time you think *incense-like* could be a compliment. "Even the Resurrection miracle isn't a guarantee, after all."

Resurrection.

Now it makes sense, you think, as you realize what ritual she was performing for you.

Life can be restored by sleeping beside a virgin, the soul called back from the edges of eternity—truly a work of the gods. It isn't quite the

©lack

same as raising the dead, but considering the state you were in, it remains an admirable achievement.

Here's the truth: The dead don't come back to life. No one living can escape death. You realize that despite having been brought face-to-face with this fact, you didn't feel any special fear. Your hands aren't shaking. It surprises you, so you look down at them to be sure.

"We aren't merely talking about life proper. We're talking about the soul."

You raise your head again, startled. The nun's calm, clear eyes aren't far away from yours. Her gaze pins you in place. It's as if she can see straight through you. In your mind, her eyes look like those of your master. Even though you know they look nothing alike.

"Heal the body as thoroughly as you wish; if the soul has no desire to return home, then you're lost."

She's practically read your thoughts.

No one wishes to experience death again and again. And many wish to live longer than their allotted span.

Wonder which I am.

It's not that you specifically desire to live. Rather, you live because you haven't died. That's how it seems to you.

"So many are like cooling ash. So many of the adventurers in this city." The nun's eyes turn away. No—her face turns away, but her eyes still follow you. "It seems you are different."

You wonder about that. You repeat the question to yourself—and think. Those adventurers who spend their time in this town and you: You're all adventurers. Where's the difference?

When you first got here, you thought you were different. You're not so sure now. Maybe you're the same—in the end, it's only whether you live or die, isn't it?

The nun smiles with a certain exasperation to see you so deep in thought. "If you have the time to contemplate, then you should spend it taking care of other priorities."

You wonder aloud if maybe she means you should thank the gods.

"Don't be ridiculous." She snorts. "It's my duty to sleep beside you in return for a donation. But it's not the gods' duty to do anything in return."

They don't work based purely on what they get out of things. But people, with their narrow minds and narrow perspectives, are so quick to think the gods are mocking them when things don't go their way.

The nun hops down from the altar, straightens up, and heads for the door with hardly a footfall. "Be thankful to everything."

You think about this for a second, then nod and begin by thanking her for performing the ritual for you.

The nun stops, glancing back before she exits the room. "You're welcome," she replies with a nod, and in her eyes is the hint of a smile like the sun the morning after a snowfall.

If, that is, you aren't just imagining it.

§

You reckon it's before dawn. The almost painfully quiet temple seems filled with a thin purple mist. The lights that flicker among the haze must be the candles on the wall.

You almost unconsciously breathe as quietly as possible, so as not to disturb the silence, and you walk toward the chapel, trying to mini-mize your footsteps as you go. As you work your way among the pews, you realize there are some people present. Adventurers waiting for their companions to be healed—or perhaps praying for the repose of their companions' souls.

Past that handful of worshippers, in front of the altar, you find who you're looking for. Female Bishop, kneeling in silent prayer—your party member.

Seeing her that way, you're a little bit embarrassed to call her a cleric. Particularly when you think of what just happened. And when you consider the effort it must have taken her to come so far...

But here in the first light of dawn, she looks altogether fit for the name.

"Oh..." When you take a few steps closer, a word not of prayer comes out of her mouth. Her vestments rustle as she gets to her feet and comes toward you at a measured pace. She must have noticed you. Her mouth works its way into a smile. "Thank goodness... You've come to. Your body, is it—?"

She regards you with her sightless eyes, and you gently nod your head. After receiving a miracle from the gods, everything should be fine. In fact, you feel bad for interrupting her prayers.

Female Bishop looks relieved when you say so. Come to think of it, she's removed her gear already and let down her hair. You don't see your other companions, either—obviously, you didn't expect them all to forgo sleep to wait for you. You know they're tired from the delve. You assume they've retired to the inn, and that's all right with you.

You give voice to your conjecture, and Female Bishop replies, "Yes," and nods. "I took a bath at the inn, then returned here by myself. Everyone was so tired... Not to mention, having such a crowd here would have simply been a nuisance."

You nod in understanding and tell her that explains the sweet smell of soap you can detect.

"Yes. Your honorable older sister said we should at least take a bath and relax a little."

It seems she dragged Female Warrior and Female Bishop with her the moment they got to the inn. By "bath," you assume all they did was wipe themselves down with cold water—no way they went to an actual bathhouse.

Gods, but that would be just like your cousin. But it takes a load off your mind, makes you happy, to know things are going along just like usual.

"I tell you, it wasn't easy when you lost consciousness. There was quite a bit of panicking..." Female Bishop laughs an audible "hee-hee." Female Warrior just about lost it when you all arrived at the temple, and your scout had to try to talk her down while Myrmidon Monk made the donation.

You mention how hard it is to imagine Female Warrior in such a panic.

"Yes, absolutely... Your older sister looked calm, though, as far as I could tell. And I was so sure it would be the other way around," Female Bishop says, but you've always known your cousin to be preternaturally steady. The nun must have looked thoroughly exasperated; the mere thought brings another smile to your face.

When you think about it, it was truly good luck that you all made it through that battle in the dungeon. Especially the way your collapse galvanized everyone: That was unexpected. There could be no more joyful thing, in fact. You don't betray any hint of these thoughts, though, as you tell Female Bishop that it would have been fine by you if she'd gotten some rest, too.

"Oh, thank you—yes, I was told 'either way's fine,' but me, I…" She looks down at the ground shyly. There's a moment of silence. Then the words bubble out of her throat like bitter water. "I couldn't do anything else to help…"

You say nothing. What should you say to her, as she stands there with her shoulders shaking?

In the end, you simply reply, '*I see,*' and sit down on one of the pews.

After a moment, Female Bishop sits down beside you. You pretend not to hear the low moan that escapes her.

"Um, leader…"

You let your gaze drift to the holy sigil of the Trade God mounted on the altar as you ask her to continue.

"Am I…am I truly of help?"

You take a deep breath. Female Bishop's shoulders twitch.

'*Was that all that was bothering you?*'

"Wh-what do you mean, *all*? You're terrible. I've been agonizing about it…"

Ahem, hmm. You nod, discomfited, scratching the back of your head. Of course, *ahem*, you understand perfectly well what's been bothering her. She's afraid that if she doesn't prove her usefulness, she'll be dumped back at the tavern, and you can't blame her.

But then—well, as a practical matter, your delves into the dungeon would be far more difficult without her. Particularly this last one. Having a confident guide allowed you all to reach the surface safely, even with you on the brink of death.

Humility aside, your party is made up of adventurers who can attempt to challenge the third floor of the dungeon. You failed your first battle, true enough, but with all the power she's gained, Female Bishop can't possibly *not* be any help.

Bit by bit, word by word, you manage to communicate all of this to Female Bishop.

"You… You really think so?"

You nod. You really do think so. Hell, now that you think about it, you're a lot less use than she is. You just stand up front swinging a big, sharp stick around, maybe tossing in a spell if you have the time. Certainly, last time out you didn't do more than that.

You tap your neck, clearly depressed as you explain all this, but Female Bishop retorts, "That's absolutely not true!" her voice urgent. "Please stay up front for us, taking the van and making the calls! Even at the tavern, I'll—!"

'There, see?'

"Wha…?"

That. You start laughing. That won't happen. Not to you, not to her.

"Oh…" As she realizes she walked right into that one, Female Bishop puffs out her cheeks and grumbles, "Gosh…"

That's right. Nothing like that will happen. She's just overthinking it.

However—to so lack confidence in herself, you think the problem must have fairly deep roots. And you think it's more than just the way she was left in the tavern to do item identification for so long. Even if her infamous experience with the goblins is at the bottom of it…

"I… You see, I…" When you ask Female Bishop about it, the words come out one by one, like slow drops of water. "I was brought up to be something of a hero."

She then adds with a grim smile: "Even though the blood in my veins is nothing special."

Her family, it seems, is descended from a Platinum-ranked hero of old. To be related to such a legend, even on just a branch of the family tree, one was expected to be quite powerful. Female Bishop tells the story in fits and starts, but you get the impression that she wasn't "brought up" so much as she was "tailored."

Before she had even reached the age of majority—fifteen years—she already possessed power and skill enough to be recognized as a bishop. And not simply through the gifts of birth or nature. She had done the work and earned the accolades.

"And yet, all I could do was use both magic and miracles. Miracles alone, there was another child who could perform them, and more skillfully..."

She whispers a name, then, perhaps belonging to one of her old comrades or perhaps to a friend from her native village. Thus, she says, she determined to become an adventurer. And yet when she did so...

"In the end, it proved fruitless. I never caught the knack of it and only slowed down my party."

She was saved. Looked after by her companions as they traveled. And then she was left again.

"I should have known it wouldn't be so easy. That making life give you what you want from it was always going to be a challenge..."

A fleeting smile passes over her face. There's no room for doubt: In her own way, she's fought, struggled, and strived to get ahead.

You avert your gaze from whatever is seeping through the bandage around her eyes, looking up at the chapel ceiling. Maybe it's a trick of the light, or maybe just copious donations, that make it look so very far away—impossibly high.

It can't possibly have been all bad things.

You then whisper that thought into existence, trying to choose your words carefully. Indeed, there are certain things you almost envy about Female Bishop.

"What...?" It sounds like she can't quite believe you. But she only needs to think about it. How many people are there in this world, really, who know the meaning of their own lives? Not many have any clue as to why they were born or what they should be doing.

You walk the path of the sword, seeking the highest heights of the blade. Doing battle with the Death down in the dungeon is just another step on your journey. But if someone were to ask you whether that's the right and proper way to use your life, you wouldn't be able to answer. The road goes ever on and on, far into the great distance; indeed, it may have no end at all.

But Female Bishop... For Female Bishop, it does.

A hero in training. A hero who can bring peace to the world. At first, it was a mission given to her, but now it's become something she seeks of her own volition.

"Oh…"

The way is dangerous, and difficult, surely…

But the way is her own, and that, you envy her—you offer these words, and then you fall silent.

"I had… I'd never thought of it that way before…"

Well, then she can start thinking of it that way now. This you say more sternly, as if ashamed of words you didn't expect to speak. She's still only partway along the path. Of course she's incompletely formed. And not just her, but all of you. Why worry so much, then? Why twist yourself into knots?

Just go on walking, silently. That will be enough.

Be thankful to all things—that's what the nun said. All things are fate and fortune. The good and the bad—what could be better than to go on walking with both of them alike?

"Still…only partway along the path," Female Bishop whispers, and you nod again that you think so. When it comes to the dungeon, you've only reached the third floor. The way ahead is long. That makes her crucial to your party, with her ability to work both spells and miracles. With her as your nucleus, you can set up any formation, respond to any situation. Thanks to her, there are more paths your party can choose.

Above all, to proceed down the road, you need a map, or else you're only wandering lost.

"Hrm," she mumbles, pursing her lips once you've said your piece. "I'm not sure that's fair. You're treating me like a child fishing for compliments."

You laugh, loud and deliberately. It's just… Well, if you don't put things this way, it will be that much harder for her to have confidence in herself. Besides, you are what you are, this time. You pound your neck demonstratively and tell her everyone must fix their mistakes.

Female Bishop looks at you for a long moment. Despite the bandage over her eyes, it's obvious she's scowling. "Very well then, ahem… *cough*." After a moment, she coughs adorably, then comes up so close her knees are almost touching yours. "In that case, I agree: I'm glad I met you and everyone."

Hrk…

You grunt. This feels a bit like a sneak attack, but then she comes even closer. "And as such, might I ask you not to—well, not to get injured would be unreasonable. But at least not to die? Otherwise, I will never forgive you."

All you can manage is another grunt.

Female Bishop giggles and says, "That's payback," then rises to her full height with an elegant movement. "All right, I'm going to go tell everyone else you're awake." She points out that too much talk could put a strain on your body and requests that you go get some rest. Her tone still doesn't sound completely relaxed, but it does seem as if a burden has been taken off her shoulders.

That could be your misperception, but you sincerely hope it's true.

"A long day and a refreshing night. Rest well."

And even more to you. Rest well.

§

"Gods above, I thought you were dead."

The next day, you and Female Bishop go early to the inn, where you're greeted by these words. Female Warrior, in civilian clothes, has her hands to her cheeks in an over-the-top expression of exasperation, which she accompanies with a sigh.

There's nothing you can say to that, so you only offer a wry smile.

This was a direct result of your inexperience.

Alive, maybe, but hungry as hell.

You physically don't have enough blood. You'll eat anything they put in front of you—so you wish they would hurry up and do just that!

This leads to you dragging the rest of the party to the Golden Knight. Thankfully, there are no objections, and even more thankfully, your usual table is still open. You sit down just as you always do, then call over the harefolk waitress, just as you always do.

"Ah, celebrating a triumph, are we?" she whispers, her ears bobbing, as she assesses the situation at a glance. You smile, sort of, your fingers brushing the bandage around your neck. You might be proud if it happens to leave a scar.

You order substantially more than usual, after which your cousin claps her hands. "I'm so glad you survived. I can't even tell you. After all…" She grins, and then your *second* cousin turns toward Female Warrior. "This means I win our bet!"

"You were betting?!" Female Bishop exclaims, getting to her feet in disbelief. Even you look at them in some amazement. How could you not?

"Yeah, yesterday. After we got back to the inn, we were all talking."

"…And someone has to lose, or it's not a bet," Myrmidon Monk says sarcastically, clacking his mandibles. He fishes inside his kimono and comes up with a bag of coins that he tosses noisily onto the table. Female Warrior likewise ruefully adds a pouch of coins.

At the jangle of money, the scout places a hand on both their shoulders, grinning. "Point is, it's their treat today!"

"Yeah, yeah. Bah, I lost out…"

So Female Warrior says, but is it just you, or does she actually sound pretty happy? Thinking you have a sense of what they bet on, you simply shrug. It's something of a superstition, to encourage good luck. If you'd died, you don't think the winners of the bet would be as pleased as they are at losing now. At least, you're pretty sure. You hope not.

You think back on the trouble on the delve and realize it might be bothering Female Warrior more than you had considered. As discreetly as possible, you suggest to your cousin that she not overdo her winning privilege.

"Of course not! They always guard us up front. I won't order too much."

It's not clear for whose benefit your cousin is saying this, but Female Warrior gives her a smile at once conflicted and on the verge of tears.

It'll be okay… Probably.

It's not easy to tell what's in the depths of people's hearts, and it may not matter whether you forgive her. Female Warrior might blame herself somewhere deep inside, but look, the two of you will be able to look each other in the eye until the day you're both gone.

You won't forget. Neither will your party members. And Female Warrior, of course, will always remember. So instead of trying to pass things off with a simple word of forgiveness—well, this is probably the better for both of you, even if it hurts.

Your contemplation is interrupted by the arrival of breakfast. Very convenient, as far as it goes. You start wolfing down the steaming barley porridge, chasing it with cheese and dried meats and wine.

"Your stomach won't stand up to that for long," Myrmidon Monk clacks, and you shoot back at him to mind his own business, then resume your focus on filling your empty belly. Everyone else smirks at your desperation to sate your starving body, but who cares? You haven't eaten anything for a couple of days, counting the time you were down in the dungeon. You feel like you could eat a dragon, skin and all.

"Gosh…," your *second* cousin says, moving to wipe your mouth, but you ignore her and offer an idea.

Let's call today a rest day.

Then you wait for a second. It's not that you have something stuck in your throat—but you take a somewhat panicked drink of wine anyway. You drink it down.

If everyone's all right with it. You choose your words carefully. Yes, if everyone agrees:

In a day or two, we'll challenge those tiger-masked ninjas again.

"……"

"……"

There's a pause. Your companions stop eating, their gazes meeting above the round table. Hmm. Did they think you would go running with your tail between your legs just because you wound up on death's doorstep once?

"Well, now," Half-Elf Scout says with a smile and a shake of his head, his tone gently teasing. "Here I thought sure you'd suggest we get new gear or train a little more or something like that."

You smile back. You're not without a plan, you inform them. Though you don't know how well it will work.

"If you have an idea, then I don't object," says Myrmidon Monk, who's already finished most of his meal and is munching on some fruit. He pushes aside some citrus fruits to get at an apple. He doesn't seem bothered by either the peel or the core. "We get in trouble again, we can just pull back. Fine either way."

"That's a good point… As your older sister, though, I can't help but wonder if that wouldn't be overdoing it. Hmm." She taps a finger against her lips as if considering a little brother who's said something particularly vexing. After a moment she begins, "Say," and leans over, setting her chin in her hands and her elbows on the table, as she looks at you. "Want your older sister to teach you a spell?"

You think about that for a second, then shake your head. You don't think you could run straight to magic just because you lost a fight with your sword. You tell her you want to try hand-to-hand combat one more time. If you're defeated again, then you'll come crawling to your *second* cousin for help with some spells.

"Heh-heh! Well, Sis will be watching from the back row to make sure you don't get hurt again, Little Bro!"

Real nice. This, when it's always your *second* cousin who's the first to come after you in any argument. You lock eyes with her, then laugh out loud. There's no problem.

Female Bishop fixes her eyes on you from behind her bandage and nods. "As for me, I'm set on coming with you." Her expression looks like she thinks she's a coconspirator in some kind of mischief. Since last night, you understand each other. Though that fact will remain your secret for now. She's going to save the world. You're going to test your sword arm. You have different goals but share the same path.

"..."

The only issue, then, is the one remaining person. Female Warrior's expression is unreadable; in her hand is a spoon she's been holding for some time. She realizes you're waiting for a response, and after a moment, she says, "Let's see... Yeah."

She nods uneasily, indicating her assent.

That's all?

"Well," she says, starting to smile, "if I objected, that would make me the villain, right?"

It's not an answer, but she doesn't appear inclined to say anything more.

Mm. You have no intention of forcing anything out of her, so the conversation ends there. A few moments later someone cracks a joke between bites of food, and with a laugh, Female Warrior joins in the chatter.

Only Female Bishop continues to stare straight at the two of you, pinning you down with those unseeing eyes.

§

Your katana slices through the air, leaving only the sound of rushing wind behind it.

Under the blue sky, the arc of the blade is like a white flash—at least, that's what you wish for, but instead you follow it closely with your eyes.

To induce your opponent to take an action, you must yourself take that action. Because the action your opponent takes is presumably the one most advantageous to them at that moment. So you step in, driving straight forward with your sword and then making a sweeping cut.

You've come back from the tavern to the inn, where you're around back, by the stables. In the end, you never found a good place to practice where you wouldn't bother anybody.

Wish there was some kind of training center around here.

Unfortunately, on the edge of town there are only huge, empty fields, and then the yawning maw of the dungeon. You could never shake the feeling that training there would put you too close to the Death and shied away from the idea. Some might even question the wisdom of doing training while you're still a convalescent, but it's precisely because you're recovering that you feel you must train. After all, within the next several days, you'll be confronting those ninjas again. You know full well that lying around for even a day or two can cost you muscle. Sinews may grow stiff, the skin inflexible, the body sore, the bones groaning. It might make only a hairbreadth of difference, but it could mean someone's death or an inability to slay the enemy.

It's in seeking that hairbreadth advantage that adventurers polish their skills and raise their level. Spirit, technique, and body: None of them can be allowed to dull or decline.

You don't claim to understand it completely yourself. To attain that understanding, you must walk the path of the sword one step at a time; that much is natural to you by now. The others are likewise training or preparing their spirits or gear. They might appear to be playing around, enjoying a little betting—but if it's in preparation for the next fight, then you have no complaint.

Then again, if that second *cousin is just lying around, she deserves a chewing out.*

Your mouth softens into a smile at the little joke, but you quickly force it away, chasing out all unnecessary thoughts. Though it hasn't been a long time yet, it hasn't been a short time, either, that you and these party members of yours have confronted both life and death together. At the very least, you trust that none of them is heedlessly wasting their time.

You assume they trust you in the same way, and you intend to rise to that trust.

Now, then…

You raise your sword over your head and focus on your technique. The thought of a powerful stroke to the neck makes you think of the "newbie hunters" you encountered before. They were certainly using crude steel weapons, nothing like the quick blade—maybe even a fist?—the ninja hit you with, but the comparison is still instructive. It was so fast, and yet you were able to block it.

Just lucky. You grind your teeth together with the renewed recognition. If you hadn't seen the Knight of Diamonds in his battered state, you might well have ended up looking just like him. Yes—as you did this last time.

You unconsciously bring your fingers to the bandage around your neck. Before, you were lucky to block the strike; this time, you were lucky that Resurrection was performed in time. Lucky to avoid death.

Would it be Chance again next time? Or Fate? Perhaps all depended upon the roll of the dice.

You think for a moment, conclude that it's not a fruitful thing to think about, and quickly cast the contemplation aside. If you have time to fret, you have time to work.

One thing's become clear after a few battles. Stepping forward to strike and then immediately falling back again isn't a realistic plan. Those who have only half-heard tales of the martial arts to go on often believe that sword combat is determined by strength alone. Or they decide that whoever is fastest, or whoever's weapon is sharpest, will always prevail.

But that's absurd.

You yourself don't know all the martial arts in the Four-Cornered World, but you know that both strength and speed are essential. And what gives rise to both of those is muscle, bone, and nerves.

After all, the body is like a mechanism, moving at the leisure of springs and levers and cogs. People often speak of transcending physical limits, but one can only perform motions that are physically possible. Swordsmanship exists within this sphere. It is a physical system for wielding the blade as efficiently, effectively, and precisely as possible in order to take another life. A way of discerning the most appropriate actions for the practitioner to take and then always taking them.

These ways are often written down in simple words that can communicate with anyone, particularly those with the talent. Perhaps it's the way of warriors and martial artists to ultimately write such things, but...

No, it's impossible.

Thus, you come to this conclusion after comparing the art you've received from your master with your own body. Dancing and pirouetting is one thing, but to cut forward and then fall back with no other preparation, no other technique, is simply too difficult.

Perhaps it's inexperience that leads you to draw this conclusion quickly, but it's all right; you have only a day or two to work. Rather than try to create some secret master's technique, better to work on what you can achieve within that time.

You steady your breathing, and in your mind's eye, you summon up the apparition of that ninja.

Right from the start, you have one overwhelming advantage against him. Namely, that down in the dungeon, you don't care who or what your enemy is.

Once you burst into that chamber, you simply have to be ready and willing to deal with whatever appears. Whereas those ninjas have no way of ascertaining if you're the adventurers from before when you come flying into their room.

If you do the same thing, they're bound to open the same way they did before.

And there—there is your opportunity for victory.

You shake out your left hand gently, then stand tall. With your feet shoulder-width apart, you feel your body move gently up and down as the breath leaves it, then flows through it again.

And now...

"Um, leader...!"

The unexpected shout causes you to break your focus on your training. You look up to see one of your companions jogging toward the stables, her footsteps slapping the ground.

"I've come to...to watch you train...!" Female Bishop excuses herself for intruding, her cheeks slightly flushed, her voice equally full of determination and readiness.

"......" With her is Female Warrior, her sleeve firmly in Female Bishop's grasp so she can't get away. With the way she's averting her eyes and scratching her cheek, she looks like a child being pulled along by her mother.

You grin and slide your sword into its sheath with a click. You'd assumed Female Bishop would be deep in the study of magic with your cousin, but here she is, and with Female Warrior, no less.

"We happened to run into each other at the temple, so I brought her with me!" Female Bishop says. You wonder if it was really a matter of "bringing," a question only made more pointed by the awkward look on Female Warrior's face. The thought of what must have happened makes you smile.

'Watching is all well and good, but there's not much to see here.'

"I disagree, sir, completely," Female Bishop says, shaking her head, sending ripples through her golden hair. She turns her unseeing eyes on you, and for some reason, she's smiling, clearly in excellent spirits. "It's always possible I might have to wield a weapon myself one day. It can't hurt to learn how! Can it?"

She looks to Female Warrior for confirmation, but the warrior only gives an ambiguous "Mm..."

Hmm? You shoot Female Bishop a probing look, and she nods emphatically at you. Ah, so that's it. Now you see. She's reading too much into things. You're not sure whether this comes from your

cousin's "instruction," or if it's a sign of Female Bishop's own matura-
tion, or perhaps of her naïveté. But if she's trying to be kind to you,
then far be it from you to let her effort be in vain.

You think for a moment, then glance around the stable, deciding
that it won't be any inconvenience to anyone else. You suggest a round.

"…You're sure?"

It's not completely clear what meaning Female Warrior's response is
intended to have in regards to your question, but after this soft answer,
she pulls back her luscious black hair, revealing her pale throat. Once
her arm passes over her head, revealing her face, you see the smile of a
wild animal baring its fangs.

"I might win again—like last time, eh?"

Hrm. You purse your lips. That was a draw—in fact, perhaps even
your victory. And even if it was a draw, fighting to a stalemate with a
spear when you have a sword is *practically* a victory.

"Huh," Female Warrior says when you inform her of this, smiling like a cat. "How about a little test, then?" She glances around,
sounding like she's playing a game. Then she kicks a nearby pitchfork
(there for feeding hay to the horses) up into her hands, grabbing it with
familiarity.

You copy her, freeing one of the long poles that separates the spaces in
the stable and taking it in your hands. Of course, including your katana
and dagger, you're now carrying three separate weapons, and that's
going to weigh you down. You loosen the katana at your hip, and Female
Bishop, seeming to understand what you have in mind, holds out her
hands. You smile at her willingness to help and give her the sword.

Perfect. You ask her, where she stands carefully holding the katana,
to be your referee.

"In the name of the Supreme God," she says, her hand to her small
chest, and she sounds like truthfulness itself. There's no one in the
world more fit to judge a contest than a disciple of the Supreme God.

Female Warrior takes in the way you look, then her lips arch into a
smile. "Now, no complaining later that it's not a weapon you're used
to, you hear?"

Goes for you, too.

You steady your breathing, move your feet shoulder-width apart, leaving your legs relaxed, then place your left hand on the pole as though it were a sheathed sword. Female Warrior twirls around and then points the pitchfork at you just as if it were her usual spear.

Quietly but firmly, Female Bishop says: "Begin!"

It's Female Warrior who takes the initiative. She dashes forward, moving much more quickly than you would expect of someone wearing sabbatons. By the time you register the grass scattering behind her, the tines of the pitchfork are already filling your vision.

You twist, stepping back with your left leg, the pitchfork passing right in front of you. Then you step forward with the right foot, your chest armor groaning as you unleash your wooden "sword." A rising stroke, upward from below. The stick describes an ascending arch cutting through the air.

By then, though, Female Warrior has already pulled her slim body back, and neither of your weapons is within range. "Ah—ha!" Laughter, a sound of genuine pleasure, bursts from her. You bring your wooden sword back in front of you, your hands slick with sweat as you try to grip it.

Avoid, cut. That's turned out to be too slow. What to do, then?

"Hey there, if you start daydreaming, I'll—!" Female Warrior launches herself forward, not giving you time to think. Your vision seems to constrict itself down to the pitchfork. Reflexively, or perhaps by inspiration, you let your wooden sword overlap with the ferocity of her incoming attack. There's a dull sound of wood and metal colliding. You brace your "sword" with your left hand to prevent it being pushed up and away. The pitchfork bites into the wood with a crack, and you lean into the weapon without thinking.

The faint chill of metal against the tip of your nose makes you realize that sweat is dripping from your brow. You might have avoided getting stabbed, just, but the move seems so much faster than that. The tines retract, and startlingly quickly, her face is there. Her expression is cold and cruel, her gaze sharp—but in her eyes there's a flickering.

"You're gonna die again," she teases. In the blink of an eye—almost literally—she disappears from sight once more. She gives you a peck on the cheek as she starts away again, and suddenly she's out of range. Your sword freed by the retreating pitchfork, you stumble a little as you regain your stance.

Twice now you've crossed weapons, and twice now you've returned to where you began.

"That one sucked for you." Your master's words flit through your mind, accompanied by her cackling laughter. One-on-one is one thing, but against a group, letting someone get the drop on you like that would mean certain death. If one person can pin you down, limit your movements, then you can be attacked by another, and then it's all over.

Just another way of saying that you were no end of lucky in your battle with the newbie killers.

Your concentration on the battle has narrowed your field of vision. Yourself, her, your sword, her spear—that's all you see. Even Female Bishop, probably watching you with some anxiety, is completely excluded from your thoughts. You have one single focus. How to overcome the hurdle in front of you, how to press forward.

After dodging, it's already too late. If you try to defend, she'll break through. The only way is to merge offense and defense into a single move…

"Have at!!"

Three times, four times, then five. Female Warrior steps in aggressively, her attacks relentless, before she expertly returns to the original distance. It's like she's dancing; to a third-party observer, it must almost look beautiful.

You, though, deliberately refuse to try to take advantage of the window of opportunity in those movements. There would be no point responding only after your eyes have accustomed themselves to her actions. And so, when the sixth round comes…

You're already moving, executing your plan. There's a dry *bam* of wood striking, and then the pitchfork flies off through the air.

Then there's only your pole, your sword, facing down Female Warrior. Her face runs with sweat, her cheeks are flushed, and her eyes are open wide.

"Is that…enough for now?" Female Bishop asks you, and that's the end of your battle. With her impaired vision, it's probably difficult to be sure.

"Aw, look, you broke it. That won't do," Female Warrior says, seemingly in response to Female Bishop's question. She sounds as if she were chiding a naughty child. You collect your weapons and replace the pole in the stable, then gather up the pitchfork from where it landed. You critically inspect the way it split. Not a bad plan for something you came up with in the heat of the moment, if you do say so yourself.

"I believe that's our leader's win, yes?"

No. You shake your head. It isn't lost on you, the way she aimed for your neck each time from outside your distance. All six times. That was the whole reason you were able to finally respond.

You murmur that it's another draw and add your thanks to Female Warrior.

"Heh-heh." She makes a pointedly triumphant chuckle, then spins the broken haft and slaps it across her shoulders. Her hair drapes over it; she looks back over her shoulder and sticks out her tongue at you just a little. "For a spear user like me to fight to a draw with a swordsman like you, that's my loss."

Sorry. Her lips move soundlessly, and you shrug in equal silence.

Probably her way of saying you owe the apology and restitution for the pitchfork.

§

"Oh, have you two made up?" Your *second* cousin's voice sounds unnaturally cheerful in the gloom of the dungeon, echoing around before it fades into the dark.

It's the day after your day of rest from the Resurrection miracle. The dungeon once again swallows you all. Nothing about that was going to change in a few days.

You're so familiar with the first floor now that you can practically say you know it backward and forward. You skirt around the dark zone, toward the ladder. If you avoid the rooms, then there are no battles to fight. The second floor likewise passes quickly, and now you're on the third level.

You try being silent for a while, but Female Warrior marches beside you with her usual inscrutable smile. In that case, you decide to focus once more on following the faint wire frame that stretches out into the darkness.

Thus, the answer comes from behind you—from beside your cousin.

"Yes, it went great!" The bright, clear voice is unmistakably that of Female Bishop. "I didn't really follow—I mean, I don't know what to make of a battle—but they definitely crossed sword and, uh, spear." You presume she's talking with her hands and body again. You can hear the cloth rustling, the sword and scales clinking. You know she can't see that well, but her movements seem swift and precise.

Already seen her fighting prowess once before, actually. You shrug, which provokes a smirk from Half-Elf Scout. "What's the matter, Cap? Don't get too tense, now."

He's right. You're on the third floor at this moment, heading for the room where you suffered that bitter defeat. You remember, when you walked through the entrance to the dungeon earlier, how the royal guard standing there seemed to want to say something. Perhaps to comment on how quickly you've returned.

Have to get right back on the horse when you fall off, or you'll end up scared to ride. You whisper something of the sort in reply, keeping your voice low so Female Bishop won't hear. Still, knowing how sharp she is, you think she might pick up even your whisper.

Then again, it's not as though you were saying it specifically so she *would* hear.

"Well, failure is experience, too," Myrmidon Monk interjects, his mandibles clacking. "If you survive it, there's a next time. And if you die, the rest of us will learn and get better."

In other words, winning and losing are all the same to him, huh? From that perspective, everything seems easier. Not that you can quite reach it just yet.

You go ahead, your footsteps lighter, proceeding through the dungeon.

Maybe we were hurrying too much during our last delve.

Now that you take your time, looking carefully in every direction, you realize how different the third floor is. Compared to the others—even if there are only two others—this floor feels…strange. For one thing, the path doesn't proceed in an obvious straight line; instead, the floor plan is made up of a complicated series of intersections.

"Just in case you didn't already know the Dungeon Master around here was twisted." Half-Elf Scout almost groans, frowning. "You let your attention slip for one second, you'll have no idea where you are."

You turn to the right, then to the left, then do an about-face to the right… The series of crossings threatens to give you vertigo everywhere you go. You fear you'll lose track of which direction you're facing.

"I'm starting to think I don't feel so good…," Female Warrior says, turning her collar up slightly. You ignore her but hear your cousin rifling through her inventory. "Want a candy to suck on?" she asks.

"Don't mind if I do," Female Warrior replies. A typical giddy conversation between women.

Then again, maybe you have something to learn from your *second* cousin's apparent nonchalance. You bite back a laugh and let the tension out of your shoulders, and you tell Female Bishop she's in charge of the map.

"Yes, sir." She nods energetically. "I've got it." But her voice sounds very small. You figure you should save a Point spell in case you get lost. Once you know where you are, you can get back again—if you survive the trip.

As these thoughts pass through your mind, the great, heavy door looms before you again.

"Word of advice," Myrmidon Monk says bluntly. "No guarantees we'll find the same thing inside as we did last time."

Goes without saying. You nod. Whatever's in there, what you do won't change.

"Hack and slash, eh?" Female Bishop whispers, and you briefly reply that yes, that's the idea. You add that your dear Female Bishop is being corrupted.

"I-I'm not being corrupted…," she protests, but you pass it off with a boisterous laugh. At least you don't have to worry about tension.

When your cousin sees this, she lets out a sigh that sounds theatrical, although it probably comes naturally to her. "As your older sister, I'm worried about how you've started to tease our party members."

How rude. It's not as if you've ever taken pleasure in tormenting a friend, and besides, you only have the personality you were born with. At the same time as you voice this objection, you put your hand gently against the door.

"Want me to kick it down for you?" Female Warrior offers in a stage whisper, and you shrink back a little before heaving a sigh. *No, no. No reason to change now.*

You're trying to make it in the world as a swordsman, even if you have a long way to go. As such, you can't let defeat lie. Nobody can have confidence in a sword defeated.

Wouldn't be able to interrogate the world with the blade, then. All the more reason you can't run away from a fight if you hope to survive as a swordsman and sell your skills. This process will repeat until the day you die—anyway, such are the words of an ancient swordmaster, according to your teacher. You almost think they make sense to you.

Then again, it's probably just your imagination. If a moment as innocuous as this were enough to achieve enlightenment, why would the swordmasters of the world work so hard to train? You suspect they're trying to recapture some inspiration they received a mere glimpse of at some point in their lives. And how could you fail to have confidence in swordsmanship honed in this way?

You take in a deep breath and let it out again. Then you spit on your palms and grab your sword by the hilt, feeling the familiar sharkskin wrapping against your skin.

Don't care what happens next.

Sometimes you just have to roll the dice.

You lift your leg and kick the formerly stubborn door as powerfully as you can. There's a crash as it falls inward, and you and the other adventurers pile into the room.

Your gaze follows the floating wire frame into the room, where a breeze moves ever so slightly. Perhaps it's what you would call an aura, or perhaps not; in any case, the darkness slithers into a solid form. If there's such a thing as palpable intent to kill, you feel it now, raising goose bumps on your skin.

Four of them.

You see them: the tiger eyes coming at you from the dark.

You must kill, and they must kill, and so indeed the intent to kill is palpable.

§

"The ninjas…!!"

Maybe it's Female Warrior who speaks. It isn't a scream, and it isn't a battle cry; you hear it only distantly. The moment you register the enemies, your body is already moving. You won't give your tiger-masked foes a single moment.

With a great yell, you thrust forward, then make a sweeping sideward cut. You hear a *whoosh* of air. You feel nothing under your hands. The ninja's figure disappears faster than the speed of sound.

Your vision blurs. The world feels heavy, as if you were underwater or struggling through molten lead. Somebody shouts, and the hair on the back of your neck stands up. But you couldn't care less. You cast aside all distractions, trusting your body to move.

At that instant, it seems a great flash illuminates the dungeon chamber.

"___!"

It's a moment's opportunity. Is it just you, or do the tiger masks seem to display surprise?

You clench your left hand and laugh.

Yes: your *left* hand. In which you're holding a dagger.

Your body groans with the effort of slicing with your katana with only a single hand, but it gave you a chance to draw and strike with your dagger. The blade bites into one of the ninjas, a critical hit, a firm *thwack* you can feel all the way up your arm.

Now, what would my master make of that? You feel sweat on your brow, but you also feel gratification, lightness of heart.

True, you've just done with intention what you did by instinct in an earlier battle, but…

In the traditional style of your sword school, you suspect one would block with the sword in the right hand, using the dagger in the left to

strike. You've done the opposite, blocking with the dagger and striking with the sword—that probably means the move belongs to some
other school. But what do you care? This is for survival. You think you
can hear your master chuckling at the idea.

Not trusting your left hand alone to carry the day, you quickly sweep
with your sword. You're slightly out of position—you're reaching. The
tip of your blade scrapes along something hard, but fails to cut flesh.
The ninja leaps backward noisily, and you glimpse chain mail on his
chest.

But what do you care, you repeat to yourself and ready your weapons once more.

Should be able to handle two of them.

Female Warrior giggles when you voice that thought, and your scout
cries, "Right!" with affected abandon.

You shout back to your companions, then charge at the ninjas again.

"—!"

"!!"

Your enemies are no slouches, though. Seeing that their opening
gambit has been rebuffed, they retreat several steps, and then a hail of
blows comes down upon you. You look swiftly ahead. From the right
comes a kick like lightning; from the left, a spear-hand strike like the
head of a venomous snake.

You act on instinct. You fling yourself forward, rolling across the
flagstones, sword arm first. There seems to be a tremendous impact
above your head. Though you don't really register this until it's all
over.

You regain your feet and stand up to find the ninjas to your left and
right have swapped. But their metal palm covers are bent, and cracks
spider across their shin guards. You rolled right between them.

I see it. In that instant, you assess what your enemies are capable
of. Yes, they're fearsome. Each exchange of blows will be desperate.
But... *We can win this.*

"!!"

With voiceless shouts, the ninjas launch themselves at you like wild
beasts. But they aren't moving in unison. Presumably, they hope to

attack not simultaneously, but for the second opponent to take advantage while you're distracted with the first.

The ninja bends his body into an S shape like a dragon. You slide back, aiming your blades at his stomach. Then you flip the blades around in your grip, using his momentum to drive them in.

"—?!"

You can feel the weapons sink in. It turns your stomach and is accompanied by a sound like a fruit thrown hard against a rock. Blood gushes out from the mask; the ninja breaks like a blossom and slams against the wall. He might have been clever enough to wear chain mail, but it won't stop an impact like that.

You have no time to admire your work, though. Words of true power are already in your mouth; you're focusing your mind and tensing your body.

There's a flash from the ninja's hand. You don't even glance at it but let your dagger overlap it.

'Sagitta quelta raedius! *Strike home, arrow!*'

There's a screech, and the unmistakable sparks of metal meeting metal light up the darkness.

"—?!"

You might be the only one there who understands what happened. The flash reverses itself, piercing the ninja, the one who threw it. The act isn't natural, of course—it's the doing of the Magic Missile spell, capable of twisting the world around it. You targeted the blade that was thrown at you with the ever-accurate spell, sending it back the way it came.

The masked ninja pitches backward with a great spray of blood, but the wound still isn't fatal. In fact, the one you stabbed a moment earlier is also getting to his feet, even as he chokes on his own blood.

But this is the perfect chance!

"Taaaake this!!" At your sign, Female Warrior gives an adorable shout, sweeping with the haft of her spear, taking her opponent's legs out from under him. Is it your imagination, or did she give you a relieved wink when you glanced over?

"You gotta be kidding me!"

Half-Elf Scout, for his part, is still okay. But then, so is his opponent. Half-Elf Scout appears to be exclusively parrying, making silly little sounds like *hiyah!* and *hoo-wah!* He's just managing to deflect the masked adversary's fists and feet with his dagger.

That's where to focus, then!

"Right! Three moves—coordinate with me!"

"I'm on it…!!"

Almost before you can shout *Now!* the girls on the back row raise their staves and their voices.

"Carbunculus!"

"Crescunt!"

As you add *'iacta'* in perfect rhythm, magical power wells up and changes the world. The Fireball spell comes bursting from both your cousin's staff and Female Bishop's sigil. Half-Elf Scout jumps backward, and the fireball trades places with him, taking up the argument with the ninja. The heat as it goes by singes your skin, sparks dancing through the air and a hot wind whipping through the enemy formation.

"—?!"

"?!"

The ninjas, consumed by an orange conflagration, flail and struggle, still voiceless. They look like human torches. There will be no escape from death this time.

The moment the room fills with the smell of cooked hair and flesh, it's all over. The only ones left moving among the drifting smoke are your six party members.

"…Guess I didn't get to do anything, in the end," Myrmidon Monk says flatly, and the atmosphere relaxes.

'Think that finally finished them off?'

"…Hmm, probably. Don't you?" Female Warrior, still not quite completely relaxed, gives the blackened corpses an exploratory poke with the tip of her spear.

Your memory of the occasion is hazy, but you think it nags at her, having let those enemies get away the last time. It looks like she won't be certain until she's stabbed each of the foes.

You leave Female Warrior to make sure everything's dead, looking

afresh around the room and then at your companions. All of you look
spent, sweat-soaked, shoulders heaving. That includes your cousin
and Female Bishop, and even Myrmidon Monk, despite his flippant
remark.

Now that it's over, you realize the fight only lasted a matter of
moments. You suspect the time your neck was slashed, likewise, was
a very brief encounter. You reflexively put your hand to your throat
as a chill runs down your spine, and your hand comes away sticky
with perspiration. If you hadn't trained with Female Warrior in how
to deliver quick, single blows to vital points, could you have continued to
defend?

You're about to thank her when you discover your throat is constricted, your tongue stuck to the roof of your mouth. Only then do
you realize how shallowly you're breathing, how fast. Your hands
on your katana feel impossibly heavy. You shake your head at the sudden explosion of sweat, the heavy fatigue in your shoulders. This is
truly the weight of the Death, and you desperately wish not to bend
under it, even if your own pride is the only thing holding you up.

So instead you look down at the scorched corpses of the ninjas and
declare proudly that the tiger-masked assassins are broken.

§

"We did it," Female Warrior says, bumping her gauntleted fist lightly
against yours.

You can't thank her enough—but the same could be said of all your
party members. When you get right down to it, this expedition was
entirely your own whim, so it must have been simple affection for you
that moved them to come along.

"I didn't really care either way," Myrmidon Monk says apatheti-
cally, mandibles clacking. "Our leader said we would win, and we did.
No complaints here."

You're grateful to hear that. When you say so, Myrmidon Monk's
antennae sway from side to side; he reminds you, "You'll recall I
wasn't any help."

"Don't worry—who knows if we might not run into another terrible monster on the way home?" your *second* cousin says, smiling—but you don't think it's very funny. She shows no sign of noticing your withering glance as she pats herself proudly on her abundant chest. "I think that was a pretty great Fireball I came up with, don't you?"

You won't deny it, but you're afraid that if you actively acknowledge it, there's no telling how badly she'll let it go to her head. Anyway, you thanked her for her help first thing. When you remind her of this, your cousin puffs out her cheeks sullenly. Oh well—she'll be in better spirits again by the time you get back to the surface. That's just how your cousin is.

"I do think there was definite benefit in studying," Female Bishop comments. You hear her whisper that it helped in this battle.

"There was something about some secret technique written in there, too. You know, controlling time and space or something or other." Your cousin always has the most unsettling things to say.

You sigh, shake the blood off both of your weapons, then wipe down the blades and sheathe them once more. Obviously, all of you remain prepared for battle. After all, one of your number is engaged in a contest even now.

Just up ahead, your scout is rifling through the ninjas' belongings and searching for any treasure chest they might have been hiding. He had to fight on the front line earlier, but this is his true battle. With that in mind, you stand next to him, careful not to disturb his thorough search.

"Feel free to talk to me, Cap; it's okay. Won't make any mistakes because of a little chatter." Half-Elf Scout seems to smile wryly. His eyes move constantly; his hands never stop. You think for a moment, then comment that perhaps he should consider returning to the back row.

"Good point," he says. "Being up front takes a lot out of you, that's for sure."

As a practical problem, if his hands were injured in combat, it would affect your income. Parties with no scout usually had their warrior open any treasure chests, on the understanding that they might simply have to absorb a trap, but that was a reckless way to proceed. There's always risk in adventuring, but that doesn't mean one should be oblivious to danger.

To this point, you've had Myrmidon Monk fight on the front row while your scout stays behind in deference to Half-Elf Scout's stamina. But if your monk, who has a Healing miracle, were to fight so hard that he no longer had the wherewithal to perform his miracle, it would defeat the point. So who goes in front—the scout or the monk? It's a difficult choice.

"Eh, I'll give it another try. Little rest should be plenty for me to work with my hands again."

You nod and voice your understanding. If he says so, he's probably right. Some people try to hide their fatigue and push ahead with their work, but he doesn't seem to be one of them. If he's going to be that diligent, then you won't contradict him.

After all, everyone followed you in this venture. You want to follow them in theirs.

"Oh-ho?" As you're thinking, keeping a vigilant watch all around the room, Half-Elf Scout suddenly exclaims. Everyone drops into ready postures, thinking it might be a trap. But Half-Elf Scout says, "All good, folks," and holds up a strange weapon in his fingertips. "Just wondered what this was. No big deal."

It's a butterfly-shaped dagger—or perhaps shortsword. Sort of like a blade with wings on it (hence "butterfly"), it has two blades in a cross shape. At first glance, there appears to be nowhere to hold it.

The effects of the earlier fireball are evident. It looks faintly scorched from the high temperature. The weapon appears to be intended for throwing rather than cutting, but how one would throw it, you have no idea.

"Looks a bit like a thief's dagger, but I'm sure I've got no idea what this is," Half-Elf Scout says, grasping what seems to be the "hilt" between the two blades and giving the weapon a pained look. The blades are so sharp that just running a finger along one would be enough to split the skin open. It's not clear why these ninjas were carrying such a thing, but the workmanship is evident. You're impressed that you were able to send it back at them.

"Would you like me to identify it?" Female Bishop asks, hustling over with evident interest and peering at the weapon. You don't know exactly how much she can see with her eyes, but she seems to be able to *sense* a good deal.

"No worries. Save it till we get back up top," Half-Elf Scout replies, stashing the weapon in his belt for the time being. From the jangling that comes from his pouch, you deduce that the take was pretty good today.

"Too bad for you." Female Warrior giggles at Myrmidon Monk. "If there'd been a trap, you might have had something to do." Myrmidon Monk jabs her gently in the side. "Don't care either way."

"Goodness gracious me," Half-Elf Scout groans, looking intimidated, and your cousin adds to the laughter. You take in a breath once more, your lungs filling with the cold air of the dungeon, and let it out. The air carries the intense flavor of the Death. But it belongs to these fallen ninjas. You and your party have come, seen, and conquered, and you are all still alive.

No complaints at all.

§

A damp breeze greets you as you come up to the surface, brushing your cheek. The sky is light, but at the same time, dark. It's around noon, but black clouds are brewing up. You suspect a storm is coming.

"Hard to tell what time it is when you come out of the dungeon, isn't it?" Female Warrior puts a hand to her cheek and lets out a breath.

For some reason, be it the miasma that suffuses the dungeon, or the tension of battle, you can't seem to rely on your body's internal clock. Even you aren't sure how long you've been down there. You murmur that you're just glad it isn't actively raining. If nothing else, it doesn't rain in the dungeon. None of you have any wet-weather gear along.

"…Rain or shine, it's all the same to us." The comment comes from the royal guard, who stands by the entrance of the labyrinth and looks up at the sky with a certain annoyance. You know her by sight now. She tells you that the guards *do* work in shifts—it just so happens that hers often comes when you happen to be going into the dungeon.

Adventurers might head down anytime of the day or night, and even if they didn't, there would be no telling when a monster might try to come out. You sympathize: It must be hard work. But the guard chuckles and waves away your comment. "Looks like you're all in one piece, again. Good, good. Not a lot of parties who really want to get down to that lowest level."

Is that so?

"You, and that Diamond whoever—that's about it. A few more who tried and never came back."

Is that really all? You nod, and after a few more pleasantries, you part ways with her.

You and your companions hurry along the road from the edge of town to the fortress city. You might have survived your adventure, but if you get rained on and then succumb to a cold, it will be no laughing matter.

"Oh, it's started," Female Bishop notes, glancing up at the sky—just as you pass through the city gate. A second later, you hear the first droplets smack against the flagstones, and soon it's a roar. "Eep!" your cousin exclaims as the deluge makes everything black as ink. "L-let's get inside somewhere…!" she cries, pulling her cape over her head in an effort to shield herself.

She and Female Bishop are the only party members not wearing armor, after all. Their soaked clothing sticks to their skin, giving you the impression that you can see the flesh underneath it.

"Yes, and I'm afraid we might catch cold…" Female Bishop doesn't seem terribly bothered by her translucent garments. Whether she doesn't care or hasn't noticed, you're not sure. Female Warrior, meanwhile, her dark hair soaked but the rest of her covered by her armor, looks more relaxed: "I wonder. It's actually kind of nice, cools you down…"

You wave her off. Now then, from here…

"Guess the Golden Knight's closest," Half-Elf Scout says. "Let's haul!"

That's it.

"Perfect," Myrmidon Monk says, his mandibles clacking, and you all go flying like arrows from a bow.

It's not long before the gentle, orange flicker of lanterns is visible through the rain, promising warmth. Though obscured by the haze of rain, they're unmistakably the lights that illuminate the sign of the tavern. You make a beeline for them, pushing through the door, water dripping noisily from you as you enter the building.

"Welcome home!"

The fact that you don't receive a simple "Hullo" is evidence that you're now firmly established regulars. A harefolk waitress comes bounding up to you, smiling. You order a beer ("I need to borrow a drying cloth!" your cousin interjects) and some hot food.

"I could sure go for some grape wine," your cousin says. "The warm stuff. And add a pinch of sugar, not pepper."

You indicate that this should be added to the order, whereupon the waitress replies, "Certainly!" and retreats to the kitchen while you take your usual seat.

"These girls are gonna eat us out of house and home, Cap," Half-Elf Scout whispers.

"Wha—?" Female Bishop sounds genuinely shocked. You laugh. Then everyone laughs.

At this rate, maybe it's more than a dream to think you'll push through the third level sooner rather than later. Then again, you can't imagine how deep this dungeon might go, so maybe it's all a dream. Even so, your goal is nothing less than to reach the deepest depths of the dungeon and destroy whatever hides there.

One must have high ideals but a careful step...

"Here you are!" the waitress chirps, pattering up with a cloth. You take it and dry yourself off as you reflect. Armor can save your life—but left soaked in rainwater, it can also rust, and even nonmetal parts can be damaged. Think about how ridiculous it would look if you were cut down because when you pulled out your sword at the crucial moment, it turned out to be a rusty squib.

"We need to do something about your hair!"

"Let's get some perfume on you when we get back to our room."

"Oh, g-goodness, thank you..."

Female Warrior and your cousin set about fussing over Female Bishop, setting up the kind of racket for which women are famous.

Female Bishop has the longest hair of anyone in your party, and the other two women are bent on drying it out a little. You grin to yourself and remark quietly that, in that respect, you men have it easier.

"True that," Half-Elf Scout agrees with a nod, but Myrmidon Monk clacks his mandibles with some hesitation. "Still, this rain," he continues. "It makes the burial mounds crumble…"

Ah. You're reminded that each race has its own particular concerns.

Just as you're about to settle at your accustomed round table, you notice some adventurers not too far away and stop. That glimmering armor and handsome aspect are unmistakable. You turn toward the third son of a poor noble family and ask what's going on.

"Ah, nothing special. We've reached the fourth floor, and we want to be sure of our map." The Knight of Diamonds wears a severe expression at first, but it softens as he looks at you. The members of his party all appear to be safe and accounted for, including the red-haired priest and the canid warrior.

You feel a twinge of regret that they've stolen a march on you once again, but on the whole, you're honestly happy for them. You say what matters is that they're all here safely, to which the knight softly replies that "safety is something, sure." Beside him, a slip of a silver-haired girl notices Female Warrior and gives a friendly wave. Female Warrior smiles a little and waves back.

"…Looks like you're doing well," the silver-haired girl says. "I was so sure you must be dead."

"Now, that's not very nice—here I am, alive and well."

Based on what Female Warrior told you earlier of her past, you think they must be old friends from the orphanage. But you don't want to stick your nose in where you haven't been invited.

How's the party doing? Has the leader proved reliable? Can she cope with slimes yet?

You cut their conversation out of your consciousness and turn toward the Knight of Diamonds.

'Awfully laid-back party for the group that's deepest of all into the dungeon.'

"To hear that from the ones nipping at our heels—I might think you're making fun of us."

The fact that he can say this laughing suggests the Knight of Diamonds doesn't really mean it.

You chuckle and reply that it only sounds that way because you're so tired and shrug. Heh—just the other day you were hearing that the stairway to the fourth floor was hard to find, and now you've been surpassed once again. That means next up is the fifth floor. Maybe you'll be the first down there this time...

"I'm afraid not. The truth is, we've already completed our exploration of the fourth floor." The Knight of Diamonds tries to sound nonchalant as he continues: "There's just one little wrinkle. No stairway to the fifth floor exists."

'*Come again?*' you ask, astonished.

The rain can be heard as it continues to pound down, now smacking against the windows of the tavern. Outside, it's dark as night—but of course.

There is nothing so dangerous as a dragon's open jaws. But knowing that and seeing it for yourself are two different things.

"Whoa-hoh!" Half-Elf Scout flies back out of the proverbial tiger's jaws—here it would be the dragon's jaws, you suppose—but you aren't as nimble as he is. At almost the same moment as you shout—you're not sure if you say *get down* or *get away* or what—the dragon roars, and its throat expands. The next instant, a great rush of superheated air fills the dungeon chamber, scorching your skin. That's both figuratively and not figuratively. The great, hot breath isn't actually fire, to be sure, but it's more than enough to swell your skin even as you watch.

"Ngh—hrrgh—hkk!" Behind you, your cousin collapses, clawing at her throat, sounding as if she's being choked. Her labored breathing makes it clear her life is in danger. You spare a glance behind you to find her not so much pale as ghostly white. You stop your feet from their instinctive urge to turn around, forcing yourself to step forward onto the front line. If the battle line breaks now—if you go to her—the only thing that waits for all of you is certain death.

Myrmidon Monk is clearly thinking the same thing; he waves his antennae, looking as agonized as you feel. "It's poison—don't breathe!!"

Dammit!

You drop to one knee but force yourself to rise again, desperate to

find some way to fulfill your duty as part of the front row here and
now.

No—you try to make yourself stand up, but the powerful poison
gas saps the strength from your body moment by moment. A burning
pain runs through you; with every breath, your lungs feel like they're
on fire. Beside you, Female Warrior clings to her spear, gasping as if
drowning even though you're on dry land. Neither of you has many
hit points left, and another swipe from the dragon's claws or jaws or
tail will be enough to finish you off.

And that's those of you in the front row, who have trained and
strengthened yourselves. How much worse will it be for those in the
back row? So you must go on. You have to try to block the gas from
reaching your cousin and the others, even just some of it.

Well, look at this.

The exact size of the dungeon never seems quite clear, but apparently it can accommodate that mountain of a body, those wings folded
atop it. You wonder how many years the scales, dark green as if covered with moss, have seen. One need hardly mention the claws and
teeth and tail that would trample the average adventurer like dust
underfoot. And above all, there's the dark red eyes that burn in those
deep eye sockets.

Down in these depths where there's no cover but only the endless
wire frame—to think you would meet a monster like this down here.
A green dragon!

Legend has it that the former hero, a Platinum-ranked adventurer,
faced such a creature all alone… The very attempt would merit being
counted among the brave.

If the dragon gets one more turn, you will die. You're surprised
to discover that, confronted with that simple fact, you're still calm
enough to reflect on old tales.

"You're…mine!!"

Just another way of saying that if we don't give it one more turn, we'll survive.

A cape flutters as it flies over your head from behind you. Half-Elf
Scout, who stopped only briefly in the gas's area of effect, drives
straight at the dragon with all his agility. The butterfly-like blade
flashes in his hand, making a whining sound as he throws it.

"Graahhh!!"

A flash of light.

To the dragon, it must have looked like a silver beam piercing through the dungeon. In reality, it's the knife lodging itself in the dragon's eyeball. The creature roars hideously, thrashing around, its neck flailing as it gazes up at the ceiling. You see blood dribbling from under the knife, and if a dragon can bleed, then it can die.

"Here I go!" Female Bishop manages to cry, perhaps emboldened by the sight of the injured monster. "*Ventus...crescunt...oriens!!* Arise and go forth, wind!!"

She manages to get just enough air into her lungs to call out these words of true power and then to blow on the horn she pulls from her belt. A tremendous gust springs up at once, filling the room and dispersing the dark green gas.

The Blast Wind spell!

Female Bishop's utter force of will was able to surpass that of the reeling green dragon and rewrite reality. You're literally seeing the fruits of all her study of magic with your cousin.

Speaking of your cousin, though, she isn't able to overcome the effects of the toxic cloud; she remains slumped on the chamber floor. Female Bishop finally manages to get some air into her delicate chest and hurries over to your cousin. "I'll leave the rest of the fighting to you...!"

"Good by me!" Myrmidon Monk clacks, then intones the words of Blessing on you and Female Warrior: "*O my god of the wind that comes and goes, may fortune smile on our road!*"

The Trade God is the deity of travel and the wind. Your blade is enveloped in a swirl of holy breeze. With this tailwind at your backs, you and Female Warrior rush forward toward the dragon.

"Yaaahh!"

One! Two! Your weapons strike out in turn at the dragon's exposed throat. Your master once told you that a would-be dragon slayer ought to aim at the weaker scales of the throat...

You're not sure if that's completely true or not, but your katana, with the vacuum around it, plunges easily into the dragon's flesh. The creature's blood is hot like molten lava as it spews forth, a dark, gruesome red.

Female Warrior, who stabbed the creature in the side, jumps back from the mess with a shout. She doesn't sound too anxious, just as normal. But out of the corner of your eye, you can see her face is slick with the sweat of terror.

"I'm fine; I'm fine…!" she says quickly, noticing your gaze. You likewise reset your blade in a fighting stance.

"Try this on for—*hack!*—size!!" your cousin calls out (interrupted only by a weak cough), leaning on Female Bishop for support. Her hair—her pride and joy—is frazzled out everywhere, her skin is red and swollen where it's visible under her torn garments, and her eyes are tearing up. Nonetheless, she sticks her hands out in front of herself, intoning the words of her spell melodically: "*Tonitrus oriens iacta!*"

The white flash of lightning drives away the darkness of the dungeon chamber. The branching bolt describes a series of geometrically impossible angles, lashing out at the dragon faster than the speed of sound.

"Hrrrgh…ghh…!" Your cousin's fingers are singed by the tremendous outpouring of magical power, but she never flinches. Even a mighty dragon, subjected to a blow like this—

"No—you've got to be kidding…!" Female Warrior cries, shattering your optimistic assessment. As the last speckles of lightning fade from your vision, you see the huge body is still twitching. The creature is bleeding from its eye, throat, and belly, smoke rises from its scorched scales, and yet it's still staring you down. Its gaze is deadly; the monster has no intent of letting you escape alive.

But…

You feel the same way.

The instant the dragon opens its jaws, you slide forward.

'*Sagitta…inflammarae…raedius.*' Three words of true power. A will-o'-the-wisp flies from your fingers and neatly down the dragon's throat.

"_____"

You can almost hear the creature swallow, and then there's a long beat. You hold your breath.

The dragon starts to swell from inside, then flames come spurting out from its wounds, and finally it explodes.

§

"Fwoooo! Sure never expected the likes of a dragon down here!" Half-Elf Scout exclaims as he retrieves his knife, which lodged itself in the wall after being flung free of the exploding monster along with copious amounts of dragon gore. Ever since he got that butterfly blade, he's shown himself to be a stalwart member of the front row. It takes a load off your shoulders to know you have another capable fighter, but he's still a bit nervous in the thick of combat, and you can hear the fatigue in his voice. When you consider that there may yet be a treasure chest to deal with after all this, you start to question the wisdom of your formation, but...

"Pshaw. Of course dragons live in the dungeon. Always have," Myrmidon Monk scoffs from the back row, and it's hard to ignore how reassuring it is to have him there. You're learning every day that there is no single, perfect way to approach an adventure.

"Yeah, maybe, when you take a dragon quest. They're not supposed to be just wandering around down here," Half-Elf Scout shoots back.

"These days, you're lucky if one doesn't jump out of the tall grass at you."

"Yeah, that's great."

You ignore the two of them—their conversation isn't going anywhere—and pat Female Warrior on the shoulder. "Hmm?" she says, turning to you. She's smiling, but her face is distinctly pale. You're not one to talk—but you do think maybe a long weapon like her spear takes a lot of energy to use. Especially against a dragon. You don't blame her for looking a little spent.

"Aw, I've still got plenty of fight left in me," she says, pursing her lips. "I guess I was just a little surprised, you know? I'd be happy not to meet any more dragons today."

You agree completely. It's time to call it a day on this delve. You inform the rest of your party of your decision, then ask Female Warrior to keep watch for a moment while you get your breathing under control.

"You got it. I've got my eyes peeled," she replies promptly, sitting down against one wall. You nod, then turn to the other members of your party. You figure you can trust Myrmidon Monk to look after Half-Elf Scout; what really concerns you is...

"Your big sis is fine; don't worry!"

…your *second* cousin.

You frown at her where she sits against the far wall of the room with Female Bishop attending to her. Her fingers are still slightly blackened from the overcasting attempt, and Female Bishop bandages them. They look quite painful.

"Thankfully, it's not a life-threatening injury—no need to supplicate for a miracle," Female Bishop mentions as she puts away her healing implements and wipes the sweat from her brow. "But those fingers will need some first aid when we get back to the surface, or they might end up scarred."

"Yuck, I don't want that," your cousin says, but her tone is lighthearted—even though it could be a real concern. You reiterate that the party will withdraw for the day and urge your cousin not to overtax herself on the way back. "Sure, of course not… Still, I'm sort of shocked that my Lightning spell didn't do the trick."

You, mulling it over, say that you don't think it's that surprising. Your opponent might not have been a very powerful dragon, but it was still a dragon. Without the wind spirit's blessing, even your and Female Warrior's blades might have hardly scratched it. You suspect it was chiefly luck that your Firebolt worked as well as it did.

The dice of Fate and Chance refuse to let any contest be decided purely by the difference in level.

"Guess you aren't the only one who needs to keep brushing up on their magic!" your cousin remarks. Still, anyone who belittles the worth of real effort can't even dream of questing in the dungeon. You grin a little at your cousin, who's suddenly champing at the bit, and remind her not to overwork Female Bishop.

Female Bishop shakes her head furiously. "Oh, it's okay! It's all very helpful—I actually asked her to include me…" She seems to be smiling. "Every time we open a spell book, we make all kinds of fascinating discoveries. It's wonderful!"

"That's so true!" your cousin says. "I'm amazed at how good she is at finding things in those old texts." Come to think of it, she *has* been studying these things for a long time—or at least, so she claims.

"But I still have so far to go," Female Bishop says. When you point out that she seems to be putting her experience to good use, she blushes and looks at the ground. "I still haven't even been able to shape a spell to extract that Demon Core we found…"

Hmm? That's an expression you don't recognize—but, well, as long as Female Bishop is around, it'll be all right. You think.

Regardless, you reiterate your warning not to overexert herself on the way home, and then you let out a breath. If your scout is feeling up to it, you think it's time to investigate that treasure chest. You've defeated the monster in this room, but there's no sense hanging around for too long.

"Yeah, they'll be here before long," Myrmidon Monk says, sensing your approach as he stands vigilant guard.

As you proceed in your delves, even you've noticed the shadows that seem to float in the corners of the chambers and the halls. An armored man, a man who looks like a robed wizard, and a young woman who appears like a priest…

The best you can hope for is that they might be skaven or ogres.

"More newbie hunters? Or maybe…rotting corpses."

"What a nasty thought… And a lot of trouble," Female Warrior remarks—whether or not they were simply attracted by the Death in the dungeon, or if they sprang forth from the Death itself.

You shrug gently and say that at least they're not slimes. Female Warrior smiles and jabs gently at you with the butt of her spear. You dodge neatly and call out to Half-Elf Scout.

"I'm on it, Cap. Good to go. Let's take a look at that chest and then get on out of here." He stands up with a nimble movement, taking a swig from his waterskin and then wiping his mouth. He works his seven tools carefully in the lock, feeling for traps—as you know by now, his technique is something to behold. As one of your party's warriors, it's your duty to stand by as he works, keeping a careful watch. Half-Elf Scout has the most dangerous job of all, and you have no desire to leave one of your friends high and dry.

So the exploration of the fourth floor went smoothly. Except for the distressing failure to find any staircase. You sigh almost without realizing it…and then yelp as Female Warrior takes advantage of the instantaneous lapse of attention to get in another jab.

The truth is, to your surprise, the fourth floor is of tremendously simple construction. Nothing more than a single long series of chambers. Compared with the first floor, with its mysterious dark zone, and the third floor with its traps, this level is almost disarmingly straightforward. Yes, the monsters seem tougher than what you've encountered above. The awful green dragon is a rare occurrence, but giant spiders, vampires, and werewolves roam the rest of the floor. It would be wrong to call it easy, exactly, but it is different.

You explore carefully, walk slowly, fight bravely, and survive all the way down the series of rooms to find…nothing. Only more of the endless loot that comes welling up out of the dungeon. There appears to be nothing more, nowhere further to go. That simple fact, more than any powerful monster, thwarts your attempts to proceed—your attempts to reach your goal.

"…Got it," Half-Elf Scout says, and you hear the lid of the chest open with a click, gold coins shimmering inside. You take it in from the corner of one eye, but you can't restrain a great sigh.

§

You return to the surface, and when you get back to the fortress city, you and your party find yourselves caught up in a dizzying spectacle. Adventurers are rushing everywhere, lights are burning though it's deep in the watches of the night, and silver and gold are veritably flying. The endless loot that comes welling up out of the dungeon has turned this into a city that never sleeps.

"Well, what with all the work we've done, maybe we oughtta consider the Royal Suite tonight," Half-Elf Scout jokes as you dodge the crowd. You aren't exactly following a vow of poverty, but it's true that you've spent all your nights thus far in the stables. The women have been afforded a large single room in the economy accommodations, but finer living is within your grasp.

After the party's shared expenses are deducted, everything else goes to your individual purses, and you can do with it what you like.

You toss back that it doesn't make much difference to you either way.

"Me, I'm…I'm quite all right where we are now," Female Bishop says, uncharacteristically (though hesitantly) voicing an objection. She walks smack in the middle of your group, and you're honestly thrilled to hear her express an opinion.

Your cousin evidently feels the same way, because she claps her hands, smiling. "Heh-heh-heh, it's fun to chat together till the wee hours, isn't it?"

Your *second* cousin is obviously tired—you chide her, saying she'd better get right to sleep; otherwise, tomorrow is going to be awfully difficult.

"Not even!" your cousin replies a touch hotly, but it's all good.

Well, not all good. But good enough.

You worked your way through a lot of chambers today. You suppose tomorrow could be spared for a day off. Thankfully, you have plenty of money. And your level, it seems, is now high enough that you can take on a green dragon. No reason to feel remotely concerned.

"Hmm…," Female Warrior says to this, favoring you with a glance. "I think I've got another day of hard work in me yet."

"Eh, when we want to rest, we can rest," Myrmidon Monk interjects before you can say anything. He fixes you with his compound eyes, and suddenly you find yourself wondering how you must look to him. How this whole world must look. "I don't much care either way," he adds, somehow both casual and weighty at once, and you take in a little breath.

You look into thin air as if you might find the words there, and finally—actually, it probably only takes a second—you open your mouth.

'*We rest, then.*'

Myrmidon Monk's mandibles clack at your pronouncement, and Female Warrior replies with an unenthusiastic, "Yessir."

"A day off…," Female Bishop murmurs, sounding somewhat melancholy. "I wonder what I should do with it."

"Studying would be good—but so would shopping!" your cousin says eagerly, and they start in on an energetic conversation. You continue forward silently, the girls' voices behind you…

"Hoh, Cap. Not gonna drop in at the tavern today?" Half-Elf Scout asks, and you suddenly realize you've walked straight past the Golden

Knight. You stop and look up at the sign. The chatter of adventurers produces a rowdy, friendly sound from within. Maybe youngsters who have just arrived in the fortress city with nothing but a dream. Or maybe a party that's fought a successful battle in the dungeon today.

Then again, maybe some inside are drinking to the memory of lost companions. Seeking the endless fortune of the depths, they come to this town, try themselves against the dungeon, fight, kill, survive...

...And eventually are swallowed up by the Death.

Is the fourth floor the true extent of that Death? You don't know. You don't know, but somehow, you can't muster any desire to drink tonight. You don't feel like seeing other adventurers, either. Least of all the Knight of Diamonds.

You let the others know that you're going to skip the tavern and get some rest, but you pass the party's purse to Half-Elf Scout so the rest of them can enjoy themselves. It's no bad thing for them to have a few moments without their leader every once in a while. You say good-bye to them and head for the inn.

"Oh..." Female Bishop seems about to say something to you, but nothing follows this short interjection. You stop for a moment but figure that if she says nothing further, it must not be that important, and you resume walking.

As you make your way alone through the city, the thing that most catches your eye is the ever-increasing number of adventurers. They've all come with an eye on the endless loot that comes welling up out of the dungeon. If the extreme end of the fourth floor is as far as they ever go, they won't care.

You look up at the sky, the starry night slightly diluted by the lights of the town, and see a thin ribbon of smoke drifting into the air. It comes from the fiery mountain where a dragon is said to live. But that has nothing to do with the adventurers in this town.

Suddenly, you're seized by the impulse to stop everyone you see and tell them that the dungeon is a dead end, that it stops at the fourth floor. You want to demand whether they understand what that means, mock them, rant and rave at them. But you know they would only stare at you with blank eyes.

It's not long before you arrive at your accustomed inn. Today's delve has left you immensely tired. Is it because of that green dragon? No; that encounter was at once unexpected and totally expected. The dive itself went largely without incident. And yet your body is like lead. Once you sit down, you feel the strength drain out of you; it's like your arms and legs are lashed to the earth, and you can't move.

Well, some days are like that. It's not such a big deal. Tomorrow you'll rest, and then it will be fine, won't it?

And nothing will change. Not even a little.

You'll dive back down in the dungeon, fight monsters, survive, find treasure, and come back home. When you think about it, isn't that simple loop enough? Even if there's nothing more?

Still feeling like the last, smoking ashes of a burned-down fire, you drift off into a restless sleep. When you open your eyes to a gentle rustling sound, you don't know how much time has passed. You see the familiar silhouette of Half-Elf Scout moving through the dark.

"Bah, just couldn't settle down in the bigwigs' room," he says with an apologetic smile, as if by way of explanation. He seems to have realized he woke you up. "Bed that soft, feels like it makes y'older instead of better."

You nod your understanding, to which he says, "Night, Cap," and throws himself down on the hay. That must be Myrmidon Monk you see in the other corner. With his compound eyes, you don't know whether he's awake or asleep. Your thoughts still leaden from sleep, you peer outside the stables. In the distance, the lights of the inn flicker faintly. You try to remember which room is the economy one.

Maybe she's not coming tonight, you think suddenly. It would make sense—you have no business together—so why does it leave you feeling so lonely?

You smile at the ridiculous question, force your eyes shut again, and try to find some sleep among the hay.

Whatever happens, dawn will break in another few hours.

Even if it won't solve anything.

§

"Let's go shopping, O leader!" Female Bishop chimes, and you drop your spoon as you squeeze out an *E-er...*

You don't worry about the spoon sinking into your breakfast bowl of barley porridge but turn slowly to Female Bishop.

Things are always a little slow at the Golden Knight first thing in the morning.

The patrons are mostly those who have finally returned from a night in the dungeon or those who are about to go back down, sipping a drink and grabbing a bite to eat. Those who have just arrived in the city look around for companions, nervous expressions on their faces. Some sit quietly as if hoping someone might come to them, but they'll learn better by nightfall, you suspect. A wizard or a monk, they might get offers, but the no-name third son of some farmer from the countryside—not happening.

"Ooh, then maybe I'll ask you to pick something up for me. Let's see, I'd sure like to eat something sweet."

"Good idea. I think…I need some catalysts. And something sweet, too!"

"Come t'think of it, we're gettin' a little low on potions. Be a big help if you could grab some while you're out."

"Makes no difference to me either way."

While you've been busy thinking, your companions have evidently already concluded that you're going out. You wish they would wait—take a step back. You tell them you can take care of those kinds of chores on your own. A party of one. That's all you need!

You think you're being considerate, but Female Warrior immediately exclaims, "Whaaat?" deeply scandalized. "The girl actually got up the courage to invite you along, and that's how you respond? Poor thing!" She doesn't seem genuinely worried; it's more like she's teasing you. She reaches out for Female Bishop, wrapping her arms around the girl protectively, even as Female Bishop protests, "No, it's fine…"

"Hrm!" your *second* cousin announces, suddenly the polar opposite of her usual cheery self. "How dare you embarrass a young woman like that!"

Hey, that's not what happened! You pick up your spoon—sunk up to the handle in your porridge—wipe it off as best you can, and make a show of resuming your breakfast. From the amused gazes that settle on you, though, you gather that this didn't come out of nowhere.

Who was the instigator? You express your doubts that your *second* cousin is capable of such a thing (you ignore her "How rude!").

"Gosh, look at this guy, am I right?" Female Warrior says, nuzzling Female Bishop's cheek.

"S-sure, you're right," Female Bishop replies with a nod, looking embarrassed but not exactly unhappy. As for you, you're certainly pleased that she's getting along so well with the other girls, but...

"Not that unusual for another party member to invite you shopping, is it?" Myrmidon Monk clacks out while you waffle. "Or what? Is there some reason you don't want to go?"

"Oh my!" your *second* cousin exclaims immediately, but forget about her. True, you have no special reason to turn Female Bishop down—and yet...

You're assaulted by an anxiety you can't find any reason for, and Half-Elf Scout cackles aloud. "This is what's called checkmate, Captain. Be a good boy and go on a quest that doesn't involve the dungeon."

Grr. It sounds like that settles it. It's true, of late you've been focusing on nothing but delving and training, delving and training. Cutting enemies down and moving forward. You'd been working on the assumption that otherwise you wouldn't be able to resist the Death that squirms in the dungeon, but now...

Maybe that isn't the same thing as Life.

On the far side of one is six. And how foolish it would be to roll a die focusing only on that single pip.

Of course, just entertaining these thoughts while you sip your porridge isn't going to be enough to change how you really feel. The head and the heart are separate things. But they can be brought into alignment. If one acts to make them so.

All right. You nod and finish what's left in your bowl in a single great gulp. You suddenly realize that everyone else has already finished eating. You're well behind.

Well, time to go. Shopping. Not alone but together with Female Bishop.

"Okay!" she exclaims, her expression bright enough to blind you as she nods eagerly. The girls exchange little congratulatory high fives—you knew this was a setup. But strangely, you don't mind. You like knowing those you're close to are thinking of you, and it would be terrible to waste such affection.

You stop one of the passing padfoot waitresses—the harefolk girl—and ask for a cup of water.

"Coming right up! Hee-hee—I heard it all, you know. Everyone needs a break now and then!" She claps her fuzzy hands, and you smile wryly. Apparently, you're just that easy to read.

But, well, it's all right. It's all good, you think again.

Just by deciding to take a rest, to take a break from your normal routine, you feel something like a trapped breath escaping your body. You nod, bring your hands together, and place the party's shared purse on the table.

Let's begin with what everyone wants, then.

§

"Come one, come all! See the dungeon's strangest mystery—this living gold coin!"

"That's outrageous. How can the identification cost the entire value of the item? That's highway robbery!"

"Oh, please—this statue is of a bear who killed millions of enemies. It'll bring you luck and profit for sure…"

"Now, now, this key is made of solid gold, you hear me? Surely you'll give me a good price for it!"

You venture out into town, the fortress city packed to the gills with people. Shouting voices are everywhere, and you can hear adventurers arguing with merchants about their wares. In this city, there's no end of new equipment to buy, nor of money to buy it with. To see this place, you would never imagine the end of the world was nigh.

You see a few people in tattered clothing whom you take to be refugees, but they look almost relaxed. Maybe it's relief. Unlucky as they are, they're still alive, and they know it. It's hard not to feel that the good wind that blows through this town is somehow generous.

"I guess we can thank the Trade God for this," Female Bishop says as she patters along beside you. She's working hard to keep up but likewise looks almost relieved. "So many refugees, though… I guess the war isn't going so well." Perhaps it's her sense of vocation that lends an extra touch of melancholy to these words. When you consider what she told you about her life back in the temple, you can hardly blame her for feeling this way.

The world needs saving. With that burden on your shoulders, one could be forgiven for lapsing into rueful rumination when confronted with the way things are. After walking alongside you silently for a moment, though, Female Bishop says, "Right," nodding with conviction. "Our shopping today will bring us closer to that goal!" Then with an enthusiastic "Let's go!" she rushes forward. Now it's you who struggles to keep up with her—you smile at the idea.

How invigorating this is.

"Where should we go first?" Female Bishop asks gaily, turning toward you and fixing her gaze on you from behind her bandage. You're not on any adventure now, and she's in civilian clothing, without her weapons and armor; she looks truly alive. She could easily be mistaken, you think, for some young princess somewhere—and it's not just because she was actually born to a noble house. Is this her true self, then? From before the goblins, even before her parents educated her in the ways of the nobility?

You suggest maybe you should start by taking a look around to see what's available. The armor, weapons, and potions should all be easy enough to get from the weird old guy whose shop you already frequent. All the other little things, though, and the treats Female Warrior and your cousin want, are another matter. Might not be such a bad idea to take a look at the shops.

She is, after all, a bishop of the Supreme God. With her ability to identify items, you won't get bilked on your purchases. You tell her you'll be counting on her, and she happily responds, "Great!"

§

Now, wander around long enough and you're bound to bump into something interesting. Among the many wares spread out in the street are several that catch your eye. A sword, for example—a classic-looking blade.

"Ah, my young lord and lady, I see you are people of discernment! Come see my collection of swords, masterworks unparalleled anywhere in the world!" The merchant, his voice heavy with some accent you don't recognize, tries to convince you to have a gander. You suspect the ordinary clothing Female Bishop is wearing today has kept the man from realizing what she is. You glance in her direction, and she gives you a wicked little look from under her bandage. She nods, suppressing a laugh, and you squat in front of the swords as if deeply interested.

Hmm...indeed.

At a glance, it would be easy enough to take these for famous works of great craftsmen. They have the right look, and when you pull one out of its scabbard, the blade gleams brightly. It certainly puts on an impressive show...

"...Would you like me to look at it for you?" Female Bishop whispers, sounding almost excited.

You remark that yes, you would. The sword you picked up bears the name Dragon Slayer. Others have names like Were Slayer and Mage Masher, but you figure you might as well start with dragons. You just felled one, after all. If you'd had this blade along, maybe it would have been a little easier.

"This one? Let's see..." Female Bishop touches the hilt with her slim fingers. She runs them up to the blade as if in a caress, an ambiguous smile on her face. You ask if it's a fake. "No," she says, shaking her head. "It's the real thing. However... How do I put this...?" She spares a glance for the merchant, her eyes hidden by her bandage, then leans in close to you. She stretches out ever so slightly, bringing her lips close to your ear, and whispers: "It has no desire to act."

Hmm.

She giggles like a child at your response and continues softly: "It was created to fell flying beings. It won't be of real value against earth dwellers."

So there are many different types of swords that might be called dragon slayers. Think, for example, of Dragon Buster and Dragon Valor, known from the old songs and legends... The fact that so many dragon-slaying swords are understood to be just normal weapons when wielded against any other foe means there would be plenty of fakes. After all, how many people are likely to encounter a real dragon in their travels? Judged against such forgeries, at least this sword has the virtue of being the real thing. Even if it wouldn't be of any special value down in the dungeon.

"If I were to pick one...," Female Bishop murmurs. "Let's see..." She moves among the wares with the grace of a dancer, her hand finally settling on one sword in particular. "Yes, this is the one I would pick."

It is a most mysterious weapon composed of several blades joined together. The make looks somewhat old, and it has clearly seen its share of passing years.

"I knew you had a good eye. That's the work of a very famous smith, sir. How about it?"

At the merchant's urging, you take the sword in hand, recognizing its unusual lightness. With his permission, you give a few gentle swipes with the weapon, and even these mild strokes produce a *whoosh* of air. Yes—this is indeed good work. With a single swing, you could rend an enemy's flesh, turning them to mincemeat. You are aware of only one shop in the city that would sell something like this. And since you're not there right now, you wonder aloud if this came up from the dungeon.

"Heh-heh, I've had a big shipment in just recently. Couldn't be happier."

You look around and see it's true; swords of all descriptions seem to be lying around. And not just swords. The cloth laid out on the ground also hosts staves, rings, and more besides.

You know a little magic. It isn't lost on you that one of the staves lolling around nearby contains a powerful fire spell. Your cousin, of course, or even Female Bishop, with their magical abilities, might find such equipment a stalwart companion.

But... You're suddenly overtaken by a strange sense that something isn't right; you set the old sword down on the cloth. The feeling is hard to articulate, and it might be nothing more than your imagination. But you can't shake it—it's the same prickle you felt stepping into the chamber with those rogues.

"Satisfied for today, sir?"

You return the merchant's pleasant smile, lightly patting the sword at your hip. You'd rather place your trust in a familiar weapon for now.

"I see, of course," the merchant says with no obvious distress—probably used to sales slipping away.

The concern, however, is yours alone. If there's anything Female Bishop wants, well, as party leader, it's of course your job to help her equip herself. So you inquire her opinion.

"_____"

Female Bishop, however, shows no sign of hearing your question, her unseeing eyes fixed on a single point. You follow her gaze to find it resting on a shiny but otherwise unremarkable ring. Even you can tell the item must be expensive. Expensive enough to make you hesitate for a moment. But you're the one who charged a dragon head-on—you won't quail at buying an item, if it's exceptional enough to be worth it.

"...No," Female Bishop says, her voice quaking terribly. "No... It's all right. I don't—I don't need it." She shakes her head several times and then promptly walks away. You hurry after her. She looks out of sorts, but her footsteps are precise and careful, as an adventurer's steps always should be.

When you catch up to her, you don't even have to ask. She says, "That ring... It's cursed."

Cursed...

You mutter to yourself, and her shoulders shake again; she looks as distressed as a child who's seen a monster. "I don't know...how to describe it... It was cold, like I was being sucked in..."

Mm. You grunt. Perhaps it's the same strange force you felt coming from that sword. It wasn't simply frightening. It was something cold, chilling, that sneaked up on you. Something this fortress city is overflowing with. Something that accompanies almost every adventurer, almost every step they take.

You stop walking, looking back over your shoulder and peering into the busy marketplace. The shop, with the sword and the ring, has vanished amid the bustle.

And yet... Say... Could it be...?

Could that have been the chill of the Death?

§

"Oh..." Female Bishop, who's been moving so quickly she almost seems to be running away from the marketplace, suddenly stops and looks up. This allows you to catch up with her and ask what's going on, but she shakes her head and says, "Nothing. Ahem, it's this way. I think..."

She turns and sets off down a side street with complete confidence despite her impaired vision. She's running, yet nothing about her movements makes you worry that she'll bump into anyone or fall. Once again you hurry to catch up with her, but at least she seems to be able to make her own way around.

Maybe she's more of a tomboy than she looks.

The thought flits through your mind, not that it serves much purpose.

Think of her, back before the misfortune befell her, before she was brought up as a hero.

Even more meaningless, such speculations.

There's no way to know what's inborn and what comes from experience. Besides, the experience is part of what makes us who we are. Here's what it works out to: She's a bit of a tomboy.

"...I believe it's this way," Female Bishop says, stopping at a crossroads and tilting her head as if listening closely, then turning down the next street. You follow after her with no idea where she might be going. You ask, but she only says, "I don't know." Geez.

Wherever it is she doesn't know she's going, though, she soon arrives there. It doesn't take long for you to realize what she's been looking for.

A young girl. A child, ten years old or so, her hair in a braid—perhaps done by her parents or maybe her older sister. Her eyes are open wide and round, her mouth is drawn up in a line, and her hands are clasped together. It would be easy to point out that she's trying to contain herself, yet somehow also embarrassing. Despite the child's best efforts, a very slight whimper is escaping her...

'You heard that?'

"Um, well... Yes," Female Bishop replies shyly, hurrying over to the child as if to say she's what's most important right now. Female Bishop kneels down in front of the girl, heedless of the dust and grime that get on her white clothes, so she's eye to eye with the child. "Whatever is the matter…?" she asks.

You find yourself simultaneously impressed, surprised, and even smiling at her in this moment. You get a rush of warm, fuzzy feeling.

But it doesn't last long.

You walk over to a man who's loitering nearby, shaking your head in an exaggerated motion and shrugging. This is pathetic. To think any adventurer would bully a little girl so badly as to bring her to tears.

"…I haven't been bullying her." The man turns to you, looking deeply distressed. It's the Knight of Diamonds.

Standing next to him is a silver-haired girl—no, the silver-haired scout, not much taller than a child herself. Her expressions—indeed, perhaps her emotions—always seem slight, but it's clear at a glance that she's quite annoyed. You mention how Female Warrior would no doubt fall on the floor laughing if you told her about this exchange.

"Hrmph!" The silver-haired scout pouts. "Then I'll make you an offer: I'll tell you an embarrassing story about *her* instead."

You nod and say you'll accept the offer later, then ask the Knight of Diamonds what the problem is. The child looks a little more at ease with Female Bishop talking to her, and you decide Female Bishop is better suited to handling that part of things than you are.

"Ahh, see…," the knight begins, "I thought she might be lost, so I tried talking to her and—"

"The very first words out of your mouth were, *Don't you dare cry!*"

Sheesh.

You join the silver-haired scout in leveling a disappointed gaze at the Knight of Diamonds. How truly pathetic.

"No need to say it again. I doubt you know how to deal with children yourself," he tells you. You've never seen the young knight look so much his age before. Still, you can't ignore what he just said. Maybe he's right; maybe he's wrong. Even as you tease him with the words of a certain wizard, you think about what to do next…

That's when Female Bishop speaks up. "Um… May I?"

You nod; she takes the child gently by the hand and guides her over to you. Well, now. You crouch on one knee so you can look the dark-haired girl in the eye. She seems quick and clever, and she's obviously doing everything she can not to be afraid—a good girl.

"My big sis and I, we...we got separated," she says haltingly. Hmm. You consider, then nod. This is a world-ending catastrophe in and of itself.

You conclude that you'll have to find this sister of hers, then.

"Right!" Female Bishop replies as if she foresaw all of this, making you idly bashful. Thus, you stand without quite meeting her gaze, gently brushing the dirt off your knees.

"——" The Knight of Diamonds and the silver-haired scout are looking at you incredulously. "Er, you see... I thought I had you figured out after that scuffle in the tavern," the knight says, and then with a wave of his hand, he urges you to forgive him. "...It turns out getting to know a person is indeed difficult yet delightful."

You laugh aloud. *Ha*—there's a logic to all things, if you look hard enough...

You know the words to say at a moment like this.

Trust an adventurer to handle it.

§

"I see, so you and your older sister..."

"Uh-huh. We went shopping, but then I couldn't find her anymore."

That leaves you without many options. Female Bishop walks ahead of you, holding the girl's hand and chatting amicably with her. Her footsteps still don't falter despite her visual impairment; the smooth flagstones of the street are nothing compared to the difficult footing of the dungeon. Her steps are sure as she listens politely to the young girl's chatter.

"I can't believe this..." Holding the child's other hand is the silver-haired scout. Maybe the little girl thinks the scout is about her own age, because she treats her differently from Female Bishop, though she clearly likes them both. As the girl talks, holding their hands, they reply "Oh" or "Hmm" or "Huh!" as appropriate. Then they whisper something back to her—and you see that though they may not be used to it, they're surprisingly good at this childcare thing.

However…

With them there, you're not sure what's left for you to do. Finding things is a scout's business, and Female Bishop seems ideally suited to keeping the child company. At least you look like you're feeling more at ease than the Knight of Diamonds, who walks alongside you. Well, you've experienced the known depths of the dungeon, and compared to that, finding someone on the streets is an absolute pleasure. Isn't it wonderful to help someone, to see the fruits of your labors, to know there's a future?

"Sounds like hardly anything bothers you… Or at least, nothing serious."

I was wondering what he might say next…

You laugh out loud. You never imagined having such insight. Indeed, it wasn't that long ago when you didn't think very highly of yourself.

It's because of your party. You tell the Knight of Diamonds that they helped you gain something difficult to come by.

"I see," he says quietly in response, the tone of his voice like a man observing a stunning treasure. "And here I thought you might be concerned about the progress of your exploration."

You reply immediately that, in fact, that is bothering you. Could the dungeon really go down only four levels? Is there nothing further? If there isn't, then is there really nothing else to do besides kill and loot for as long as one can survive?

The Knight of Diamonds looks for a moment like he doesn't have an answer, then he grunts. "Mm. We're continuing our search, as well… It's undeniable that there's a lot more white space on the map than there was on other floors."

You start to nod: That makes sense. You already know that the dungeon isn't a square—or perhaps you should say a rectangular solid. After all, you already know that the coordinates for the stairway down from the first floor are different on the first floor than they are when you arrive on the second. You don't know if it has something to do with the dungeon's physical construction, or if some magical distortion of dimensions is involved, but it doesn't matter.

You know, she was the one who noticed that. You glance in Female Bishop's

©lack

direction. She's smiling and chatting with the little girl, making sure the child doesn't fall—you think you're seeing the real her. You can only imagine how much of a burden she must have been bearing to have shrunk into herself the way she had when you first saw her at the tavern.

Perhaps… Perhaps there might be some clue on one of the other floors, you muse.

"Certainly possible. Maybe it's time to start from the proverbial square one again…"

But there's no time. The Knight of Diamonds doesn't have to say it for you to understand.

The fortress city burbles with an unusual liveliness, a hustle and bustle. The energy of adventurers, merchants, and refugees who arrive with an eye on the endless loot that wells up from the dungeon. This is the very cusp of the danger that threatens the entire world, yet it draws each of them near.

It's entirely possible that tomorrow, yes, even tomorrow, the Death will crawl forth out of the dungeon and destroy the world. But no one seems to pay the chance any mind. Maybe they're just pretending not to see it, or maybe they really don't care. The whole place is like a pile of guttering ashes, giving off a faint glow.

Or, you suppose, maybe there really is no Death down in the dungeon.

"And we're on a complete wild-goose chase, utterly off the mark, looking for something that doesn't exist in a place that produces endless treasure?" The Knight of Diamonds laughs aloud. "I guess it's a little late to worry about that."

You laugh, too. Female Bishop and the silver-haired girl look over at you, but you wave to them, indicating it's nothing.

If you truly have another mission to accomplish, then this right now is sheer idleness.

'*Still, it's impressive you talked to her instead of abandoning her.*'

"What do you mean?"

You respond that you mean the girl, nodding in the direction of the dark-haired child. The knight might not have been exactly sure how to handle the situation, but he did what you would expect from Lawful Good.

The Knight of Diamonds goes silent for a moment, makes a face, and finally musters an awkward, "Hardly..." You glance at him but don't have anything in particular to say, so you wait for him to go on. "I myself have a younger...a younger sister," he says. That, he concludes with a note of self-deprecation, is why he couldn't ignore the girl.

He's looking at Female Bishop talking to the child, but he seems to be looking past them, through them, to someone else beyond.

"You believe one of every pair of twins is cursed?"

You think for a second, then reply that you doubt it. You think it's nothing more than a superstition. A misguided response to an extreme roll of the dice.

"My father didn't agree," the Knight of Diamonds spits. "There's no going back, for her."

Seeing the way he stares fixedly at the silver-haired scout, you only offer a quiet word of acknowledgment. *Sometimes you simply have to let someone go.*

You don't think there's anything more for you to say. Judging another person's emotions is so immensely difficult. The more so when the person who's cut loose is a family member. Any number of things might drive someone to recognize that "this is as far as we go." Even this self-proclaimed third son of a poor noble house has a past, and indeed, has a present. As one who knows nothing of them, you should simply accept everything you're told at face value.

"Oh...!" Suddenly the little girl's face begins to shine, and she rushes forward at a quick trot. Female Bishop tries to clamber after her and take her hand at the same time, but only succeeds in confusing herself and coming to a halt.

"Hmm," the silver-haired scout mumbles quietly, and you follow her gaze.

"*There* you are...! Oh my gods... I told you not to go wandering off on your own!" calls a clear voice, overpowering the little girl's "I'm sorry!"

You recognize this new girl. You've heard her voice before. She looks familiar, but you can't quite place her. She must be the little one's older sister.

When she turns toward you, flicking her long hair back, you suddenly realize. The fairly generous chest is contained in civilian clothing, so it took you a moment. At the same time, the royal guard—the one who's always standing outside the dungeon entrance—recognizes you, too.

"Hey," she calls out. You and Female Bishop smile, while the Knight of Diamonds and the silver-haired scout both pull faces for some reason.

"Ah-ahem. Thank you, um, I'm sorry for any trouble my sister might have caused you…"

"Think nothing of it," the Knight of Diamonds replies with a disgustingly suave wave of the hand. "Any adventurer would have done the same."

You can only smirk to hear him mimic you, but your uneasy expression matches that on the royal guard's face. The two of you smile slowly at each other, and she seems to relax. "Again, I'm sorry for the trouble. Come on, say thank you."

"Thanks…very much!" the girl says politely, with an exaggerated bow. You tell her not to worry about it, then say you didn't realize the girl was the guard's little sister.

The royal guard chuckles. "Surprised?" she asks with a mischievous wink. "Even I'm off the clock sometimes."

So she is indeed. The fact that she's literally face-to-face (you suspect) with the threat to this world's very existence doesn't change that. What's world peace worth if you have no time to spend with your family?

The guard and her sister bow to you all once more, then walk off hand in hand. You watch until they vanish into the crowd.

"…Well, I'm glad," Female Bishop says, after a short breath of relief. "I'm glad she wasn't afraid."

Hmm. You don't take her meaning immediately, and Female Bishop looks at you awkwardly. "I mean… You know, because of my…scars." She offers her best smile and a tilt of the head. She looks almost sweet.

You tell her not to be silly, following up with a laugh. Who cares what random people think? It doesn't matter how pretty your face is; if you have so much as a scratch, some people will point and jabber. It's practically a hobby for them, and paying them too much mind will drive you out of yours.

"I wonder… Oh, which is to say, I'm certainly happy to hear you say so…" Still, the words don't seem to have been much comfort to Female Bishop.

You wonder what the problem is, but as someone who isn't very caught up in his own appearance, there's not much you can offer. Female Bishop looks somewhat fragile but beautiful; her body isn't voluptuous but has curves and is otherwise fit—you've never noticed much more about it than that. This is definitely more a subject for Female Warrior, or (though you hate to admit it) your cousin. You suspect you might make things worse instead of better.

"Hmm…" The silver-haired scout is watching and listening to the two of you, and then she pulls on the knight's sleeve. "Come on, let's go. Aren't you going to buy that sword you saw at that shop?"

He nods seriously. "Ah, yes, unmistakably a fine blade. It's not my kind of thing, but it would certainly give our party more prowess in battle." Now that you think about it, did his party have any other warriors?

You tell him to hurry and find the fifth floor. You'll never be able to stop looking, otherwise.

The Knight of Diamonds graces you with an earnest laugh. "Fair enough. Nothing will change if you rot down there."

Same to him. You nod, and he nods back.

You all look one last time into the crowd of people, the denizens of the fortress city among whom the sisters have vanished. Merchants, adventurers, and refugees are each seeking their daily bread and their own entertainments.

The wind comes blowing by in a rush. A good wind, sent by the Trade God.

"I know one thing: We have to save this world."

You say nothing.

The Knight of Diamonds has already said it all.

§

"…Perhaps if I were a bit bigger. I don't think of myself as that small, but…"

You never know what she's going to say next: This time it's about body type. The firm muscles revealed by the royal guard's civilian clothing showed a build well suited to wearing armor and swinging a sword. Considering how even Myrmidon Monk sometimes stands on the front row, Female Bishop seems to be taking the matter to heart. Especially now that she talks more with Female Warrior.

Your master always insisted that body type had little or nothing to do with anything...but you think you'll just get yourself in trouble if you say that. You tell Female Bishop she should ask the others when you get back to the inn tonight.

"Yes. I'll do that." She nods eagerly, flailing her arms as if waving an invisible staff.

Yeesh. Female Bishop doesn't notice you trying to suppress a smile. Her footsteps are light. In fact, the same is true of yours—and your shoulders, which are feeling far less burdened than they were before you went out. Maybe you should thank her—though you feel expressing formal gratitude would be not quite appropriate.

You picture the faces of your party members, waiting for you at the tavern, and your face relaxes into a smile. Challenge, fight, carve a path. The very same things you've been doing all along. So you're not as sure where you're going to go next—that's not something to panic about.

Acting like an amateur...

As twilight settles upon the fortress city, you and Female Bishop stroll down the street. The two of you exchange idle chatter, talk about the day's shopping, and about the lost little girl you helped. It seems to have dissipated the lethargy you've been feeling in your body.

That's all it really takes, in the end. Your friend asking you to go shopping. A little girl who needs your help. Small things that give you a feeling of accomplishment like tiny adventures, things that help you move forward the slightest bit.

It's about time. The answer comes to you suddenly, and you announce it with insufferable pride: If the source of all this evil isn't down in that dungeon, then you'll just keep adventuring until you find it. If it's all over with the fourth floor, then fine. You'll forge ahead to the next thing. It's as simple as that. More fool this villain is, if they think they can run away from you and your party.

"Goodness…" Female Bishop, swept away by your grand declaration, puts a hand to her mouth and laughs. The sound is clear as a bell and echoes deep into your heart. "Yes, I suppose you're right. Then until we find the source of the Death, I—"

Female Bishop smiles, but you never find out what she was going to say.

"_____!"

For suddenly, someone calls her name.

"Oh…" Female Bishop stops, taken aback by the friendly exclamation. She looks as if she's seen a ghost. You turn to discover another girl who's the spitting image of Female Bishop. Vestments and all. But her body has the fullness that Female Bishop's lacks, and her face is as alluring as a blooming flower. Above all, there's light in her eyes. She shines like a star that has never known pain or suffering.

"Ahem, ah…" Female Bishop's voice grows scratchy and shrill, like a child who fears she'll be scolded no matter what she says. "So you're all right… Thank goodness…," she finally manages, with real feeling.

"Ha-ha-ha, of *course* I'm all right! Would I ever get lost?" The other girl, in contrast, laughs loudly and produces a map from her pouch with a flourish. She unrolls it to reveal a diagram that's noticeably detailed and easy to read. Perhaps not as excellent as Myrmidon Monk's work, but then, he's the best mapper you know.

She's in his league, though. Yes, that much is true.

The girl waves the map around, causing the ring on her finger to glint brightly, then quickly rolls it up again and puts it away. "How about you? Not getting lost around town, are you? I'm sure you're working hard to remember all the streets."

"Y-yes. I'm managing…"

"I know how easily you get lost in new places," the girl goes on without losing momentum, as if she hasn't even heard Female Bishop's hesitant response. "I *always* had to trail you everywhere you went."

You suppose you're grateful the girl doesn't seem to have noticed you; you study her carriage and behavior closely. The generous interpretation might be that she doesn't try to hide who she is; the less generous, that she has no filter.

She seems to genuinely care for Female Bishop, as far as you can tell.

After all, otherwise, why would she follow her around to make sure she didn't get lost? It's easy enough to misjudge this girl—although that might be a misjudgment in and of itself. It's difficult indeed to read people on your first meeting.

"Hey, the guy next to you—is he from your party? ...Nah, couldn't be. We told you to wait at the tavern." The girl rolls on with her own conclusions before you can get a word in edgewise. She turns with an almost poetic motion and calls to someone behind her: "Heeey!"

You seize the opportunity to take stock of Female Bishop, who's looking at the ground, obviously deeply uncomfortable. You don't know what happened between her and these people, but all her cheerfulness has vanished in an instant. Maybe she would have been better off staying by herself at the tavern, doing identifications?

Hmm. Just that small acceleration of breath causes Female Bishop to quake as if pierced by a thorn. You produce a wry smile and tell her she doesn't owe these people anything. That alone won't be enough to comfort her, of course, but it does get a nod from her.

A moment later, someone appears before you—no, before Female Bishop. A young warrior with an easygoing manner. "Oh! Thank the gods! We were just heading to the tavern!" From the scratches on his armor and equipment, you can tell he's no novice but an accomplished adventurer. A sword hangs at his hip in a red-lacquered scabbard, which he grips with a hand bearing a ring. He wears a tightly bound metal forehead protector, and his expression is one of relief; he doesn't try to hide that he's out of breath. "We were coming to get you! Come on—let's go adventuring!"

He smiles broadly as he speaks.

§

"Wow, talk about self-important."

"Hey, we did kinda poach her. Fair enough."

"As your older sister, I think I object to your attitude...!"

"Well, you *can* be that way sometimes." *Giggle.* "But we knew that already."

"So what did you do?" *Clack, clack.* "Not that I care either way."

§

Female Bishop stands stunned by the young warrior's words.

Don't blame her. Adventurers from this fortress city disappear all the time down in that awful dungeon. Parties are lost, in other words. They hit trouble down in the depths, and though sometimes they can make camp and hope for help to arrive, there are limits. Female Bishop may have hoped they were still alive, but she would have known it was past time to give up, realistically speaking. Even if they were alive, there was every reason to think they had simply left her behind.

If she's hardly able to keep up with this sudden development, well, it's only natural.

"Look, you... I mean..." The warrior stops, finding the words, carefully adopting a cheerful tone. "Training takes time, you know? We wanted to be sure we would be strong enough to protect you."

"What...? I...I had no idea..." Female Bishop's voice is still vanishingly quiet. Her hand grips at her chest. The symbol of the Supreme God whom she serves floats there, and she looks like she's supplicating to it.

You wait silently for her to come up with the words. The young warrior likewise doesn't interrupt.

"...Why did you never come to see me?" Female Bishop asks finally, her voice quaking audibly.

A good question—that was foremost in your mind as well.

The other girls might know about Female Bishop's past, but you don't—not in any detail, at least. You don't think it's the business of an outsider to aggravate that goblin-inflicted wound. Thus, perhaps it was consideration on the part of the young warrior to leave her at the tavern and go on ahead. Did he never imagine how she would be treated, left behind to earn her keep by identifying items? You don't think this qualifies as watching over somebody.

"We thought if you were at the tavern...you'd be safe..." This response comes from the priest, the one who looks just like Female Bishop—it sounds like an excuse, and she can't look at you as she speaks. At her neck is a sigil of the sword and scales, hanging from a blue sash. She serves the Supreme God, too.

It's often said that once humans had taken over the scales of the law, the judgment of good and evil belonged to them, not the gods. She probably also thought this would be for Female Bishop's benefit, after much agonizing.

"I know it was for training, but we had to do so much killing—we didn't want to…"

"We didn't want to see you until our penance was done… We thought that would be best," the warrior adds. "We're really sorry." He bows his head deeply.

Neither the priest with her boundless enthusiasm, nor the warrior with his willingness to speak so frankly to Female Bishop, has a shadow on their face. It's not yours to judge the actions of others. But you do register how direct they are. Though you don't know if that's good or bad.

"B-but that's… B-but I…!"

Even Female Bishop herself doesn't know what to say. You don't blame her for that, either.

And yet, what could you personally say to these people you've only just met this very moment? You've been listening silently until now, but even with this thought, you decide it would be all right to put in a few words here. After all, this concerns you, as well. Whether you like it or not, you have the right to speak.

You're perfectly happy to wait for Female Bishop to talk first, of course.

After a moment's thought…

'You should do what you like.'

Short, to the point.

"What…?" Female Bishop looks at you with all the shock of a child who's been slapped by her parents. Needless to say, as the leader of your party, it's not that you have no compunctions about her leaving. But that's not for you to say now, to push it on Female Bishop when she hasn't even asked.

Yes, you are your party's leader. You are definitely not Female Bishop's guardian, nor do you speak for her. Thus, you must respect her free choice. It's her life and her decision. So you repeat: She should do what she likes.

'And whatever decision it is, don't worry about it afterward.'

Because you are the leader of your party, you are her friend and companion.

"Do what...what I like..." Female Bishop looks at the ground, her shoulders slumped weakly. Silence reigns between you for a long time.

"—" The young warrior opens his mouth to say something, but the priest jabs him with an elbow, and he closes his mouth again with a grunt. The priest plays with the blue sash at her neck and sniffs quietly, waiting for her friend's reply. You pull your conical hat down farther over your eyes to hide the fact that you're trying to hold back a smile.

"Um..." After a long time, the single syllable starts a flood of others. "Did I—was I ever able to...to be of help to you?" Female Bishop asks, her voice trembling.

Your answer is immediate. Yes.

Of course she was. You never once questioned it.

Magic, miracles, mapping, item identification, today's shopping trip, talking things over with the rest of the party. Any one of them was already a major, important contribution. You wouldn't want anyone else on your back row.

"I...I see...!" Female Bishop wipes at the corners of her eyes behind her bandage. She opens her trembling lips and takes a deep breath, filling her small chest with air. And finally she says, in a single clear utterance: "I'm sorry. I'm going to stay with this group."

And then with her face clear as the blue sky, she stands beside you.

The priest, Female Bishop's double, is the first to respond: "Whaaat?! You're kidding—I can't believe this!" Her tone is aggressive, but she appears more shocked than anything. You think somewhat flippantly how easily her motivation might be mistaken.

"Forgive me," Female Bishop says. "But I want...I want to try getting by on my own strength."

"Really? Are you sure about that? Are you sure about *him*?"

Easy to misjudge, indeed, you think, the thought coming back to you like a boomerang. The girl, needless to say, is staring daggers at you. In her eyes, you're probably some con man who found her poor, naive friend at the tavern and talked her into joining your party. You know you can't shoot back anything rude, so you just pull your hat over your eyes again.

"...Come on, that's enough," says the young man with the lacquered sword. He probably doesn't realize he's standing up for you.

"But..." The priest purses her lips but can't seem to find a leg to stand on despite her desperate wish to object further.

"You've only just met him. At least be polite."

"Yeah, you're right..." She shuffles back, nodding, and the warrior turns toward Female Bishop. His expression is hard. But not from anxiety or anger; rather, he doesn't seem quite certain what expression is appropriate. After a moment, he settles on a gentle smile. "Very well, that sounds good. You work hard...and we'll be rooting for you. Just don't forget that we're your friends—if you ever need anything, ask us."

"I will! Thank you...very much!" Female Bishop, clasping the sword and scales to her chest, nods. She has all the enthusiasm of a small bird or a puppy, and the warrior smiles, then looks to you. "Er...I take it you're in her party? You'll have to excuse my companion there."

You smile and wave it away. She spoke from her heart, and there's nothing to rebuke in that. Indeed, you feel you ought to be the one apologizing for effectively stealing a very capable bishop from them.

"She is an excellent bishop, isn't she?" the young man says, beaming proudly. "Be good to her. She's a dear friend of mine."

"If you let anyone put so much as a scratch on her, you'll pay!!" the priest adds hotly.

You nod: of course. They hardly need to say it. The dungeon is a dangerous place, and you can't make any guarantees, but if it's remotely within your power, she will stay safe.

At the same time, you feel utterly relieved. You tried to say the best thing you could think of, but you don't know what you would have done if she'd actually decided to leave your party. You're grateful that she chose to stay, and that you can go on exploring without regrets.

You weren't sure how it was going to go for a second there, but now it's finally settled...

§

"No! No! I won't allow it!!!!"

§

Apparently, it's not so settled after all.

"I won't let you run off to some other party!!"

Red-faced and shouting is a girl about the same age as Female Bishop and the others. Judging by her equipment, which you evaluate as she comes rushing up, she's probably a scout. She's human, but her movements are nearly as efficient as your own Half-Elf Scout's. Maybe she comes from the eastern desert. Her clothing and tanned skin look vaguely familiar to you. She's of slim build, her chest slight, her leather armor not thick at all. And she, too, wears a ring.

"Er, I'm sorry, I—"

"No! We're supposed to be friends!" Her sheer passion is part of the problem. If the priest earlier was too blunt, leading to easy misinterpretation, well, there's no mistaking this young woman. She looks in your direction with a disgust you would normally expect to be reserved for rogues in the dungeon. It's like having a weapon pointed at you: It's not for talking; it's for stabbing.

You can only groan. Since this young woman used to be Female Bishop's friend, and a companion of this warrior-priest, you can't imagine she's a bad person. She probably means well...but you still have a decision to make.

"Please, stop. Getting emotional will only make things harder for everyone."

The cold, rational words seem to speak for you. You look and see a black-haired youth, seemingly another warrior, appear following the sand-bandit girl. Perhaps another former—yes, former—member of Female Bishop's party.

From beside you, Female Bishop speaks the black-haired warrior's name in a small voice.

"But...," the sand-bandit girl protests. "But she... But I...!"

"What are we supposed to do with you yelling and shouting?" The black-haired youth sounds like he's trying to talk the sand-bandit girl around now, and on his hand, too, a ring shines. His attitude is outwardly conciliatory, but you can see in his eyes that he isn't sure about you, either.

You can't help a wry smile. You're honestly happy to know they care so much about Female Bishop, but you think it might kill you to have to explain as much. Not that you would regret it, here and now. You didn't and won't interfere with Female Bishop's decision, but once she's made her choice, it's your duty as party leader to support her in it.

However… You observe the other party carefully. The young warrior with the lacquered sword, the priest girl who looks just like Female Bishop, the sand-bandit girl, and the other warrior, with dark hair. In terms of its makeup, this party doesn't seem entirely suited to delving the dungeon. Certainly, it's not always possible to get exactly the adventurers one would like in one's group, but still…

"Now, now, we can't go saying such things…" As if in answer to your question, there's another voice, like a flickering shadow.

The last party member.

That makes five—now you see it; they do have an entire complement.

"——…" Female Bishop turns her bandage-clad eyes toward the voice. This last adventurer is dressed in a manner most unusual. The voice sounded like a shadow to you, and indeed, the adventurer looks like one. It's a man dressed all in black. If you had been asked to describe him, that would have summed up your entire observations. He wears a black conical hat, and his entire body is hidden by a full-length black cloak. Glimpses of pale skin are visible in a few places, while his eyes burn like will-o'-the-wisps. But for all that, his voice is impossibly mild, like a breeze blowing through the grass in the dark of night.

Indeed, he is like a shadow. But he has more…force than just that.

"Teacher!" the sand-bandit girl exclaims. "Say something to her, Teacher! She's being so selfish!"

You smile. Selfish—so that's what it's come to. Female Bishop, meanwhile, says, "Teacher…" in a voice tinged with wonder. "Who is that? Who…are you?"

"Oh, yeah. You haven't met yet," says the young warrior with the lacquered scabbard. His face softens into a smile, and he spreads his arms as if introducing someone he respects deeply—or rather, not *as if*, he does seem to respect this person. "Let me introduce you to the man who taught us to train ourselves—a wizard and our teacher."

"A pleasure…" So saying, Teacher—that is, the man with the black hat—brings his hands together in a gesture of greeting and gives a languid dip of his head.

You bring your own hands together and bow back to him, and you each give your names. Proper introductions are important.

But…a wizard? A wizard…? He certainly doesn't seem like any wizard you've ever met—he comes across as rather more intimidating. Nonetheless…

Very capable.

His footsteps, the movements of his eyes, even the slight twitches of his hands and fingers—every motion he makes is utterly efficient. He has no blind spots; no matter where he was attacked from, or when, he would react. It's clear he's a high-level adventurer. How long, you wonder, would one have to spend down in the dungeon, fighting and winning, to achieve this sort of level?

You can tell at a glance that he's in a place you can hardly imagine.

"Intimidating, hmm? Intimidating…" The way he strokes his chin as he speaks, he might as well be talking about the weather. He hardly seems to take any real notice of you. No—that's not true. Just like you, he's taken stock of his opponent—and determined they're of no consequence. "We could settle this here…but I think it would only lead to greater strife."

Agreed. You reply as carefully and guardedly as you can without arousing suspicion. Female Bishop has made her choice clear, but it seems not all members of her party are prepared to accept it. It's very rare to run into another group down in the dungeon, but to go adventuring with a grudge hanging over your heads would be unsettling. Though you aren't so uncouth as to worry that the other group might set an ambush for you in the dark or any such thing.

For one thing, both of you would regret your attitudes, and that would blunt your movements. To have any personal distractions while in the dungeon is practically to invite the Death upon you.

"So what do you say? Shall we have a little contest, here and now?"

Contest…? Your hand is instantly on your sword, and you're settling into a fighting stance. A single exchange, right here. Unless he means something else?

You don't have to look over at Female Bishop to know that she's clasping the sword and scales, no doubt with reluctance. She's a combat-tested adventurer now. As are you, you hope.

"Oh, I wasn't imagining anything so violent," the man in the black hat says. "Well... Perhaps a *little* violent." He gives a diffident wave of his hand and smiles, showing his teeth. "We've just been exploring the fourth floor lately. I presume you have, too?"

Mm. You nod.

"How about we see who finds the way to the fifth floor first?"

The fifth floor...?

You're not sure what to say—you don't mean to refuse, but admittedly the wager is perplexing. You had been wondering only shortly before whether such a thing even exists. Yet, this man before you sounds completely confident that it does.

"No objections here!" exclaims the sand-bandit girl. "We'll prove to you that our party is superior!"

"I d-don't think there's any...particular problem," Female Bishop says slowly but with conviction, shaking her head. "It's just...ahem. This party... I *decided*..."

"It's true, Teacher. She said she would join them, I heard her. I don't think there's anything we can do," says the priest girl hesitantly—although she doesn't sound pleased about it.

"That's how *she* feels," the man in the black hat says coolly, casually. It occurs to you that it's the aloof tone wizards so often take. Perhaps the man realizes it, too, for he smiles. "But how *you* all feel...that matters to me."

"I...I want—! I want..." There's a creaking sound. You see the young warrior has again grabbed the scabbard at his hip with the hand bearing his ring. Perhaps the scabbard cried out when he gripped it too hard—or perhaps it was the sword within. "I want a contest...!" He stares straight at you, the words squeezing out of him. "I want to... know if I can trust...my friend...to you...!"

——? A strange doubt seizes you, and you take a half step back. The look on the face of the young man challenging you is the precise opposite of the calm reserve he showed earlier. Maybe that can happen with human emotions sometimes, but...

"Ah, youth, so passionate!" The man in the black hat chuckles as if those few words explain everything. "Perhaps it's best we settle this? Strife between adventurers is exactly what the master of that dungeon wants, after all."

The man still wears the same indulgent smile. He's right; what he says is true. And yet... Shouldn't Female Bishop's own desire be respected? You try raising the objection.

"Surely you aren't telling me you're not confident in yourself?"

You shake your head. No, that's not what you're saying. But now you can no longer back down. The anxiety that assaulted you until a moment before seems like a distant memory now. Whatever the obstacles, whatever the barriers, you will break through them and prevail. The details don't matter to you. If any would laugh, let them.

"Just a little competition. Nothing more." When he sees your resolve, the man in the black hat places a heavy, cold hand on your shoulder. The sort of easy, intimate gesture one would share with an old friend. "Win or lose, nothing in particular will happen. Now, shall we go?"

"Yes, Teacher...!" the young warrior and his party say, with the alacrity of disciples responding to their master. Then they follow the man in the black hat.

You stare after them until they're out of sight, and then you place a hand on the shoulder the man touched.

"Um... Are you okay?" The concerned voice comes from just slightly below that shoulder. You exhale, nod at Female Bishop, and then answer aloud. Your entire body is soaked in an unpleasant sweat, your clothing clinging to you. You've encountered someone profoundly uncanny. A powerful opponent indeed...one to be wary of.

The young man with the lacquered sword—and the wizard in the black hat. You clench your fist as you follow them into the hubbub of the town.

No choice but to accept this challenge.

"Listen...I'm sorry. It's my fault things turned out this way..." Female Bishop looks at you pitifully, her voice smaller than a flea. She bows her head, shrinks into herself, and looks, to your eyes, just as she did when you found her in the tavern. How much must this gentle girl's heart be hurting? Even you can easily imagine.

You smile, say there's no reason to worry so much. Tell her that you're the one who should apologize. You set out with the intent to respect her volition but ended up accepting this silly challenge.

"But... That was..."

Your response is prompt and firm: It's nothing—you were going to keep exploring the dungeon anyway.

".......Right." She smiles, maybe in part for your benefit. It's a gossamer expression, as if it might vanish into the twilight.

That's right: Things won't be any different from before. You'll get through that dungeon. You'll cut down the monsters. You and your friends will battle the Death. Nothing different. Though now you must succeed for Female Bishop's sake as well... But in the end, that's exactly what you were doing anyway.

At that point, you suddenly have a thought, and you laugh out loud, practically cackling.

"——...?" Female Bishop looks at you, startled, but you wave a hand; it's nothing. Nothing important. Hardly needs to be said. In fact, you *should* be used to this. After all, this is the second time you've almost drawn your blade against another adventurer in Female Bishop's defense. You think you were a lot calmer this time than that day in the tavern, if you do say so yourself.

So you know it's true, then. You are indeed making progress...

§

It's the next day. On the way to the dungeon, you tell everyone about what happened the day before.

"...Huh, quite a story," Female Warrior murmurs, licking her lips innocently. "So that's why you were so late getting back..."

When you finally returned to the tavern after everything that happened, you and Female Bishop were both too tired to explain. Though you suspected that unlike the men, who slept in the stables, the girls in their more comfortable accommodations might hear some bits of the tale.

"And here I thought for sure you were just having a nice little walk together!"

You ignore your *second* cousin.

Perhaps your choice was a bit hasty, you wonder aloud.

"Eh, seems to've got you back on your game, Cap, so it's all good," Half-Elf Scout says, making sure he's speaking loud enough for Female Bishop, still worried about the situation, to hear him. "We were gonna look for the next level of that dungeon, anyway, so what's the difference?"

"If we haven't attained the proper strength, though, it could mean death for us. And anyway, we don't even know for sure that there is a fifth floor." *Clack.* Myrmidon Monk is curt, as usual. He isn't wrong, either. But strangely enough, no one in the party seems to doubt the existence of another level. "Personally, I don't care either way," Myrmidon Monk adds.

"Your older sister wants her little brother to learn to be nice to a girl now and then," your *second* cousin says. You don't even think that's the point at issue.

"I don't know; I don't think it would make him any less troublesome." Argh. Now even Female Warrior is piling on. You sigh dramatically, your eyes settling on Female Bishop.

"Hee-hee…" The characteristic banter has brought a slight smile to her face. To your surprise, she doesn't look depressed at all. Maybe the girls did have some salubrious chat in the simple accommodations the night before.

It seems neither Half-Elf Scout nor Myrmidon Monk has any objection to this dungeon exploration contest, either. You find yourself giving thanks to the Trade God for the blessing of fine companions.

Gotta make a donation at the temple when we come back from exploring.

"This wizard, though… He bothers me. From what you say, he sounds pretty high level. What's your take?" Myrmidon Monk says.

"How should I know?" Female Warrior replies with a shake of the head. "I don't hear much talk about wizards. Never thought I'd have to look for another one."

You grunt: *Mm.* It's odd that your two companions, both of whom have been adventurers longer than you, have never heard of this man.

Even considering how many adventurers come and go in the fortress city every day, a wizard who helped other people get more powerful would normally attract attention.

"Were you able to scare anything up about them?" your cousin asks Half-Elf Scout.

"Hrm," he says, folding his arms. "I tried asking around between adventures, but they're just another party. And if they were training, they'd be down in the dungeon most of the time anyway, right?"

You nod. At least, if you take them at their word, they would be.

"Long story short, not a trace of 'em. Even though there ain't that many parties able to get down to the fourth floor..."

You nod again. By no means do you suspect Half-Elf Scout of having overlooked anything. But the matter does nag at you. Yes, they had a high-level adventurer accompanying them, but you're still surprised that they've progressed as far as you have. Unlike most of those who come to the fortress city, you and your party haven't focused on making money but have single-mindedly dedicated yourselves to exploring the dungeon. That's why you're veritably able to keep up with the Knight of Diamonds and his party, even if they may be slightly ahead of you. And you can't imagine there's any place so deep in the dungeon that's suited for basic training...

"Well, we won't learn anything new just by thinking about it," your cousin says, sweeping away your doubts. "We need to keep exploring, just like we always do!"

"You said it, Sis! Same job as always!"

Mm.

You nod firmly, then look up at the entrance to the dungeon looming before you. You check the fasteners on your sword, then make sure your equipment is secure. Your other party members do likewise, and then you double-check everything for them, as is your duty as leader. You need to know everyone's situation, check everything over, and finally have someone check you: That will put everyone's minds at ease.

"Oh... What about medicines and such?" Female Bishop asks, pulling a potion from her pack, but Female Warrior makes a face. "I'm always afraid those are going to break."

Yes, maybe it would be best not to entrust them to the front row. But then, considering the possibility—may it never come—that your clerics may have to move up a row…

"That leaves me!" your cousin says, raising her hand and grinning. Yes, yes it does.

She takes the bottles from Female Bishop and hugs them to her chest as if she's going to bury them there. "Just leave everything to your older sister!"

Well, if your *second* cousin is so eager, at least it means she won't be as nervous.

Right—time to head down.

When the royal guard at the dungeon entrance sees you, she gives an elaborate bow. "Thank you for yesterday."

She's referring to the little girl—her sister. You reply that it was nothing, but she tells you it was quite a lot. "Make sure you come home, now. I don't want to have to tell the kid what happened if you don't come back."

You laugh, your footsteps light as you venture into that abyss where only the wire frame is to be seen. Beside you, Female Warrior giggles with a sound like a bell. "Same job as always…"

Very much so.

Whatever you've been challenged to, and whoever challenged you to it, in the end, what you have to do hasn't changed.

§

First floor, second, third.

Avoiding the dark zone, slipping through the rogues' den, braving the hallways full of traps…

You've been this way many times before, and now you travel it with a minimum of danger.

This dungeon that has buried so many adventurers, with all its monsters and trials, is now merely a place you pass through. The monsters you have to deal with aren't terribly threatening, so long as you're careful as you enter each chamber. Soon you're descending the rope ladder, rung by rung, carefully, down onto the fourth floor.

"Now, what do we do today...?" Female Bishop asks, and you hear her unrolling the map.

After a second, you respond. Maybe you should start with a quick tour of the level. There might be hidden doors you've missed. You need to have a look around.

"So I just take a little look-see at the walls and whatever?"

"What? Ugh, that sounds so boring..."

The responses from your two vanguards are quite distinct. You're used to the arched eyebrow of displeasure you receive from Female Warrior. After all, if this doesn't turn up anything, you'll probably be compelled to start over again from the first floor. All of you are hoping that this time you'll discover something, anything.

Thus, you proceed into the first chamber without hesitation. You knock down the door, and there, on the other side, it waits for you. An odorless gas floating in the gloom, a chilling thing to encounter.

Odorless? Is it really? Wanting to know whether the eerie feeling you have is warranted, you take a sniff. It's sweet. The aroma that drifts toward you is something like flowers or perhaps incense...

"Here it comes!" Myrmidon Monk clacks, his antennae flailing. Almost immediately, your weapon is in your hands; you're in a fighting posture and ready to go. The darkness seems to slither toward you, and out of it emerges—no, that's not right. The Shade, the darkness itself, attacks you.

"Wha—?" Half-Elf Scout exclaims, his voice scratching. "The hell is this?!"

You can't hide your own confusion. It's completely impossible to tell what you're trying to attack! The way it seems to swirl and writhe makes you think of a living gas cloud, but...

It's like there's nothing there...!

You swing your sword but cut only the air, and all you hear is a sort of wheezing laughter. You smell something sickeningly sweet, and your head spins like you've had too much to drink.

"Haagh...?!" Suddenly, there's an anguished cry. It's Female Warrior. You look over to find her bent double, leaning on her spear as if she can barely stand up. Her eyes are watery, and her cheeks are so red you can see it even in the gloom of the dungeon. Her breath comes in quick, hard gasps. Each time the darkness shifts, she thrashes, her equipment rattling noisily.

You don't have the chance to call out to her, though. The moment you open your mouth, the darkness enters it. It fills your lungs, a tickling sensation. It's not entirely unpleasant, but it is terrifying. You almost find it hard to breathe, like in that beautiful moment after you've shared a kiss with a woman you dearly love.

Strength...bleeding away...!

No...it's being sucked away. Somehow, you're sure.

You force strength into your legs, taking a shoulder-width stance, gritting your teeth so hard it feels like they might crack. You convince yourself that you have to resist, somehow, even as you feel the caresses of the miasma working its way under your armor. You feel floaty, drowsy.

Your attention wavers for an instant, and you discover a blank in your consciousness. If you slip into it, you'll fall asleep. Everything will be easy. But...you doubt you'll ever come back from it.

"Cap...this is...bad! Gotta stay sharp, or we'll die...!"

"Hngh... Ahhh!"

Half-Elf Scout's warning, Female Warrior's anguished cry—they both seem far away now. She swings her spear as if she's a child having a tantrum—but it only sweeps through the darkness.

You think you might say something, that you know or to calm down. Then, in front of you, you see the silhouette of a woman. Her hair is red as flames, her skin pale, her body voluptuous as a ripe fruit. On her back are two wings, all bone and flesh—but when you try to focus on her, get a closer look, she seems to melt into an unsteady haze. You blink, she appears; you blink again, she disappears; her shape shifts, and at times she looks like a young woman with black hair wearing black armor.

Is this an illusion birthed by the dark mist, or is it the true form of the creature attacking you? There's an irresistible whining in your ears. The inarticulate whispers of the dark women. You almost think that, if you listened closely, you could make out what they're saying, yet ultimately you can discern no meaning in the cacophony. You feel like you're drowning; you want to open your mouth.

Someone is shouting behind you, but you don't understand them anymore.

No… This isn't right…

"O my god of the roaming wind, carry our hearts there and their hearts here!"

A wind comes rushing through, and the women scream. With shrill screeches, the darkness recedes, and you suck in gasping breaths.

"Well, well… Looks like they don't know what to do with *my* heart or mind. Damn succubi," Myrmidon Monk clacks, making a complicated sigil with his hands. That was the Transfer Mental Power miracle just now, you're sure of it. So even the succubi, whose stock-in-trade is drawing people's desires out of their dreams and thus leading them into darkness, can't pierce the veil of a myrmidon's heart. The great bugman glares at the dark clouds where they've drawn back, wiggles his antennae in their direction, and spits, "Not even worth setting up a sanctified space to catch them. Can you stand?"

"Hey, standing's my favorite thing," Half-Elf Scout says with as much conviction as he can muster, and you likewise reply, more briefly, that you can do it.

You reach out to Female Warrior where she's still slumped over, and after a single full-body twitch, she nods. "Sorry. I'm fine…!" She wipes away her sweat and tears, getting to her feet with the help of her spear on the one hand and you on the other. Good.

As for you, you bring your katana to bear and steady your breathing. You keep your eyes on the darkness, widening your stance. Succubi, you've heard, are quasi-incorporeal creatures that exist in the realm of the dead. This is what makes them so terrible when they enter dreams and illusions.

But we know what they are now. Armed with that knowledge, awakened and alert, you won't be taken in so easily again. At the same time, you know your sword can't touch them—so spells will be the deciding factor.

"You can count on us! Let's do it!"

"Right! I'll…I'll do my best!"

One of the girls responds to your instruction with eagerness, the other with seriousness. At the same time, the darkness howls.

"SUCCCCUUUUUUUBBBBB!!!!"

It's some monstrous incantation you don't recognize, presumably in the tongue of some monstrous realm. A spark, a hellish flash of light, sweeps through the dungeon—you recognize the effect, at least, as the Lightning spell.

But your women, concentrating on the Force while you and your fighters prepare your bodies, are one move ahead.

"Magna remora restinguitur! An end to magic!"

"Lord of judgment, sword-prince, scale-bearer, show here your power!"

Your cousin's powerful voice causes the magical clouds to disperse, while Female Bishop's incantation causes the very logic of the air to rewrite itself.

A blast falls as if from the heavens above. A great flash from the gods that reaches all the way to the depths of the dungeon. It is Holy Smite, springing from Female Bishop's outstretched sword and scales.

"——?!?!"

The succubi, subject to the judgment of the gods, give an other-worldly screech. The darkness writhes and skitters backward, and for the first time, you see it: ectoplasm scorching and igniting, stuff that thumbs its nose at the laws of physics.

"They may whisper sweet nothings in our ears, they may beg and plead for mercy, but I shall not forgive!" Female Bishop, her face illuminated by the white light, is impossibly cold and clear. "Demons, succubi, and vampires are all living things…and their cries are only those of animals!"

Even if the monsters truly do repent of their actions, a crime demands a punishment. That much is immovable. If these creatures who hide in the darkness truly wish to become people, all the more reason they must accept their just deserts. For the gods have delegated to people the judgment between good and evil.

"They're no better than goblins…"

You pretend not to hear the last words that squeeze out of Female Bishop's mouth. They mingle with the last rumbles of thunder and are soon swept away.

§

An unpleasant smell of ozone in the air signals the end of the battle. No other traces of the darkness remain in the chamber; there's only your party standing there—no, wait.

"Man, oh man, never expected demons like that to show up...," Half-Elf Scout says, wiping away nervous sweat as he eyes the treasure chest the creatures have left behind. You nod agreement while listening to Half-Elf Scout's lockpick scrape in the keyhole. As terrifying as that dragon was, at least it was a creature of this world. You don't think it's normal for succubi, creatures from another realm, to just appear like that.

"Do you think it's really the Demon Lord down at the bottom of the dungeon, then?" your cousin asks with an uncharacteristic note of discomfort, frowning as she waves away the black smoke.

Female Bishop shakes her head slowly, uncertain. "I thought that was just a story... Even considering the miasma of the Death." She sounds less like she's seriously objecting and more like she doesn't want to believe it. You know how she feels—but facts are facts. If there wasn't some connection to the world beyond this one, you wouldn't have encounters like the one you just had.

"Speaking of stories...they talk about archmages... Hrrmm..." Your cousin puts a finger to her lips in thought. You say nothing. She knows what she's talking about; she certainly knows more about magic than you do.

Even if the things that come out of her mouth can be dubious.

Anyway, there are more important matters. You turn to Female Warrior, who looks into the empty space in front of her as if her mind is elsewhere.

'Doing okay?'

"Mm, I'm fine. Just a little shaken." She looks annoyed for a second, then shivers. She blinks, then repeats a couple of times that she's fine, rubbing her face with her hand. So hard she turns red, in fact. "Hey, maybe I could get a drink. My throat's so dry."

You nod and toss her your waterskin. Down in the dungeon, it's easy to lose track of when you're hungry or thirsty. If you notice the pinch of thirst, you should absolutely drink.

Glug, glug. Female Warrior's pale throat rises and falls as she swallows the water, and you avert your eyes. "Something's going on, whatever it is." *Phew.* She places her hand to her bountiful chest, finally answering your cousin's whisper, which had gone without a response until now. Whether they came from a door to the nether realm, or if they were produced by the upwelling of the Death, those weren't opponents to be trifled with.

"Gate is a lost spell, after all. And even your big sister doesn't understand it very well yet." Though, your *second* cousin insists, she gets the theory. You only briefly acknowledge her comment. Since you have indeed been confronted with actual demons now, though, perhaps you'll eventually be needing that Demon Core after all.

"Demon Core…" The words drop into the air like pebbles in a pond. Female Bishop seems to be mulling them over. She looks intensely serious.

You wave it away: You were just joking, you tell her, and try to change the subject by asking how the map is coming.

"Oh, right! It's right here…!" Female Bishop nods quickly, pulling the folded parchment from her bag and trotting over to you. Both vigilance and rest are called for while Half-Elf Scout does battle with the treasure chest, but at the same time, you need to decide where you are and where you're going. You glance at Female Warrior, who acknowledges you by taking up a fighting stance with her spear and moving toward the wall by the chest. Then, while expressing your appreciation for Myrmidon Monk's miracle, you also ask him to come over and have a look at the map.

"It was no big deal," he says, glancing over your shoulder. "So what do you think?"

"There certainly don't appear to be any doors on the fourth floor…," Female Bishop says. The three of you study the map, which rustles as you unroll it. Female Bishop's diagram, your memories, and Myrmidon Monk's observations all agree.

But there is obviously empty space. A quarter of the floor or perhaps more. The shape of this floor is very odd compared to those of the previous three.

"That's true." Female Bishop nods. "Of course, we don't know for certain that all of the floors in this dungeon are perfect squares."

"The other three have been. I think it's a safe assumption to start from," Myrmidon Monk says, tapping a pointy finger against the as-yet-unmapped portion of the fourth floor. "And I think that entails the assumption that there's a way to get here and a way to continue farther down."

'From the upper levels?'

"Possibly. Possibly not." Myrmidon Monk's mandibles clack. "I don't much care either way."

It has to be—there's no other possibility.

This is your conclusion after a brief moment of consideration. The third floor, the second, the first. You need to check them again. If nothing else, it will be better than sinking into depression because there seems to be no way forward.

Just having a marker has changed everything—you mention that, in that sense, you're grateful to *them*, too.

"Wha—? Oh…" Female Bishop looks confused at first, but then a pleased smile softens her face. "Yes…you're very right."

You don't have to hate each other. You'll just take things as they come. Who knows but that years from now, you'll be telling this story over drinks somewhere.

"Yes, got it!" Half-Elf Scout cheers.

Ah. You fold up the map and hand it back to Female Bishop, then hurry over to the treasure chest.

A sword—a sword—is there any sword? It's fine if there isn't. You don't mind either way.

"Hey," Myrmidon Monk grunts from behind you (you pretend not to hear), and you peer down over Half-Elf Scout's shoulder. There's the usual mountain of gold coins and several items that look like equipment.

"There y'have it, Cap. Gotta have those items identified when we get back up top." But he thinks there's something more important to say. "Captain, what kinda woman those succubi look like to you?"

There's a whistle as the butt of a spear comes flying through the air. "Yipes!" Half-Elf Scout cries as he goes tumbling backward.

"Come on, boys. Can't let down our guard when there might be traps, can we?" Female Warrior, with her black hair and black armor, is smiling at you both. Half-Elf Scout looks at you. You nod.

Mm, well, yes. True enough.

First things first: You want to go back up. Then you look for a way down. You jump into action immediately; the others share a smile and then follow you. Another day, and you still haven't found the stairs. But you're starting to think maybe having a day like that every once in a while isn't such a bad thing after all.

§

The days pass, full of the deaths of monsters and your survival and the piling up of treasure.

For the fortress city and the Golden Knight, there seems to be neither day nor night.

You work on your breakfast, not quite watching the dancing girls who shout and twist their hips on stage. The red-and-green frog costumes are ridiculous, but their very comical quality has an air of the salacious about it. The form-fitting clothes are obviously welcomed by the adventurers back from their quests.

As for you personally? Well, you don't mind having something to enjoy looking at while you sip your barley porridge and wait for your companions.

"Hmm. Here I thought I might find you pouting because you don't know where to go next, but you're in quite a good mood, I see." There's a cackle of laughter, and a wind rushes through the tavern. A young woman, squinting like a cat, slides up next to you as easily as the breeze. You glance in her direction, reply that you're doing all right, and sip your porridge.

"Well, at least you haven't let it get to you. As a big-sister type cheering you on, I have to say I'm happy to see it." A hand emerges from her cape, and the woman—the informant—waves for a waitress. "One lemon water, please. Put it on *his* tab."

Fine—you don't mind. At least she might talk to you while she drinks. You have a few questions you'd like to ask.

"Oh-ho," the informant says, her eyes sparkling as she takes the glass from the waitress. "Curious about how to get down to the next level?"

You laugh. That's not really one of your questions. You already plan to search the whole dungeon from the top down again. But if she has something to share on the topic, you're all ears.

"Heh-heh. I love a man who lets his imagination run wild." The informant giggles, then looks you over as she savors a sip of her lemon water. "But I think you've already got some ideas of your own, am I right?"

Mm. You nod, and you open your mouth. You and the informant say the same thing at the same time:

"The dark zone."

The shadow of the Death that lies like a tomb upon the first floor of the dungeon. The lightless space even the miasma of the crypt can't seem to penetrate. It's literally dark. *Terra incognita.*

None who have entered it have ever returned. To be quite honest, you strongly suspect it of housing some very unpleasant trap. The very least you can say is that no one who goes down into the dungeon purely for the profit goes anywhere near the dark zone. Plenty of money to be made fighting monsters in better-lit places. One is already in a fight for one's life. What need to go throwing oneself directly at the Death?

"But *you*…," the informant woman whispers sweetly. "You're different, aren't you?"

You correct her: Not just you alone. Everyone in your party.

"Well, isn't that fine. Yes…I think I like it."

You reply brusquely that you're glad she approves. The words of praise might even be heartfelt, but you feel somehow embarrassed to accept them as openly as they're given.

The woman seems pleased by your reaction. She puts her chin in her hands and laughs again. "All right, then, a little reward for you, from me. I'll tell you anything you want to know."

Anything?

"You heard me. Anything at all…"

What to do? You dip your spoon into your porridge and bring it to your mouth to distract yourself from those searching eyes. There are so many things you wonder about. But some of them probably aren't things you should ask.

You don't mind asking, however. Nor do you mind keeping it to yourself. You could even choose your own question to ask.

You're an adventurer. You came here to this fortress city because you'd heard rumors about the terrible Dungeon of the Dead, and you wanted to brave its deepest depths. It would hardly be to your credit, then, to rely on others for every last thing. You've chosen this path—now you must choose how to walk it. Thus…

"Hmm? The party of a guy with a red-lacquered sword?"

Mm. You nod. You choose not to ask about the dungeon, or about her, but about this. She looks at you for a second, blinking in surprise—you can tell even in spite of her hooded cape.

"Hmm. Well, now." The woman mumbles happily to herself, then leans coquettishly over the circular table. "I actually don't know anything about them," she says, tilting her head to one side and looking up at you. "And that's the problem, right?"

Yes, of course. A party on the cusp of discovering the fifth floor of the dungeon can't possibly be anonymous. The only ones you're aware of are the group with the Knight of Diamonds—and, not to brag, your own.

Trading rumors about adventuring parties is as common as talking about the weather around here. It's a matter of public record that you've saved other groups, crossed swords with the scruffy men, and arrived at the fourth floor of the dungeon.

But they're different.

It might be one thing if a famous party had shown up in the city on their travels. But this group worked with Female Bishop once—you dare say their level isn't that different from yours.

"And yet they're not such a different level from *you*."

Yes, that's it. Even if they were delving before you, it seems beyond strange. This isn't a matter of jealousy or envy. Even your group, if you put in enough time—no. You never imagined you would eventually reach a point where you could go toe-to-toe with a dragon.

"Heh!" The woman smiles like a cat that's fond of its master, then brings her glass to her lips. "I do know where they got so powerful, though." The informant sips her water again and swallows noisily. You suddenly remember Female Warrior's gesture from earlier and reply simply, no.

"Huh." The woman licks her wetted lips and nods. "Only one place, right? The dungeon." She snorts as if this were the most obvious thing in the world. You bring another spoonful of porridge to your mouth, chew, then swallow it before turning to her. You tell her you need to know more.

"What do you want? According to legend, the Platinum ranks are practically beyond human understanding." That's her first gambit. To speak of the heroes now gone from this world. Great adventurers said to have saved the world in their shining chain mail. Sometimes it was believed they could even transcend death, returning to life to punish evil.

But now they're gone.

"And now we've got this dungeon beneath our feet. What's down there? The Death."

Hell. The afterlife. The Death. Old dwarven legends tell of a force of destruction that sleeps in the depths of the earth. You remember your master telling you about all of them, what feels like ages ago now. Is she there, too, then, down underneath the earth?

"And if you delve into the depths and stand on the border between life and death, and come back to the surface... Then what?" The informant woman puts the straw (when did she get that?) in her glass into her mouth, chews it thoughtfully, and looks at you. "Isn't it the Death coming back all over again?"

Well...

You're lost for what to say. No—in fact, you understand. You see the answer, as if a marker has been placed in your mind. It's an immovable fact, the imitation of a heroic act that transcends human knowledge. As one who has had a taste of magic, you can understand it. Imitation doesn't stop with physical mimicry.

Yes: The Death is power.

Adventurer, monster, killer, killed, one survives. That's power.

A good night's murder in the dungeon, killing and killing, could raise your level before the sun rises.

The dungeon is a place beyond human knowledge, where it's possible to imitate the works of the great superhuman heroes.

However.

Beyond that pile of corpses—beyond that great height—what is there?

©lack

"'Fraid I can't rightly say. I'm not an adventurer." She smiles ambiguously at your question and shrugs.

You didn't expect an answer. She doesn't owe you any more of them anyway. If you want to know the answer, you'll have to go and find it. You think you know where it lies now.

"The dark zone." The informant's small whisper and your own convinced declaration harmonize with each other. She stands up slowly. "Thanks for the drink," she says, her smile disappearing into the shadows under her hood.

You ask if she's leaving, and she says, "Yeah," and nods. "Believe it or not, I'm a busy gal."

That is what it is, then. You've already gained quite a bit from her. Certainly, more than the price of a single lemon water.

"Oughtta at least thank me, then," she says with an ear-tickling giggle. Of course: You bow deeply toward her.

There's a sound like another pleasant gust of wind through the tavern. As it brushes your cheek, she leaves you with a sharp sound and a "But remember…someone who only cares about weak or strong, winner or loser… They might not even be an adventurer anymore."

That's the last thing she says.

§

"The dark zone…" Myrmidon Monk is the first of your companions, finally arrived at breakfast, to speak after you do. "Guess it is the only place left to look."

You nod: *Mm*.

Regardless of how you've reached the conclusion, there's a distinct possibility that the dark zone is the key.

You've had many of these strategy meetings over late breakfasts, and each time, as you stuff yourselves with food, a strange presence seems to be with you at the table. It's the words you haven't said, the unknown space sitting in the first floor. The great, yawning tunnel of the dark zone.

You can never see very far ahead in the dungeon corridors, but there's at least a modicum of illumination. But not in that one place.

There's only a lightless expanse that threatens to swallow adventurers whole.

Some say that a mad wizard lurks within, conducting unholy experiments in an attempt to open the door to the netherworld.

Some say that a den of the dead lies within, that it's the purview of the Death and connected directly to hell.

Some say that no one who has set foot in the dark zone has ever returned.

You presume it's not a place that would be of interest to those who have come to the fortress city purely to make their fortune. The only ones who might be willing to try themselves against it would be reckless fortune hunters seeking the biggest score of all—or else those attempting to make the dungeon's deepest depths.

In other words, you and your friends.

"Most people don't even seem to remark on the strangest thing around here," Myrmidon Monk says, his mandibles clacking.

"What's that?" Female Warrior asks.

"The endless treasure."

He means the loot that wells up from the dungeon. You think of the treasure chests, no small number of which your party has found. When you destroy the monsters in a room, one always appears. Many adventurers lust after them. They're the basic ingredients of hack and slash.

"Do you think there really is such a thing?"

One might argue that of course there is: It's what built the place you're sitting in right now. You know that's too simple, too convenient, but you say it anyway. Just as Myrmidon Monk and your other companions do for you.

"Say you're right. Still, something doesn't come from nothing. The world doesn't work that way." Somewhere, there has to be something, some resource, feeding it all.

"But ain't it just fine that there's a mountain of money around?" *Hmm.* Half-Elf Scout stuffs a piece of bread into his mouth and goes for some liver and onions. "True, it's pretty weird, but it's not like there's blood on the money."

"But it built this town." Myrmidon Monk shrugs slightly, the way clerics of the Trade God sometimes do. "It's all money here, every-where. It's obscene. Eventually it'll overwhelm everything, and then it'll all be over."

"Adventurers and our work are like bubbles, huh? A dream within a dream." Half-Elf Scout chews his liver and onions, then swallows. "…I see what you're saying. And I guess…that makes it seem most likely there's something behind it all." He folds his arms, grunts, and frowns.

It doesn't change the fact that the dungeon is a dangerous place. You like this reaction better than simple wholehearted agreement.

"Me, I just don't want to be afraid…" Thus, you're grateful for Female Warrior's strained whisper. She's resting her chin on one hand, stirring her porridge listlessly. You can see how uneasy she feels. After all, even though you only met after you arrived in the fortress city, you've gotten to know her quite well. "…I'm afraid to die, you know?"

"So you want to spend the rest of your life pottering around the fourth floor?" Myrmidon Monk clacks back at her. He tears off a piece of meat from some beast you don't recognize and swallows it. "I don't care if you do, myself. Though I'd have to find myself another party."

"…I didn't say that," Female Warrior replies, her eyes shifting around hesitantly. Finally, she lets out a small breath. "I'm just won-dering if we're really going to be okay."

Well, truth be told, you can't answer that.

"I was hoping you'd say we'll be fine…even if it wasn't true." At length Female Warrior giggles, and you relax.

True, you well know the dungeon is a profoundly dangerous place, but adventurers are the people who take those risks. The knight-errant in the old song might warn against recklessness, foolishness, and care-lessness, but still you must go. The true master of the sword is he who sees the charging horse come down the path and simply steps out of the road. But this doesn't mean to face only opponents you know you can beat, to challenge only places that are ultimately safe.

However…

You wonder what your cousin and Female Bishop are up to. Those are two women you would normally expect to put in their two cents on a matter like this.

"Hrmgh?" Your *second* cousin looks up blankly; both girls have their noses buried in a thick book. It has a weathered leather cover incised with characters from some other land. A mysterious tome indeed. You think it must be a spell book the girls purchased somewhere along the line...

"What, this? No, no. Look, remember those demons we ran into a while ago?" Your cousin adopts a tone like an older sister explaining something to a particularly dense younger brother.

She's right, you suppose, that succubi are a type of demon. They use human dreams as the medium to usher themselves into this world. Your sword was able to cut that which it can't normally touch because the women (you think they're women) are inhabitants of the other realm. You wouldn't want to encounter a Greater Succubus, a creature with the power to maintain a physical manifestation in this world, while you were asleep.

"So I thought we needed to do a little research about summoning, the Demon Core, and the Gate spell." Summoning demons was one kind of thing, but those other two—they were a forbidden art and a lost spell, weren't they? Your tone is slightly exasperated. And your cousin has even got Female Bishop tangled up in this now.

"Oh, but..." Female Bishop shakes her head, very serious. She turns her sightless eyes on you, her fingers still running along the page, reading the characters. "I think...it's going to be very necessary to help us move forward."

Hmm.

Impressed by her demeanor, you relax a little, even as you contemplate what she's said. All her considerable force of will is focused on moving the party forward. Any hostility toward her former—yes, former—party members, any anxiety about you and your new group, is gone. That's something you're very happy to realize.

You tell her that although you'll be on the first floor of the dungeon, you yourself will handle any goblins you encounter, so she should just focus on her magic. You don't forget to add that you'll deal with any slimes, too.

"...Hee-hee," Female Bishop chuckles, then nods and says, "Right." Good.

"Ugh!" Female Warrior exclaims, puffing out her cheeks; with her long legs, she manages to give your shins a kick under the table. You squirm with pain, while your cousin admonishes you, "You shouldn't say things like that!"

These ladies are tough. You tell them they could stand to be a little more gentle…or at least show some discretion.

"Dunno, Cap, I think you were the problem there."

"Doesn't matter to me what they do."

How cruel. Your mumble is only greeted with a wave of Myrmidon Monk's antennae. "So," he says, "we *are* going, aren't we?"

Yes, you're going.

"That's settled, then." He raps on the table with one carapace-clad hand and stands up.

Half-Elf Scout sticks his hand in the air. "Check please, miss!"

"Yes, sir!" the harefolk waitress says, bustling over, and there's a jangle as money changes hands. They only exchange a few words, but he shows his quick wit and sensitivity in them.

"Let's see here. We should be fine on potions and other provisions. Your big sister has been taking good care to keep everything stocked up." Your *second* cousin puffs out her generous chest proudly.

"And if we're going into the dark zone, we'll need a map," Female Bishop says, clenching her fists to indicate determination.

Gods. The hint of a smile passes over your face. Look at these stalwart adventuring companions.

So—how about it?

Female Warrior, her chin still in her hands, just glances up at you. "Mm. 'Course I'm going." She squints like a cat and giggles. "Besides, you look like you couldn't stand to go without me."

Do you, now? You stroke your chin. Female Warrior grabs your sleeve and pulls you toward her. "If we run into any slimes…well, I can count on you, can't I?" She grins. You nod.

And so you all prepare your equipment, and prepare yourselves, as if this were any other trip into the dungeon. The dark zone waits for you, a place unknown and untried. But you don't think about how you might not come home. That possibility has always been there, since the first time you went down into the depths.

§

To step off a familiar, well-trodden path is an act of courage. It's practically reassuring to encounter your usual foes, like goblins and slimes.

"Ugh, I hate those things…" Female Warrior sniffles, patting a slimy shoulder—but you're thinking these thoughts about how the encounter is almost comforting.

You look back over your shoulder and ask if everyone is all right, to which Female Bishop replies, "Y-yes, I think…," in a strained voice.

"You just let Big Sis handle this," your cousin says. You know you can rely on her at moments like this. You nod and exhale. You reflect that long before you worried about the dark zone or rogues or ninjas, the first floor of the dungeon was your sorest trial. An experienced adventurer could practically walk the halls alone, but that first adventure—you remember now how exhausting and dangerous it was.

"Okay…I'm all right now," Female Warrior says with one final pat of her shoulder, and you turn to your companions. You don't want to waste energy on random encounters if you don't have to. You don't want to use any spells. And yet you'd be embarrassed to run away.

Although if it came to that, the situation would probably be worse than embarrassing—and certainly more draining.

Taking it cautiously from one end to the other, that's the best way to go about this. At least here in the dungeon.

"Sorry… Thank you, I didn't mean to cause trouble." Female Bishop takes the waterskin your cousin offers her and drinks gratefully. It is what it is, what with first goblins and then slimes appearing in quick succession.

More seriously, you mention, it would be ideal for people about to go into the dark zone to *not* start out that way.

"…If that happened, I think I would cry," Female Bishop says. She sounds like she might be joking—but then again, like she might not—and you respond with an ambiguous smile. Then again, the fact that she can talk this way means she's probably fine. You ask if you can trust her to find the way.

"Yes," Female Bishop says with confidence, pulling her beloved map out of her bag and unrolling it. "We head north. Then we go through the intersection and toward the far door. After that…left."

"So no chambers this time?" Half-Elf Scout asks, peeking over Female Bishop's shoulder at the map. She nods. "That's right. We can ignore them… In fact, I suppose we have to."

"Man, guess there won't be a lot of profit this time out," Half-Elf Scout quips, provoking a giggle from your cousin.

"Who knows, but there might be a mountain of treasure somewhere in the dark zone," Myrmidon Monk clacks, and this time it's Female Warrior who smiles. "I don't want to have to carry any more than I already do, so whatever we find, you handle yourself, all right?" she says.

"Er, sure…"

There's a good rapport here. You let out a breath, grateful that everyone is keeping their wits about them even though you're about to go into unknown territory.

"Don't you want some water? Don't strain yourself, now!" Female Bishop must have taken your exhalation for fatigue, because she holds out your cousin's waterskin to you. You take it appreciatively but can't quite ignore the fact that Female Bishop put it to her lips only moments ago.

Blasted second *cousin…*

"What, too embarrassed to take a drink?" Female Warrior's voice tickles your ear, and you glare at her, then take a defiant gulp of water. The liquid is hardly down your throat before you thrust the waterskin back at your *second* cousin.

Geez. Just…geez.

"Heh-heh-heh, if only you were always so forthcoming," your *second* cousin teases with a grin, thoughtless as ever.

"—? What's going on?" Female Bishop asks, confused. You can't imagine having to explain with Female Warrior standing right there, so instead you say it's time to get going.

"Mm. Ready when you are," Myrmidon Monk says.

"Same here," adds Half-Elf Scout. The party regroups and sets off.

You go down the stairs, then directly north. Turn the corner, kick down the door. You come to an intersection, where you would normally turn to the west—to the left—and head toward the stairs to the second floor.

But not today.

Today you stare down the abyss that looms directly ahead of you, to the north. It is, quite literally, dark. You're used to being able to see only the faint wire frame down here in the dungeon, but in that abyss, you can see nothing at all. If the dungeon were a living thing, this would be its throat, prepared now to swallow you and your party.

"...We really goin' in?"

"I think it's a little late to be getting all afraid," Female Warrior says.

Half-Elf Scout laughs. "Yeah, that's right. I'm a little scaredy-cat. So you can take point, Sister!"

"Oh, for..."

Female Warrior clicks her tongue quietly. You smile, then inform them that it's the leader's prerogative to head up the column. And also to kick down doors.

"Not that there are any doors in here," your cousin offers, and meanwhile you hear Myrmidon Monk grumble, "Just do it already."

You advance forward, step by step. One, two, three, four.

But that's as far as you go. Everything is black ahead, as though the entire world a single step in front of you has vanished. First, you try sticking the tip of your scabbard into the darkness. As you expect, it vanishes. You pull it back out.

"...So I guess it didn't, uh, just disappear," Half-Elf Scout says.

"But what if there was no floor or something?" Female Warrior asks.

She's not wrong, but you know you have to take that next step. You offer a prayer to the goddess who controls justice and the scales, as well as to the one who brings good fortune and the wind. An old text says that prayer has nowhere to go in the dark heart of the fortress, but it can't hurt to try before you embark on this venture.

Then you focus your resolve and veritably jump into the void—to discover your feet land on solid ground.

That's the only thing you're sure of, though.

Darkness.

Your vision is a single, undifferentiated blackness. Ahead, beside, above—even when you look back over your shoulder, you can see nothing. You know only that you yourself exist, as the feeling of the hard stone under your feet tells you. If that sensation were to disappear as well, you wouldn't even know whether you were standing up. You could be floating in the sky. Or drowning. Or falling. Your body starts to sway as if you were on a ship at sea.

You stretch out a hand and touch something cold, and for a second your heart skips a beat. But it's nothing. The stone wall of the dungeon. You unconsciously touch your face, rub your cheeks. It's all right. You're still here. Even if you can't see your own hands.

"Captain, you okay?" Half-Elf Scout calls. He sounds strangely, startlingly near. As if he were just on the other side of a curtain. Feeling supremely odd, you reply that you're fine, and slowly you start to hear the party's footsteps. Then there's a collection of *yipes* and *eeks*.

First comes a conversation between Half-Elf Scout and Myrmidon Monk:

"One strange place we've got here..."

"The dungeon never was a place where you counted on your eyes anyway."

"Yeah, but you got those antennae there."

"Is this place really that unusual...?"

That final voice must be Female Bishop. If anything, she might be your best hope in this place. Certainly, nobody else could continue making a map here: You were right to trust her with the task.

"Yes, sir. I'll do my best!" she says forcefully when you tell her so, and you smile in the darkness.

"We'd better move really carefully so we don't get lost, though. I guess we can't exactly hold hands..." Hmm. You don't have to be able to see your cousin's face to know she's frowning hard. And it's not just her: You figure you can pretty well guess the expressions of each of your party members. For example...

"All right, let's go nice and slow then, shall we? And *no* touching 'just because we can't see.'" That's Female Warrior, the heels of her boots clicking on the stone.

"Man, don't wanna think about what would happen if we ran into any monsters in here...," Half-Elf Scout says uneasily, and you hear him carefully following Female Warrior.

When it comes down to it, for you and your party, this darkness means nothing more than that you can't see anything. And for some reason, that makes you very happy.

§

The party works its way through the absolute darkness in formation, slowly. You advance a short way, then call out. Advance, call out. It was your cousin who suggested the system, and for once you readily went along with her. However familiar the first floor might feel to you by now, this is still unknown territory. You have no idea what might be in here. Stay together, that's the key.

"...Sheesh, seems like there's nothin' at all," Half-Elf Scout murmurs, and you know the choice to speak now and say this is deliberate.

Not long ago, there was discussion of using a long pole to get around, to which Female Warrior had curtly replied, "You're not using my spear."

"I was sure some crazy old man was gonna start flinging spells at us the moment we stepped inside," Half-Elf Scout says.

"Could the mastermind behind all of this be right here on the first floor?" Myrmidon Monk asks, and you can hear his mandibles clacking. "Not possible, is it?"

"Oh, but it would sure be convenient for going out and shopping and stuff," your *second* cousin says brightly, clapping her hands. You sigh pointedly.

"Yeah, going up and down all those stairs would be a pain." Female Warrior giggles. As for you, you just can't understand the things women worry about.

But then again, nothing is impossible. No one knows what the Death truly is; there's nothing to say it might not be lurking here on the first floor of the dungeon. And who knows? You might even run into a villain going out on a shopping trip.

"Do you really think someone who's tried to spread plague all over the Four-Cornered World would be that friendly?" Myrmidon Monk asks, his mandibles clacking in a distinctly annoyed way.

That makes five of you who have now spoken. So what about Female Bishop?

"..."

There's no response. But you can feel her aura, if such things exist. Maybe she's thinking about something. "Anything wrong?" you hear your cousin ask softly.

"Oh, no..." Female Bishop looks up and shakes her head—you can tell from the slight sound of her hair shifting that reaches your ears. "We're almost off the edge of the map, though... I might need to attach more paper."

"Oh, you want some help?" your cousin says, to which you hear Female Bishop reply, "Perhaps you could hold this, then?" The two of them work by feel. Your cousin may not seem like much, but the two of them get along quite well.

Is this the end of the corridor?

You mutter this to yourself as you listen to the rustling of the paper. What happens when you go beyond it?

"This might be just what we were looking for," Myrmidon Monk says solemnly, full of caution. "Perhaps the idea of the mastermind being on the first floor isn't so ridiculous after all."

"Hey, we can't be sure." Unlike his easygoing demeanor on the surface, Half-Elf Scout sounds vigilant and concerned now. "The one thing we know is that the master of this dungeon is twisted. Who knows what kind of traps there might be around here?"

"Or if he might send us flying off somewhere with magic." Female Warrior chuckles, but Myrmidon Monk replies tartly, "It's not funny."

Whatever else it might be, this is not a place to let down your guard—that's the one thing you absolutely cannot do here.

That's when Female Bishop—or is that your cousin?—says, "All right, we're done." Down here in the dark, Female Bishop's map is your only lifeline. If you lose track of where you are, you'll never get back out. That, at least, gives some credence to the story that no one has ever returned from the dark zone.

Come to think of it, wonder what happens to the corpses of those who die down here.

It might seem a strange thing to think about now, but maybe you're inspired by the unusual odor that's presently tickling your nose.

"...Do you smell something...weird?" Female Bishop asks.

"Smell?" your cousin replies, clearly confused. You can easily picture her sniffing the air, but as for you, you put your hand on your sword.

"Hey, what *is* that?" Half-Elf Scout says.

"…Think it's coming from in front of us?" Myrmidon Monk asks. Each of them is on guard.

"No," Female Bishop whispers. "It's from the right."

"Makes no difference to me either way," comes the clacking response.

Carefully, but blindly, you reach out to the right—and touch the wall. No, wait…

"May I, Cap?"

You nod, taking a step back in the darkness, hoping that will get you out of the way. Somebody—of course you know who—moves forward in your place, and you can sense him moving for a few seconds, working.

Then there's a breath of a breeze. You hear a soft clicking sound, and the breeze increases. A fetid, unhealthy wind.

"Okay, got it," you hear, so you reach out for the wall again, and this time you feel—nothing. Where you expected stone, there's only an open space. A hidden door, a branch in the path.

"Interesting stuff…," Half-Elf Scout continues. "What's the plan—do we do it?"

Forward or right?

You and your companions can continue to push boldly forward, or you can turn down this hidden passageway—either is fine. It might be a trap. Then again, this entire space might be a trap. Maybe it's a little late to be worrying about traps.

Deciding to grasp the clue you have, you urge the others to follow you, then take a decisive step to the right. There's the floor. Good start—you're able to go in this direction. You have the sense that this might be a particularly long hallway. Slight shifts in the air tell you your companions are nodding, and you continue forward through the utter blackness.

"Wait, I………." It's Female Warrior's whispering voice. You can hear the tremor in it. "I've smelled this before."

Everyone falls silent. But none of you stop moving forward. As you continue in the silence and the dark, the hallway begins to twist like a snake, first left, then right. It almost feels like you're being pulled along. You start to think you probably couldn't get home if you wanted to.

Finally breaking the quiet, you ask if things are okay with the map.

"Er, ah, y-yes," Female Bishop says in a high, trembling voice. "It's… It's fine."

Fine, then. After your response, there's no further conversation.

In the blackness, the only information you have is the sound of everyone's footsteps, the breathing, the sensation of the stone beneath your feet—and the smell. As you walk along, it starts to register with you, too. Maybe from some time long ago.

It's just like Female Warrior says. You've smelled this smell. Perhaps Female Bishop has, too.

"What a nasty stench…," your cousin mumbles, accompanied by a rustling of cloth. She must be holding her cape over her mouth, not that it will do her any good. The smell is sickly sweet, stomach turning. Like a trash pile, the odor of overripe waste left forgotten.

The source of the stink seems to be at the end of the hidden hallway. When you reach out your hand this time, you don't feel a wall. Perhaps another door. It's obvious that the odor is coming through the door, from something on the other side.

"…Let me check it out," Half-Elf Scout says, sounding slightly nauseated but nonetheless stepping forward again as you take a step back.

The last time you smelled this smell was—yes, it was during that fight on the second floor.

You move slightly to make sure you're out of the way of your scout, then slowly draw the sword from its scabbard at your hip, holding it steady.

"Doesn't seem like there are any traps…"

You nod, slick the hilt with spit, get your hands in position. You check that your equipment is all in one piece, then slowly you raise your leg.

This smell—it's the smell of the Death.

§§

There's a chamber on the other side, simple as that. But you've never seen a chamber so blasphemous as this one.

Corpses. All corpses.

Dismembered, rotting, left unburied, forgotten, bodies overflowing the place. The doors to several small rooms stand open, piles of bodies pouring through them. There are no flies, maybe because you're so far underground, but that is your one and only saving grace.

There are bodies of men. Bodies of women. Elves and rheas, padfoots. Others are too rotted to tell what they used to be. And all of them—young and old, male and female—have only the slightest scraps of equipment left to prove that they were once adventurers.

This is the sight that greets your eyes when you kick that door open, the chamber's faint illumination the first light you've seen in what feels like an age.

"...!" Maybe it's your cousin who swallows audibly, or maybe it's Female Bishop. Or maybe Female Warrior—or maybe you yourself. The reek of the bodies makes simply breathing an assault on your lungs.

To take the first step into that room, so full of corpses that there's hardly anywhere to put your feet, takes as much courage as stepping into any monster den. But you steel yourself and enter. Underneath the door you kicked down, you feel the soft *splorch* of crushing flesh.

"Gotta watch out for corpse-eaters down there... Really don't like doing this, though..." Half-Elf Scout tries to joke as he jumps lightly into the chamber, not making a sound. Maybe, with his training, he doesn't need to walk on the bodies. Or maybe he isn't thinking about it.

"........."

You watch Female Warrior enter the room without a word. Maybe it's the dim light that makes her slim face look even paler than usual. She hardly seems to have any blood in her cheeks. You don't say anything about the way she's viciously biting her lip but simply tell everyone not to do anything reckless.

After all, seems pretty obvious this room isn't connected to any lower levels.

"This is unbelievable...," Female Bishop whispers, her breath ragged in her throat. "What's going *on* here?" She's gripping the sword and scales so tight her fingers are turning white. Maybe she can tell how obscene the scene is even without her eyesight. Maybe it's a blessing that she can't see this.

When you see that she looks like she might topple over at any moment, you're about to call out, but your cousin moves first. She doesn't say anything, just places her hand over Female Bishop's. Then she looks at you and gives a small nod. You nod back. You hate to admit it, but this is one of those things about your cousin you have unalloyed respect for.

"Captain, wanna come have a look at this?"

You tell Female Warrior to keep watch, and she nods, then you head over to Half-Elf Scout. He's crouched, examining the bodies. You squat beside him. A burst of humid air hits your face, along with the wafting stench.

"...If our lady back at the temple saw this, she'd start screamin' about apostates."

You force yourself to smile a little at Half-Elf Scout's joke, even manage a chuckle. Many adventurers lie "saved" there in the temple, but...they were alive. Their bodies purified, in hopes that they might someday be healed. There's a respect there. You know your alms aren't going to waste. How would that nun and her colleagues ever accept blasphemy of this sort, you ask Half-Elf Scout.

"Good point... So about this one here." Your scout wields his butterfly blade like a scalpel, indicating a wound in one corpse. "I've been with ya this whole time, Cap, so I think I recognize this. What about you?"

The wound was obviously caused by something very sharp. A blade driven powerfully into the body and extracted with a twist of the wrist. The point wasn't to get through the chinks in the body's armor but to stab a vital point. This was caused, you say without hesitation, by a katana.

"...Ya think so, too, huh? Yeah, I kinda had a feeling..."

However, you don't think a simple blade did this. Cutting all the way through this armor. When one performs a "helmet-cleaving strike," usually one considers it a success if the blade sinks into the helmet. To slice through flesh and bone, along with armor—that's not normal.

Preternatural, in fact.

Some of the corpses were cut down with a katana. Others with a more typical sword. Still others have been burned with magic. Many kinds of wounds, many ways of killing. What's more, you can see one wound, older, that appears to have been fatal, but there are others as well, overlapping with it. Newer ones. This isn't how the wandering monsters of the dungeon work. Nor do you think it's the MO of the newbie hunters.

You think it might, in fact, be the doing of adventurers.

"I see, so that's the story," Myrmidon Monk spits, playing with his curved scimitar. "That's how a group appears virtually out of nowhere. How they gain enough levels to make the fourth or fifth floor..."

That's right.

You remember the words, words that have been bothering you ever since you heard them.

"I know it was for training, but we had to do so much killing—we didn't want to...

"We didn't want to see you until our penance was done... We thought that would be best."

What had they been killing? What had they been repenting of? How had they been training?

What had they done that they felt couldn't be forgiven?

"These were how they trained."

The answer comes slowly, like something out of a nightmare. A form pulling itself to its feet, like a clown shrouded in rags. You would have been alert enough if there had been just one of them. An unknown enemy. You and your party could have taken your time, battled methodically, single-mindedly.

But the situation doesn't allow it. There's a scraping of flesh and bones, wet sucking sounds coming from internal organs. First from one place, then another. The door you kicked down begins to quiver, and another emerges from beneath it. If all of the corpses in this room should rise and come after you...

All we could do would be to laugh.

"Don't you think maybe we should be getting out of here?!" your cousin calls, sounding uncommonly panicked, but you shake your head. You can't let creatures like these out of this room. And anyway, the last thing you want is to be surrounded in the dark zone.

You look around quickly, shouting for everyone to circle up as you slide toward the center of the chamber.

"R-right!" Female Bishop says—perhaps she's able to take the initiative thanks to your cousin. You cover them as they move together; meanwhile, you use your free hand, the one not holding your sword, to take Female Warrior's arm.

"Oh…," she mutters distantly, an expression of surprise on her face. Her arm is thinner than you had expected, more delicate. You reprimand her for this brief lapse of attention as you pull her toward you. You have to make this stand—or die.

"Right… I'm sorry," she says, then raises her spear before giving her head a shake. That's good enough for you.

"…Do you know the story of the ants and the adventurer?" Myrmidon Monk asks, sounding as poised as if nothing special were happening, his antennae waving in your direction. "It's a simple parable: Does the adventurer push through purgatory first, or is he overwhelmed by the never-ending flood of insects?"

You see now. His story has a point.

"Yeah, real instructive—maybe I'll thank you later…!" Half-Elf Scout says. He and Myrmidon Monk already have their weapons out and are moving to reinforce the sides of your formation. The four of you confront the undead in a square shape, with Female Bishop and your cousin in the center.

Really wishing we had that extra warrior instead of a scout about now.

"Real nice, Cap!" Half-Elf Scout chuckles when you say this aloud, taking your attempt at a joke for what it is. But from Female Warrior, who would usually get in a jab at a moment like this, there's nothing. Half-Elf Scout shrugs. "If you're gonna kick me out of the party, at least wait till we're back at the tavern to do it!"

You nod. You'll take it under consideration. Then you look at the corpses shuffling toward you. There are enough of them now that you could hardly swing your sword without hitting one…

"…Shall we use a spell?" Female Bishop asks quietly. She's grasping the sword and scales, ready to begin a chant at any moment. But you shake your head. It isn't time yet. This isn't the fifth floor; it isn't even the fourth. The real fight is yet to come. Somewhere deep in the dark zone.

"But if our backs are really against the wall, your big sis will cast some magic!" Damn *second* cousin. The corner of your lip twists up. You say that if your backs are really against the wall, you'll count on her. "You got it, Little Bro!" You assume she's puffing out her chest proudly. Taking Female Bishop's hand, no doubt. No anxiety at all, then.

"Practical point. I think after diving into this first chamber and cleaning up, we ought to go back home," Myrmidon Monk says, mandibles clacking. Not that any of this matters to him. "Undead ought to be susceptible to Dispel. Buy me some time to concentrate."

You nod. Steady your breathing. You're ready. You just have to start swinging.

The vestiges of adventurers pile in like an avalanche.

§

Some statue, perhaps once venerated here, has been smashed to pieces, the incense burner abandoned somewhere nearby. But you don't have the wherewithal to watch your feet, to make sure you don't stumble over whatever it is.

"MUUUUURRPPHH!!!!!!" The corpses of the former adventurers groan inarticulately; they seem to have no intelligence left. Whatever levels they once possessed have been taken from them, and they wield neither weapons nor magic, but only try to grab you with outstretched hands.

"...Hrgh...!"

Obviously, rotting fingers aren't going to break through your armor. Female Warrior lashes out with her spear, sweeping several of the enemies away.

But then you hear a sound. *Scritch-scritch. Scritch-scritch.* It's the monsters' claws and teeth scratching at your equipment.

Each time something grabs you, you shove it away. You slice through the occasional internal organ as well as any flesh that spits back rotting juices at you. It starts getting hard to see. Even the instant it takes you to wipe the slime away from your eyes isn't enough for these creatures; you have plenty of time to regain your stance and strike again.

You start to slip on blood and grease. The goo is even on the hilt of your sword, making your hands and fingers slip.

But none of it matters. You put more strength into your legs, grasp your katana tightly, and strike into a monster's face from above. Nothing dramatic happens—you don't cleave it from the skull down its spine or anything. But you do literally break its brain. You don't know what that means for a creature in this state, but the enemy crumples.

You steady your breathing again. Each time you inhale the disgusting stink, you're struck by the inescapable feeling that your lungs are being polluted.

"Sons of... They don't give up, do they...?!" Half-Elf Scout exclaims, wielding his butterfly knife relentlessly. You don't answer.

He's right. It's not so much that these undead are especially powerful. One or two strokes of the sword is more than enough to deal with them. Their rotting flesh presents no serious threat. Frankly, they're no stronger than goblins or slimes. Considering how ineffective they are even despite their numbers, maybe they're even weaker than those enemies.

But fighting them induces a sort of hypnosis. Mechanically cutting with your sword can hardly be called combat. You slice the creatures down like wheat, find more opponents, and then repeat the process. It isn't even physically challenging. It just makes you feel...sluggish. Your head starts nodding with each repetition, each time you do the same thing over again. Your vision starts to blur and darken, your breath grows shallow.

The martial artist's virtue of "no mind" has such a nice ring to it. But it's a fact that even thinking has become a challenge.

Slowing down... Too slow.

You aren't growing physically tired, nor even mentally fatigued from all the slaughtering. The hands that hold your weapon never slacken; the enemies simply keep coming, and you keep killing, keep cutting them down.

The goal isn't survival. It's not even loot. This is murder for its own sake. As the bodies pile up, you feel your heart grow colder. Something in your mind dulls. A fire is going out. A smoking ember is all that remains among the ash.

This isn't an adventure. This is simply work.

"…!" From behind you, your cousin makes a choked noise. You look forward to discover a corpse, all four of its limbs in a brutalized state. You did that. But the body rises once more, as if suspended from an invisible string. It seems like a hunk of meat in vaguely human form, something terrible and indescribable, a creature uncanny and bizarre.

"Oh…g…oh gods…," Female Warrior whimpers like a child, shaking her head in horror. She falls back on her behind with a clatter of armor, right there in the middle of the fight. You've known something was up with her from the moment you stepped into this room. She must have finally reached her limit. You open your mouth to say something, but…

At that moment, the sword and scales, sharp and true, come driving from beside the unsteady warrior.

"Please… You must stay strong!" It's Female Bishop. The sword and scales smash into the corpse that's trying to grab at Female Warrior, and Female Bishop shouts out, "Your foe…may be hideous…! But don't do them the dignity of being frightened…!"

Don't. Don't give them the dignity.

Her eyes are bandaged, and she's striking from the back row with a long weapon. She's not going to land a finishing blow. Nonetheless, Female Bishop grits her teeth, wielding her sword and scales against the corpse. Perhaps she wouldn't show such bravery if she were facing a goblin. But maybe that's why she's so stalwart now. If she weren't, she wouldn't be here.

You, Female Warrior, Female Bishop—all of your party members are exactly like that.

"Maybe we can't win…! Maybe we're afraid…!"

Still, we have to stand and fight.

Female Bishop grits her teeth, bites her lip, and then stabs at the monster.

Argh…

It may be faint, it may be cold, it may be guttering—but some here still have a spark. You pat Female Warrior gently on the shoulder, then take a step forward and brandish your blade, ready to fight enough monsters for both of you.

The corpses are dried-out husks; cutting them down sounds and feels like chopping wood. This is the moment you most need to stand firm. You laugh out loud, calling to Half-Elf Scout.

"I gotcha, but man, this is tough! I'm getting exhausted!" He's veritably begging you to trade places with him, but you tell him to try someone else. There's a despairing cry.

It's just like always. The light voices, the easy banter. Truly, these are stalwart companions.

And yet. And yet it's true that you've had just about enough of this. Surely something has to happen soon.

"Hold out just a little longer," comes the merciless clack of the mandibles. "We die down here, nobody knows, nobody cares."

Yeesh, good gods. You wonder aloud how a cleric can be so intimidating.

"I—I don't think he's that scary...," your cousin ventures in reply.

Well, no. You shrug slightly, then glance at Female Warrior. Your eyes meet hers, which are vague and slightly unfocused. "......" She seems to be trying to say something, but then she closes her mouth and looks at the ground. Her eyes are red.

Do you remember how she once talked about seeking a Life? That's what she whispered to you that night, when you were alone and you asked her about it. If the Death is down in this dungeon, then perhaps its opposite is here, as well.

But this can't possibly be that Life.

"Oh..."

You don't know if the words you speak reach her or not. There are too many enemies to worry about it. They aren't very strong, though, so they're mostly just a lot of trouble.

"Gosh... You just don't know how to treat a girl, do you?" your *second* cousin whispers. She's kneeling by Female Warrior. Even though you're fighting with your back to both of them, you can tell she's smiling.

"Can you stand?" your cousin asks.

"......Yeah," Female Warrior says weakly. You hear cloth rustle. Probably her sleeves, wiping her eyes. "I'm...sorry about that."

"Hey, it's fine, no problem! I would have been surprised if you *hadn't* been scared of that!"

Now you hear fasteners clinking—Female Warrior standing up, although slowly. You call out to her, briefly. Is she all right, is she okay—something like that.

You don't get a definite answer. But beside you, she says softly, "I can hold out a little longer."

That's all we need.

You face down the swarm of undead from dead in front of them. To reiterate, this is just a chore, not a battle.

Something you heard once flashes through your mind—that the slow accumulation of life and death is what makes an adventurer strong. Perhaps there's a certain logic to that. But what value is there in accumulating *this*?

"All right, I'm ready! Let's try Dispel on these things...!!" Myrmidon Monk's magic fills the chamber with a fresh breeze, and the corpses are reduced to dust.

Even there, in the midst of the dancing powder, you can't understand what all this work was worth.

§

"Let's take a break!" This suggestion comes, of course, from your cousin. You don't know where she gets the resilience. She claps her hands as if suggesting you should all have a picnic. Whether from the relief or the exasperation, your feeling of fatigue vanishes immediately. You would never tell her this because it would go to her head, but this is one of those things about your cousin you have unalloyed respect for.

Maybe the one slight wrinkle is that all this is taking place in a room piled with the dust of vaporized corpses.

"Not sure how I feel about takin' a break right in the dark zone," Half-Elf Scout comments.

"I don't mind," says Myrmidon Monk. "All the same to me."

"Huh...," Half-Elf Scout mutters softly, and you can almost hear the rueful smile, but you understand where the monk is coming from.

There's too much dust to move it aside, so you all settle in the middle of the room, sitting on the floor.

"I'll establish a barrier…" Female Bishop promptly produces holy water from her bag and starts sprinkling it around the room.

There are no guarantees that the undead won't show up again. A barrier to keep monsters at bay could be crucial. You tell Female Bishop that when she's done, you want to go over the map, too. "Right," she says brightly.

As she works, Myrmidon Monk hefts himself to his feet. "Mm. Suppose I can help here…"

"Sure, and I'll keep an eye on the entrance," Half-Elf Scout says, hopping up. He holds his butterfly knife with both hands and moves without a sound. "You mean to keep going, right, Captain?"

Yeah, pretty much.

If nothing else, your resources—your health and spells—are untouched. Besides…you want to see the face of whatever freak thought it was a good idea to make something like this.

"I'm with you there." At your comment, Half-Elf Scout's words are brief, but he's certainly in agreement. You watch him position himself by the door, then let out a breath and start into motion yourself. As soon as she sees you move, your cousin smiles and holds out a waterskin. "Here."

Oh, for…

"What is it?" she asks, looking at you with a perplexed smile. You feel like you want to say something, but instead you just shake your head. You don't mean to attack her head-on. Instead, you simply thank her. "Sure thing. All right, Big Sis is going to be getting her spells ready. For next time!"

Next time. Somewhere deeper in the dark zone. Before you worry about next time, though, you need to check out the corner of this room. Female Warrior is there, sitting with her knees pulled up to her chest.

You sit down beside her, saying nothing. The walls and floor of the dungeon may be ambiguous and difficult to make out due to the miasma, but when you touch them, they feel like cold stone. You lean against that chilly presence and are silent for a while.

"…I wanted to help her," Female Warrior says. She speaks in a whisper, not looking up. "My sister."

You acknowledge her gently. You remember this story. Her sister is at the temple. The Preservation miracle was—if not futile, at least too late. You might even remember that this situation inspired Female Warrior to visit the temple regularly.

You sip some of what's in the waterskin. It's tepid and doesn't taste like much. You wish you had some alcohol. You remember your master. A withered flower, thin and bony. Perfumed with wine and medicine.

People die. That's what they do.

Anyone alive must one day die. Even elves are no exception. It's an immutable fact. Incontrovertible. The truly dead can't be brought back to life, not even with a miracle. And the idea that the deceased live in our hearts? Foolishness. Memories fade and change. They can even be made up. Above all, what a person thought and felt, how they lived and how they died, can be known only to that person. The deceased in our memories are nothing but convenient simulacra.

Meaning the Death—and the Life—can't be like that, then.

That's all you say, and then you fall silent. You catch the scent of a woman, and a soft weight leans on your shoulder.

She doesn't smell like your master, nor like your cousin.

"You really..." Her voice is quiet, almost pleading. "...don't have any idea, do you?"

You tell her to forget about it, then you press the waterskin into her hand. Her face twists into a smile, then she brings the water unsteadily to her lips and drinks.

You don't notice anything. If your shoulder is damp near her face, that must be the water spilling from the pouch.

You doubt any of your party members notice anything, either. Each is busy at their own task. You're sure they don't hear the quiet sobs.

This is just a quick break—nothing more and nothing less.

§

Your party returns to the darkness. In the dark zone, even something as simple as going back the way you came is a sore challenge.

At least, it would be, without the map.

"O-oh, I don't deserve all the credit… I just draw the path as we walk it." Female Bishop sounds self-deprecating, but consider the darkness. Forget drawing a map—just reading one must be hard enough.

You follow Female Bishop's directions as she guides you all through the blackness. You glance over, but in this place, you can't see the face of Female Warrior beside you—which is both just as well and disappointing. She'd regained her composure by the time you set off, walking lightly. No need to worry about her—perhaps.

"…Heh-heh, what is it?" she teases, but you shake your head, saying it's nothing. If you need anything, you'll speak up.

Then you continue walking. The hallway seems to go on and on. You could almost be convinced that it has no end. Or that space wraps around on itself here. So when you finally hear Half-Elf Scout mumble, "…Hrm?" you're downright relieved. "Somethin' here, Cap. Right in front of us."

"A monster?" Myrmidon Monk asks with caution in his voice, but Half-Elf Scout replies, "Don't know."

You stop and think, then tell everyone to get ready and draw your sword. You can't see what's happening in the dark, but even after the chore that passed for a battle earlier, the weight of your sword feels reassuring in your hands.

From the left, the right, and behind you, you hear metallic rasping as people prepare their weapons and equipment.

"How about spells?" your cousin asks, to which you decide to ask her to have something ready to go, just in case. This is unknown territory. There may be new monsters here. You need to be ready to strike as hard as you can.

But as you advance forward with utmost caution, you come to see that you've jumped to conclusions. A door reveals itself to you, floating in the hazy light of phosphorescence. It almost looks like a single solid sheet of metal, but the seam running down the middle indicates that it must be a pair of doors. The light comes from four crevices notched in a column alongside the door. Each appears carved in the shape of some strange character, and the topmost one is depressed, as if buried in the wall.

You only realize you've stopped moving when Female Bishop asks, "Did something...happen?"

You briefly explain the door to her, then ask your scout to investigate it. "On it," he says and steps forward.

"Heh-heh... Not even you have the balls to kick this one down, eh?" Female Warrior chuckles, her tone deliberately the same as always. So just the same as always, you reply that you have to give your scout a chance to shine.

"Hmm... Don't think this door's booby-trapped, but...what is this? It don't make any sense to me..."

"Oh!" your cousin says, peeking from behind you as Half-Elf Scout stands flummoxed. "Maybe this is that elevator!"

"E-le-vay-tor?" Female Bishop asks, clearly unfamiliar with the word. "Yep!" your cousin says, puffing out her ample chest. "It's like, uh, a box supported by strings. People get inside, and it moves them up and down."

"...Ah, a dangling room," Myrmidon Monk clacks. "An ancient trick you find in ancient ruins sometimes, I think. You step in, and the weight makes the rope break, and down you go."

"You don't think that's just because they're so old? They have a big one of those in the arena in the city," your cousin says.

"Oh-ho..."

You're only half listening to the conversation, enough to get the gist. The important part is that this thing goes up and down...

"So it could go to the fourth floor...to someplace we haven't explored yet."

You tell Female Bishop that you're thinking the same thing. There are four nooks. If the depressed, topmost nook represents the first floor of the dungeon, then the lowest must be the fourth floor.

Female Warrior watches your fingers play over the buttons and says uneasily, "...What if it really is a dangling room? What will we do?"

Much as you hate to say it, if that happens, you'll simply have to rely on your cousin's Falling Control spell. Much as you hate to say it. You really hate to say it.

You ignore your *second* cousin's *Hmph!* and try to breathe evenly.

You are an adventurer. Risking danger is what makes it an

adventure; you didn't come here just to make some money on nice, safe work. But as to whether the others will come with you...

"Heh, now that's the captain I know," Half-Elf Scout says, sounding genuinely gleeful (even as he adds that he *is* scared, though).

You check your armor and equipment, adjust your grip on your sword, and give it an exploratory swing.

Let's go. Down to the fourth floor.

"You're in charge. I—"

"—don't care either way, eh!" Half-Elf Scout laughs. "Anyway, we haven't made any cash today. Gotta earn a little something."

"In that case, I want to try staying in the Royal Suite one of these days!" Your cousin grins, adding, "Y'know?" You finally have no choice but to laugh.

"I bet we could afford one night," she says. "Consider it a celebration!"

"Celebration? Um, of getting through the fourth floor, I guess?" Female Bishop asks.

"Nuh-uh!" your cousin burbles. "Of winning the contest!"

"Oh..." Female Bishop puts a hand to her mouth as if this is completely unexpected. She seems nearly taken aback—almost a little flustered. If that bandage weren't there, you suspect you would see her eyes widen. She leaves her mouth covered as her cheeks flush with embarrassment. "...I'd forgotten all about it."

"Boo!" Your cousin puffs out her cheeks, but she actually looks perfectly happy.

Female Bishop seems completely aware of this. "I'm sorry," she says with a laugh. "But anyway, you're right. We have to do our best to win the contest." The way she grips the sword and scales, you think, makes her look quite stalwart. You hope that you, likewise, have grown some since that first venture into the dungeon.

Now, what's left...?

"......"

Female Warrior, at some point, has fallen silent, the same way she did in the tavern when you suggested fighting the newbie hunters. And just like at that time, you wait patiently for her reaction. Your party members do the same.

To go ahead—to turn back—nobody forces the decision one way or the other. You're adventurers. People who adventure because that's what they want to do. You've decided to challenge the dungeon, to save the world. You know Female Warrior hasn't forgotten the reason that has brought you all here.

"…Mm."

So when she gives a small nod of her head, that settles it. You press the lowest button. The doors of the elevator open, and you step inside.

It's like a coffin.

Cramped, claustrophobic. Once those doors close, you may never come out again.

These thoughts pass in the space of a breath, giving way to the recognition that the many rooms down here, and the dungeon itself, are the same way. The rest of the party piles in, and you find that even with all six of you aboard, there's still space left over.

Once you're all inside (how it knows this is mysterious), the elevator doors close.

There's a feeling as if you're floating. The elevator begins to descend with a sensation as if the floor is dropping away from you. Everyone shifts uncomfortably at the unfamiliar feeling, unconsciously touching the walls of the box.

It's almost like you're tumbling into an abyss. At that moment, you see Female Warrior's red lips move ever so slightly. *Fwoooo…boom!*

§

The doors once again open soundlessly, and you find yourself in what feels like the quintessential dungeon chamber. At the end of a long hallway, occluded by the miasma, something or someone waits. All you can see is the wire frame extending endlessly, but you know they're there.

You're not sure whether intent to kill is really something that can be concretely sensed. But you feel a kind of pressure. The air is heavy, like you're underwater, making it difficult to breathe. Another reason to believe something waits for you.

"But for all that…no monsters," Half-Elf Scout mumbles from one side of you.

"Yeah… It's a little too quiet," Female Warrior agrees from the other, and you take one very cautious step forward. You hear only your own heavy footfalls echoing through the hall. You take a single breath of the thin, cold air.

Guess it wouldn't be any better if they'd rolled out the red carpet.

"I wouldn't mind some music or something," your cousin says with the best smile she can muster. "You know, *ba-baaa* or *da-daaa* or something."

"You mean, like *dum-dum-dum, dum-dum-dum-duuum…*?" Female Bishop's voice is a little strained, but she tries to get in on the joke nonetheless.

"I don't know what kind of music that is," Myrmidon Monk says, his mandibles clacking, "but be careful. We don't know what our enemies are up to, but it can't be good."

Well, you knew that already.

You blink your eyes, which had become accustomed to the dim light of the elevator, and start vigilantly down the corridor.

At the end of the long, straight hallway, you discover strange stone steps that look like a twisted altar. A fell pattern is carved into the floor, a wild profusion of nongeometric lines feeding off one another. It glows with a faint orange light, clearly some manner of magic.

Even you, with your fairly minimal knowledge of the true words, with your limited ability to read the logic of the world, understand what it means. This artifact represents control, it represents arcane knowledge. There can be no question. This, this very diagram, is the center of this maze, the heart of the maelstrom.

When you step into the fearsome space, a bell—it doesn't sound like an alarm bell—jingles somewhere. And then, out of the center of a wind of Chaos…

"…Hey there. Looks like we win the bet."

There's the warrior with his lacquered sword and his party, looking as calm as anything, waiting for you.

"Hrk… I knew it…," Female Bishop says, swallowing.

Beside the warrior stands the priest who's the spitting image of Female Bishop, holding high the sword and scales. Then there's the black-haired warrior with his sword, and next in line the bandit girl, holding her dagger in a reverse grip. And standing behind the party is the wizard in his black hat and cape.

Their gazes all seem to focus piercingly on Female Bishop. She bites her lip but nonetheless takes a brave step forward. "...I didn't imagine you would go so far as to lie to me."

"Aw, we didn't lie," the young warrior says, frowning and scratching his cheek in embarrassment. "We just found a way to get to the depths of the fourth floor before you guys."

No. You shake your head. The bet was on who would reach the *fifth* floor first, you note. Beyond the altar, though, you see a door, shut fast. Another elevator, you suspect. If they haven't yet boarded it, there's every chance they haven't yet won.

The bandit girl narrows her eyes and howls at you, "That's just a stupid quibble!"

"Look who's talking. You're the ones who came up with this little contest," Half-Elf Scout mumbles. Then he shrugs and reaches out a slim arm to pat Female Bishop on the back. She looks at him in surprise, and he flashes her a toothy grin. "Just ignore 'em. Give 'em a piece of your mind. Luck's on our side!"

"...Right!" Female Bishop nods firmly, then takes another step forward. With her bandaged eyes, she looks at her former friends. "I don't know what you must be thinking. Are you really so desperate to spring ahead that you would even manipulate me to do it?"

There's a beat before they respond. You don't know if she's guessed right. She might be speaking in part from the pain of being left in that tavern. But the fact remains that they aren't able to answer immediately. Not affirmatively, not negatively.

"We thought if we said that stuff, you'd give up," the black-haired warrior replies, but it sounds like an excuse. "We didn't want you to put yourself in any more danger. To get hurt any more..."

"I'm the one who will decide what hurts me!" Female Bishop says, her words as sharp as the sword and scales. The trembling girl you met in the tavern is gone; she now speaks firmly and clearly. Be she abused by goblins, be she tormented in the tavern—even so she has come every step of her life to challenge the dungeon. Working her way to this day, this moment. You know that. Your entire party knows that.

So Female Warrior can say bitingly, her lip curling, "You never believed she would get this far, did you?" She has to push for the facial expression; she's so tired—but still, she knows her friend well.

"Me personally, I don't really care what the story is," Myrmidon Monk says with a merciless clack of his mandibles. His compound eyes, inscrutable to those who don't know him well, appraise the other group. "But I guess those *things* on the first floor were your punching bags."

"…We did it to save the world," the young magic knight says. He almost doesn't seem to realize he's speaking the words. He glances at the ground for a second, then his face fills with a tragic resolve, and he looks squarely at you. "We had to get stronger, so we could go on adventuring… So we could save the world."

"So y'figure it's okay to cheat if it's not just for your own benefit? Interesting."

"Let us sin, if it's to save the world! We—"

"That won't do at all!" your cousin exclaims. The same words she used to scold you with when you were young and had been bad. "You're just telling yourselves that! It's not your decision to make!" She takes Female Bishop's hand, squeezing it tightly. One of the things you respect about your cousin is that no matter what's happening or who she's talking to, she'll always say what has to be said. "You think you can do something wrong just because you're going to apologize for it later? That's absurd!"

"If we fall, there will be no one to save the world!" their priest insists, her voice almost breaking. It isn't about logic for her. Just about feelings. Her face is flushed, her breath harsh as she's flooded with emotion.

So similar, you think. She and Female Bishop are both walking their own paths as best they can.

"A girl who can't even defeat some goblins—how is she supposed to save the world?" the priest asks. So, she says, they wanted her to wait. Somewhere safe. Alone. Always. Forever.

You think the words are spoken from the heart—the heart of a friend. One who has known Female Bishop since they arrived in the fortress city. Their feelings haven't changed since the moment they left her alone in the tavern to go do the dungeon.

"No... No!" Female Bishop shouts. She places her hand, still clasping that of your cousin, on her slight chest, and steps forward, supported by Half-Elf Scout. "We don't have time to bother with those little devils! Goblins aren't the problem here!" she says, picking up on what Female Warrior and Myrmidon Monk have already mentioned. "And why? Because I...*we*...are going to save the world!" Then she stabs forward with the sword and scales and demands: "Now, move aside! You're in our way...!"

That's when it happens. You feel a cold prickling on your neck, and faster than thought, you whip your sword out at Female Bishop.

"...?!" Female Bishop, who has been looking directly forward, never wavers. The sound of metal on metal rings throughout the chamber. The gloom is illuminated by the flash of sparks. The *whoosh* of wind follows just after.

You remember this feeling. The shadows in the four corners of the room squirm and rise. At your feet is none other than a twisted throwing knife. You're confronted by two men in black clothing and bizarre masks—ninjas.

Of course, you know nothing of what the other party is thinking, or feeling, or even what they want. You have no way of knowing why they've decided to work with these ninjas. All you know—all you can understand—is the path you've walked to get here. The accumulation of everything that has brought you and your companions to this moment.

There can be only one conclusion.

They think if they don't do this, they won't be able to save the world.

"......So I see we have no choice," the young magic knight murmurs, readying his lacquered sword. The black-haired warrior draws a longsword and the bandit girl her dagger, while the priest and the man in the black hat begin weaving sigils with their hands.

Hmm.

It seems you've been chosen to be among the honorable sacrifices that will make the salvation of the world possible.

"I hate when people...get their heads...so far up their own asses!" Female Warrior spits. Her face is pale and gaunt.

The air of the room is still heavy but now seems sharper somehow.

Against seven adventurers, you are six. A disadvantage in numbers. But the feeling between you is no different from that when you step into a room and confront monsters within. Female Warrior has her spear at the ready, Half-Elf Scout has his butterfly dagger gripped in both hands. Your cousin has raised her staff and is focusing her spirit in preparation for a spell, while Myrmidon Monk is intoning the name of the Trade God.

Meanwhile, with katana in hand, you ask if everyone is ready. But you don't doubt the answer.

"...Yes," Female Bishop, clinging to the sword and scales, replies after an instant's silence. "Let's—do this!"

And so the fight begins.

§

"*Omnis nodos libero!* Release and unbind all things!"

"*Perfecte placidum donum!* Perfect silence give us!"

These spells become the first salvos of the battle. The man in the black hat describes bizarre symbols with his hands and unleashes one set of true words, while your cousin thrusts forward her short staff and intones loudly. Their words, able to rewrite the logic of the world created by the gods, explodes into the chamber, tearing the air.

A fearsome blast of magic that destroys all things is met with a declaration of absolute silence. Into the ether that bubbles between them, you step without a moment's fear.

Your foes are seven. By a simple calculation of combat strength, you are beaten. Caution you must have, but he who hesitates is lost. If nothing else, you have more spell casters than they do...

"*O my god, ruler of judgment, watch over my sword that it judge only those who are evil.*"

It's only moments before your expectations are overturned. The black-haired warrior steps forward just as you have and intones a holy supplication in a clear voice. The sword in his hand glows a faint whitish color, showing how effective his invocation has been.

A lord...!

"*O my god of the roaming wind, banish all cold winds, that our feet not tire!*"

Myrmidon Monk isn't intimidated by the sword with its blessing but promptly intones a protective spell of his own. A refreshing breeze blows through the underground room, wrapping itself around your bodies. More than anything, you appreciate the feeling of being protected.

Female Bishop, sensing the divine aura from the back row, exclaims, "When you were with me, you hadn't yet—!"

So it seems she's got the higher rank. You suspect the biggest issue is going to be the enemy priest, but battle is joined before you can follow the thought to its conclusion. You look left, then right, from under your helmet and decide to focus on evening the odds a little bit. The enemy front row consists of a magic knight, a lord, a sand bandit, and two ninjas.

Can't let the ninjas get to the back!

"Leave it to me, Captain…!" Half-Elf Scout shouts, then raises his knife to meet the men in black costumes. Female Warrior gives a quick swing of her spear to make some space, then leans forward. "I can handle a couple of them, too, I'd say!"

"Dammit, don't get in our way…!" The sand-bandit girl gives a cluck of her tongue and jumps at you, while the black-haired lord shouts, "Don't rush in by yourself!" and follows her. Female Warrior takes the first exchange using the haft of her spear against the blessed sword and the dagger. She sweeps with her weapon as you even your breathing.

In that case, you have just one opponent.

"…You should stop this. You're going to die." The young magic knight stands before you, his sword at the ready and glowing red. You hold your katana in front of you and give a derisive snort. Once the blade is drawn, the only outcome is life or death. It is your duty to the sword to be completely committed when you use it. It would be shameful if you weren't prepared to kill or to die. That has been among your most important tenets since the day you came to the fortress city.

One comes here bearing a grave responsibility: his party's fate. The magic knight seems hardly to feel the weight.

And he's adventuring without even understanding that?

"This is exactly why I can't let you have her…!" The first strike

comes, a great, long reach. You predicted it long ago, so your movement is almost instantaneous; you dodge by a hairbreadth. A sharp
spike in air pressure brushes past your cheek, and you swing out with
your sword even as you step back.

"*Pfft, real nice.*"

You suddenly hear your master taunting you in your mind. You'll
never be able to contain your opponent if you aren't constantly prepared to destroy them.

The red sword collides with your katana, producing a screech of
metal on metal. You brace yourself against the stone floor, holding
your stance, then take a fresh look at your opponent.

He's young, his gaze is directly ahead, and his agitated countenance
looks, it's fair to say, almost childish. His equipment isn't yet weathered; only the sword in his hands is clearly distinguished.

A newcomer who happens to have picked up a master weapon.
That's how he looks to you. However…

He's capable.

You can still feel a slight tingling in your hands from that first
exchange alone. It reminds you of the giant man you battled when
fighting the newbie hunters. To be able to produce such speed and
power despite his small frame—that's impressive.

"Face meeee…!"

A sharp acceleration of breath and you meet his attack without
flinching. He strikes hard and fast, aiming precisely at your vital
points. Throat, side, elbow. Then he slaps the hilt of his blade with the
palm of his hand in a whirlwind move, reaching for the hollow of your
neck, just below your helmet. Each of these is an important point not
protected by armor, and you have to repel them with your sword and
dodge by stepping away.

Yeesh. Kämpfergeschaft—*warrior's work*—*isn't easy.* But one thing is for
certain: You recognize this fighting style. Unless you miss your guess, it's
the same as that which marked the undead you fought only shortly before.

So that's where he learned it! You groan. He's used to this—to killing
people. This style is adapted for murder.

"I've fought and defeated more enemies than you; I'm sure of it…!"

As the magic knight speaks, you step in with a downward swing from above. He freezes for an instant as if taken by surprise but then neatly raises his blade to meet yours. They ring out clearly as they come together. You push another step forward—strike again.

"…Wh-why, you…!" There's an unmistakable note of irritation in the boy's voice now. His left hand moves in a flash, producing a card. "*Kiraṇa dāna agni!* Light, grant ignition!"

There's a blinding flash and an impact assaults you. The exploding card was his best gambit.

That's awfully tricky, using magic in the middle of a hand-to-hand battle, but two can play that game—you're an adventurer, too.

Sagitta…sinus…offero! Gift a curve to arrows!

Still protected by the breeze of the Trade God, you make three successive sigils, then stomp hard on the floor. You deflect the exploding card, and it is this on which you stomp, using it as a springboard to fling you forward.

"Grr!"

Obviously, this isn't an enemy you're going to defeat just by gaining a little altitude for your next cut. He sweeps with his red blade, in a move that can only be considered a strength move, but which nonetheless has startling speed and power. When his blade meets yours, it doesn't move an inch but absorbs and deflects your blow.

You use the force of the impact to push yourself backward, leaning into the landing and rolling along the stone floor to make some distance. Otherwise, you're sure his sword would have sliced into your neck at that instant.

"Never let down their guard… No openings…!"

Not necessarily. Been on the edge of death any number of times.

You take a moment to assess your companions' situation and check on how the overall battle is going.

The first to exclaim is Half-Elf Scout, facing off with the two ninjas. "Cap, how'd you ever manage to take on two of these guys?!" He's parrying desperately with his daggers in both hands, but even so, his enemies don't exactly have the advantage. They move like vipers, but he dodges their fists and evades the kicks that come his way. "Whoops!" Although he's avoided any serious injuries, you see scrapes and scratches on his cheeks and arms. From that perspective…

"Hiiyah!"

…Female Warrior, keeping her two enemies at bay with broad swipes of her spear, is in much the same situation she was before. In a contest between a longer weapon and a shorter one, only a significant advantage in skill would allow the wielder of the sword to fly past the spear and attack its wielder.

"Dammit! Pole weapons—that's cheating!" the sand-bandit girl howls.

"Little late for that!!" Female Warrior replies, jabbing down at her opponent. As much as she tries to appear like she has technique to spare, however, you can see that her face is set and she's sweating.

"You're mine…!"

After all, this isn't one-on-one.

As the sand-bandit girl jumps backward, the point of the spear thwacks against the floor, at which instant the black-haired lord dives in. He strikes, fierce as fire and fast as lightning, a move that the knight of legend was likewise supposed to be proficient in. Female Warrior pulls back her spear and braces herself with it, leaning backward like a dancer to avoid the blade. The tip just grazes her chest armor, passes over her nose, and leaves the slightest nick in her forehead as it goes by.

"Oh, for…!" Female Warrior says, almost petulantly, then kicks forcefully off the floor with her steel-toed sabbatons. The lord doesn't appear to have been expecting this. "Wha—?!" he exclaims, but even so, he manages to dodge backward, exhaling sharply, so that he's just a fraction of an inch out of range of Female Warrior's foot.

"What do you think you're doing?!" the sand-bandit girl hollers.

"Sorry," he says. "I'll get her next time!"

As for Female Warrior, she doesn't respond. Her breath is coming in shallow gasps, and she leans on her spear, only just able to stand. She wipes furiously at her eyes, as if trying to wipe away the Death she's just so narrowly avoided, even though what she's really wiping at is the blood running down her face, along with something at the corners of her eyes.

"I can…still…hold them…!" she squeezes out, and if you didn't know better, you might think she sounded like she was crying. Is she talking to you or to herself? She was already emotionally spent; if her physical endurance is running out, then she's going to have a hard time on the front row. The same with your scout—front-row work isn't his real business. Even if he is managing it for now.

One step forward, one back. You haven't managed to strike a decisive blow. And without that, numbers will eventually tell—against you.

But…

—.……

Something feels off to you about this fight. A small doubt, too small to call it a proper opening. You would have to be crazy to gamble on it. And yet no matter what path you choose, it's impossible to know what lies ahead. No, that's not quite true—at the very least, you know it's victory or defeat, life or death.

No need to worry about the details, then. Only go forward with all conviction.

If it means being destroyed in this battle with your friends at your side, so be it. If stronger or smarter or more accomplished party members might have been available to you, you wouldn't have picked them. You have no regrets. You feel purely comfortable—and you haven't the slightest intention of losing.

To pursue a single chance of victory, to follow a single path to its bitter end, is like challenging the Death.

This is good.

"What are you smiling about?!" the magic knight wails. He drives in with his red blade with all his might, and you meet him in kind. There's a crash of metal on metal, and a shock runs through your hands. You have to be careful not to drop your katana.

In point of fact, you don't have as much leeway as you try to pretend. If things go south, your adventure might end here.

That's when you hear Female Bishop call out, her voice clear: "Give me a turn!" But of course.

You add a comment of *'Better have the scout focus on opening the treasure chest, then, eh?'*

"Whoa, there…!" Half-Elf Scout reacts to your words immediately, but the blank faces of the opposing party show that they have no idea what you mean. Half-Elf Scout spins his butterfly blades in his palms, catching the knifehand strikes flying from the left and right. At the same moment, he rolls to one side, opening a path to the back row for one of the antagonists. "That's the way it goes—passing one to you!"

"Interesting move...!" Myrmidon Monk clacks, and almost simultaneously, one of the ninjas thrusts at his throat.

But there's a *clang*, and the ninja goes from lethal agility to reeling, an astonishing transformation.

"First meeting with a myrmidon's something you don't forget," Myrmidon Monk says and laughs. The hard carapace around his neck has stopped the knifehand cold.

The ninja immediately, silently tries to kick Myrmidon Monk in the torso to make himself room to retreat, but Myrmidon Monk grabs his arm in his long fingers. The tiger mask makes it impossible to see the man's expression—yet, for a moment, it seems he might be quaking in fear.

"*Sagitta inflammarae raedius!*" Your cousin shoves the end of her staff squarely into the ninja's stomach and mercilessly releases a bolt of flame. Charred flesh flies everywhere, steam hisses, and the ninja hits the ground, a lifeless corpse, before he knows he's been defeated.

"...Scary lady," Myrmidon Monk mutters. Your cousin puffs out her ample chest, a smile of triumph on her face, and says, "Heh, I think this is the part where I say, 'Take that!'"

Spell casters do more than just fling fireballs and lightning bolts, but when they do start slinging spells, you don't want to be in their way.

Now that your scout is one-on-one, he shows himself as capable as anybody. "I've got you...!" His butterfly dagger flashes, catching the kick that comes in with the force of a tiger. The ninja's eyes widen to find his ankle caught between the blades, at which point your scout's hand comes off his dagger and grabs empty air.

"Hiiiiiiyah!!" Your scout shouts as he unleashes a knifehand, which immediately thereafter pierces the ninja's throat. Blood comes spraying out accompanied by a sound not unlike a whipping winter wind. As the ninja collapses to the ground, though, his head is still attached to his body—the hit wasn't critical.

"Huh! So much for monkey see, monkey do...!" Half-Elf Scout gives a wave of his right hand, catches the butterfly dagger back out of the air, and jumps at the ninja. It's a simple matter for him to finish off the writhing, suffocating man.

Five left now. Still the same number on the front row, but you've made up the difference in combat strength. You've got the advantage now; they're the ones at the disadvantage.

"Feh!" the bandit girl shouts as she realizes what's happened. "Finishing this girl off won't change anything!" Then she leaps at Female Warrior with a movement like a carnivorous beast. Female Warrior cries, "You little—!" and sweeps at her.

A beat later, the lord thrusts in with his sword. "You don't know when to give up…!"

"You're…not so quick on the draw…yourself!"

Barely—just barely—Female Warrior has managed to meet his sword with her spear, her feet unsteady. The keening blade is the work of some master of days of old. Female Warrior has the less distinguished weapon.

At that moment, the tip of her spear makes an unpleasant sound and gives way, cracking with a screech.

"D-dammit all…!" Nonetheless, Female Warrior grabs the haft with both hands and swings it at the lord with all her might, forcing him backward. There's distance between them now, both of them breathing hard. His face is hidden by his black hair. Hers is pale and soaked with sweat.

Female Warrior's eyes waver ever so slightly. What should she do? She glances in your direction. You nod.

"As if you had the time to be making eyes at each other…!" the lord exclaims.

No, and you don't even have time to communicate. It's only the barest instant. The slightest movement of your lips.

But for the two of you, it's enough.

Can I ask for one turn?

"——!" Female Warrior's eyes flash. Her sabbatons kick gracefully off the chamber floor, and she throws herself forward with all her weight.

Toward you.

"Wha—?!"

You don't spare even a glance for the young magic knight, who watches you in astonishment, but only fling yourself toward that spearpoint.

©lack

For the briefest of moments, your katana crosses paths with her spear as if they were about to exchange a kiss. Female Warrior passes by you, her face startlingly close, and you can see her skin stippled with small scars that make it look as if she's wearing rouge. It's the result of tiny shards of blade flying off during fights and lodging themselves in her face. An occupational hazard of being a warrior.

As you pass by each other, you see the slightest of smiles on Female Warrior's face. Your own face softens. Your own scars tingle.

And then each of your weapons, now well apart, drives forward with the force of a loaded spring. You hold tight to your katana, which has accelerated like a shooting star, while you draw the dagger at your hip with your left hand and whisper three words: *Sagitta...quelta...raedius.*

"Hngh?!"

"Eeyagh!"

At the same instant as the dagger, released from your hand, pierces the lord, your sword slashes the sand-bandit girl, reaching farther than she ever expected. The feeling of cutting a woman's flesh, notwithstanding her defensive equipment, is a disturbing one. The blood that flies back at you is slightly sweet.

Meanwhile, behind you...

"Gurgh...?!"

"G-got him!"

Female Warrior's spear tip has been smashed to pieces by the red sword, but nonetheless, it's made contact with the young magic knight's forehead. Blood spews out of it, as the boy struggles to process what just happened.

The switch.

Half-Elf Scout and Myrmidon Monk—and you and Female Warrior. You all simply changed places. The other party, though, never expected it. *How did two of them each fight us at once?* That's what they're wondering.

You saw it, during the battle. How their leader, the magic knight, never gave a single instruction. How each of the other adventurers was fixated only on their own opponent, their own objective. There was no unity, no cohesion. Yes, they might be powerful. You have no idea how much training they've done against those undead.

One-on-one, their levels might be higher than yours. But they weren't a party. They didn't fight as a party.

They've only ever faced limitless, squirming masses of undead. They weren't adventuring—they were doing work. You're sure they never thought about it. They just wanted to be stronger than the enemy in front of them, stronger than anyone. So maybe they've never needed to fight together. Maybe it had always been enough simply to bring down the opponent in front of them.

In other words, *that was all they had done* to save the world. How did that make them any different from the monsters that wandered the dungeon? They were powerful monsters, yes, but nothing more, just six or seven of them waiting in a chamber.

Once you realize this, you see they aren't even worth being afraid of.

"But how...?!" the priest on their back row—now their front row—exclaims.

The only response is a word from Female Bishop: "*Ventus!*" She holds high the sword and scales, a terrible whirlwind forming in her hand. It screeches, a magical maelstrom not of this world, like the howling of some beast.

Your cousin, recognizing the spell Female Bishop is intoning, opens her mouth but can't produce a sound.

"...! *Lord of judgment, sword-prince, scale-bearer—*"

"*Lumen!!*"

The other party's priest begins to intone a spell, but she's a step behind; the second powerful word is already out of Female Bishop's mouth. This is the difference in speed between one girl who was unable to see an opportunity to use a spell in the chaos of combat, and one who was prepared to do so.

An uncanny pale light shines around the chamber, floating through the dark heart of the maze. Everyone sees it: those looking for their next opponents, those laid out on the floor and trying to get to their feet. It's the overwhelming, primeval power of the nether realm, exerted by the Demon Core.

It's too much for a single young woman to control, but Female Bishop brings it to heel with Overcast. Her fingertips are singed black, and she bites her lip against the pain, so hard it bleeds.

©lack

She isn't doing this for self-gratification. Not to lord it over the others or to show off. She simply knew she would have to push herself to her utmost limits. And the priest across from her, the subject of the unyielding gaze from behind the bandage, is the same. Her beloved friend, someone with whom perhaps she's never had so much as a serious argument until this moment, is coming for her. If she doesn't meet her with all her own strength, then what use is friendship? What use are companions?

Her soul-shattering prayer certainly reaches the heavens, for the sword and scales begin to glow with the menacing light of the gods.

"Show here your pow—"

"Libero!!!"

There's a wail of lightning and a rush of wind.

§

The ear-shattering roar is in fact an agonizing silence. Burning wind scorches your skin, and the light blanks out your vision, your eyes feeling as if they've been gouged out.

You have no idea how long it takes you to get a grasp on the situation. At first, you aren't even sure if you're standing or on the ground, but at last you realize you're pressing your hands against the floor. Your katana—it's there. Still held fast in your right hand. Good, that's good.

The first thing you hear is your cousin coughing, then complaining: "Argh... I can't believe you! Using a spell we still don't fully understand; that's outrageous!"

She may sound mad, but she rushes straight over to Female Bishop. The young woman has been brought to her knees by the overwhelming spell, her breath coming in small gasps. Your cousin takes her hand. It's the very opposite of that other scene (which one was that, again?), and for some reason the thought brings a smile to your face. Female Bishop says something back to your cousin; you know because you can see her lips move slightly, but her voice doesn't reach you.

That's not a problem, though.

You manage to get unsteadily to your feet. Strangely, it's now that your sense of smell comes back to you. The scorched air isn't that bad, but for some reason it threatens to turn your stomach.

You look around to find Myrmidon Monk helping the toppled Half-Elf Scout to his feet. They're both heavily wounded and obviously exhausted, but neither is in danger for his life. Thus assured, you reach out to Female Warrior, who crouches next to you.

"......" She looks vacantly from you to your hand and back, then slowly takes your proffered hand. Her own seems so small and is still trembling faintly. "...Thanks."

Don't even mention it. You grasp her hand firmly, helping her make it to her feet. Female Warrior wobbles unsteadily but finally gets her balance by leaning on her spear. Then her gaze goes to the tip of the weapon—or rather, the space where it used to be—and grins. "Broke, huh?"

Well, it happens.

You're looking critically at your own beloved blade, which has survived the intense battle, then you slide it gently back into its sheath. It isn't the work of any famous master, but it rose to the occasion when its master needed it, and that makes it a good weapon.

From that perspective, even Female Warrior's spear served her to the bitter end—a good weapon, you tell her.

"...Mm, you're right," she murmurs, in a tone of gentle happiness. Her hand runs along the shaft of the spear as if to comfort it. Her lips move, forming words of deep fondness and emotion: "My older sister..." You decide to pretend you didn't hear. Your ears are still ringing, after all.

"Ugh... We...we lost..."

Instead, you turn to the young lady lying spread-eagled on the ground (a most unladylike position): the priest from the other group. Her cheeks are puffed out in a pout, her singed hair splayed wildly about, and her lips pursed in obvious displeasure.

"That whole thing seemed pretty unfair, didn't it?" the priest asks from the ground.

"No...it wasn't," Female Bishop, finally able to stand with your cousin's help, says. She adds a teasing laugh. She bears no visible scars, but her exhaustion must be extreme. She doesn't look like she could walk without assistance. Yet, even so, she summons all her strength to put one foot in front of the other, working her way over to her precious friend. Finally, she smiles and says: "I only did the best I could."

"Are you saying my best wasn't good enough?"

"Oh, I don't think so." There's no trace of disdain in Female Bishop's voice, only conviction—and it's accompanied by another giggle.

"Hrm," the priest grunts as if she doesn't really believe Female Bishop, but then she runs a hand quickly through her own hair. It hardly looks like it could ever have been neat in her life at this point, but she hasn't lost her cheerfulness and sweetness. "No changing it, I guess... We lost." The priest gives a great, deep sigh, then calls dispiritedly to her companions: "You guys dead?"

"...I'm alive," comes a boy's voice, although he sounds awfully put out. It's the young magic knight, who presses a hand to his forehead and groans from where he's lying on his back on the ground. The red sword has fallen from his hand; it must have rolled away somewhere, but you don't see it. The young man seems more worried about the blood that still drips from his wound, frowning and muttering, "...At least, so far."

You say kindly that he won't die. Foreheads just tend to bleed profusely.

"Hrm...I don't know. I gave him a pretty good whack!" Female Warrior says, but the chuckle with which she accompanies the comment suggests she doesn't mean much by it.

After a moment, to let out his frustration and disappointment, when the magic knight's next question comes, he sounds resigned: "What about the others...?"

You wonder—you look around the chamber and especially at the blackened altar. The wizard in the black hat is seated against one wall, his shoulders shaking. He appears to be laughing with untrammeled joy—in any case, he is obviously alive.

You assume the ninjas are dead, but as for the other two party members, they're probably safe. You check the fallen lord and sand-bandit girl to see if they're still breathing, thinking back over the fight. You'd made sure your Magic Missile hit somewhere that *wasn't* a vital point, and as for the slash with your sword, well, you didn't hit very hard.

"...All good, then."

"That's right," the priest says, almost indifferent. "We're alive... That means there'll be another chance."

"Another—another chance," the magic knight murmurs to himself several times before saying, "That's true." He nods. "She's right... We may have lost this time...but next time, we'll win."

Mm. But it remains that you and your party are the ones who will reach the deepest depths of the dungeon first, you tell him.

"Guess so," the boy says, smiling ruefully. "If you ever make my friend cry, I'll never forgive you."

'Who needs your forgiveness? We won the fight, so I can do what I want to her.'

Female Bishop turns bright red at that, and the priest exclaims, "Why, you—!" Your cousin bursts out, "Dummy!" and is off and angry again, while Female Warrior gives you an especially vicious jab with her elbow. You groan aloud, provoking a chuckle and an "Oops" from Half-Elf Scout. Myrmidon Monk looks as if he's trying to ignore the whole thing.

Argh, that was embarrassing. The magic knight looks genuinely relieved seeing how uncomfortable you are; he lets out a bellow of laughter. Huh—so you didn't resent one another after all.

Strange as the situation may have been, the fight is over now, the outcome clear, and so that's the end of it. The boy exhales once he stops laughing, wiping at something that moistens the edges of his eyes as he says softly, "Hey, Teacher. Train with us again. And then next time—"

§

"Too bad! I'm afraid your adventure ends here!"

§

The change is dramatic.

"Wha—?!"

The confused exclamation might come from Female Bishop or perhaps the priest. Or maybe you yourself—you don't know. But the next one clearly belongs to the young magic knight.

"A—agh... Ahh... Agghh?!" His moaning is so hysterical that at first it almost seems ridiculous—until you see first his face, then his torso, then his limbs go limp, then wither away, crumble, and finally turn to ash. When he tries to move, his clothing crumples soundlessly, ash flowing out of the sleeves.

Whispering shadows gather in the depths of the room: "Ahh, a mistake, a miscalculation. I never dreamed your level was so high already..." Darkness billows up as if shrouding itself in the miasma of the dungeon. Before you is darkness itself, incarnate in a humanoid shape.

Then you see it; you're sure of it: In the man's—the black-hatted wizard's—hand is the red blade, glowing brightly. A blade unnatural.

"Teacher! Help me, Teacher! Why...? What did I...? Why...?!"

"Hmm, well, let's see, here. I thought you were a young man with real potential—I never meant to deceive you," the wizard says, adopting the tone of a teacher who's made a mistake in class. He scratches his cheek as if embarrassed, as if the whole thing is a simple misunderstanding.

That's when you notice how strange he is—you couldn't miss it if you wanted to. Even though he was hit full force by Female Bishop's spell, an attack into which she threw everything she had—he isn't so much as scratched.

"But you see, it's a real failing not to know your history. Haven't I been saying so all along?

Never equip a random ring you picked up."

These words are like the key that sets off the chain reaction.

First there's a clattering of armor as the lord's flesh turns to ash where he lies on the ground. The sand-bandit girl is the next to lose her body and soul. She turns into a pile of ash as if to hide the blood, leaving behind only clothing and equipment, and your dagger perched in the middle of it all—the old, famous sword and the knife.

And lastly, two dull-colored rings.

"Teacher...! Tea—" The young magic knight's voice can no longer form words. Now that the transformation to ash has reached his throat, he probably can't even breathe. The young man who stood against you, fought you, and might have become friends with you meets his end as a pile of dust. Strangely, there seems nothing dramatic about the way his life concludes.

"No! How could you...? Ah—Agghh?!" the priest shouts.

Female Bishop, unable to stand it any longer, calls out the priest's name and reaches out to take her hand—and maybe she would have. But the moment their fingers touch, the priest's hand falls away, dissolving into ash.

"Ah—ahhh—ahhhhh...!"

All that remains in Female Bishop's hand is a fistful of ash, the dust of her former friend. There are ash-filled vestments on the ground and a single lolling ring. That, and the blue cord the priest had worn.

As Female Bishop scrambles desperately to gather the dust to herself, the miasma of the dungeon carries it away. Finally, Female Bishop is left on her knees clutching an empty outfit, the cord in her hand.

She has to admit it now. Her friend is finally and utterly lost.

Your cousin stands beside her, her wizardly gaze surveying the detritus coolly. "This ring... It's cursed, isn't it? It's the kind that drains life energy..." She just manages to grab the ring, which now sits in her delicate hand. It's a simple gold band, unremarkable, but just for an instant something written on it shines with a dark, reddish light, then vanishes again. "...Was that your plan all along—to steal the life from these children?!" Her voice shakes as she squeezes out the words. Still, she manages to keep a hold on her emotions, her affect mostly flat.

The man of darkness—the man in the dark clothing—doesn't answer. His only response is a voiceless laugh. He seems to be saying there's nothing left to talk about. Instead, he claps his hands and says: "Ha! Congratulations, brave adventurers!"

Bastard...

"Now, now, don't look at me like that. I would've thought you'd be a little more pleased..." As he speaks, he sways from side to side like one of the ancient nazgul of legend. He seems almost made of darkness itself, but his smile forms a horrifying red slash across his face. His mouth, like a blood moon on a lightless night, opens and closes in a way that doesn't look human. "Have you not proven your strength, just as you wished to do?" He speaks as if this were the most obvious thing in the world. The red sword dangles from his hand. "You've gotten stronger. Is this not the power you wanted?"

Well... You try to speak, but the words won't come. You defeat enemies, you get stronger. That is what you wanted. But that—it wasn't the only thing you wanted.

"Are you him, you son of a bitch…?" Myrmidon Monk asks, never letting his vigilance lapse for a moment. "Are you the Dungeon Master?"

"You think it's him…?!" Half-Elf Scout sounds shocked; he's already bringing his butterfly dagger to bear.

"…Hrrrraaaaaahhhhhh!!" Female Warrior, summoning all the strength left in her body, dives at the man. She tries to make the iron haft of her spear substitute for the broken tip. In your eyes, the move itself is ravishing, a killing strike imbued with all the fury of her heart. Into it she pours everything she has, everything she is, all her pain, all her feeling.

"Wha……?"

The man doesn't dodge the strike.

No—it *looked* like he didn't dodge it.

Instead, he takes a half step. The slightest movement. Enough to evade the blow completely.

At the same time, he jabs the hilt of the sword gently into Female Warrior's solar plexus.

"Ah—hrgh?! *Hack—!*"

It's enough to send her flying like a dead leaf. She skips across the ground with a series of dull thuds until she slams against the far wall of the chamber. It must be a serious shock to her internal organs: She twitches, and blood mixed with spittle dribbles out of her mouth.

"H— Hggh… Agh…gh…"

She's alive. You bite your lip as you hear her broken voice. You want to rush over to her, but instead you confront the man. You're closer to him than any of your party members at this moment. You can't leave this spot. A single stroke will have to settle—no…

That's not enough to bring him down.

You don't believe you'll be able to land the blow. The way the man in the black outfit holds himself is simply too perfect.

He's just standing there, not too much weight on either foot, with the red sword in one hand. That's all. And yet…

No matter where or how I strike, I'll be the one who gets cut down.

©lack

That seems the only possible outcome.

Even so, you grasp the hilt of your katana. You drop your hips deep, then rise.

Your vitality is running low, you see no chance of victory, your companions are behind you, but you simply cannot run away.

A familiar voice sounds in your head: *"You are a master. So is your opponent."* You never thought you would hear that voice again. *"Your opponent carries a master blade, while the weapon in your hand is just a lump of iron."*

Her eyes seem to be watching you, piercing through you: mellowed with drink and yet the eyes of a tiger, never to be mocked.

"So. What do you do?"

"Ha, you've come so far... But there's still so far to go."

Before you can find the answer to the question in your mind, the man speaks, sounding like a child who's grown tired of playing with his toy. He strikes his shoulders with the flat of the red blade as if giving himself a little massage, and then he moves, swaying. Not toward you and the others, but toward the great, thick door in the far wall.

He reaches out, and the door opens without a sound.

Whoosh—a terrible wind, so cold it seems not of this world, fills the dungeon chamber.

"I'll be waiting for you...," the man says, as casually as if he were going for a stroll, though he stands on the brink of an abyss. "Please, come find me anytime you like. But I urge you to hurry. For otherwise...

"...your little world is done for, eh?"

The man in the black outfit sounds practically giddy—then he flings himself into the depths of the darkness and disappears. The doors hang open, and you have no way of knowing where the blackness within them might lead.

No, that's not quite true. One thing is clear: This abyss must lead somewhere, and wherever that is, something is waiting for you.

The Dungeon of the Dead.

A labyrinth of magic and murder calls to you...

AFTERWORD

Hullo, Kumo Kagyu here! I hope you liked the second volume of *Dai Katana*. I gave writing it my all, and I would be thrilled if you enjoyed yourself.

So "you" and your party have gotten through the first two levels, and now the challenge of the dungeon begins in earnest. Fearsome ninjas await, along with the heart of the maelstrom. Even in this most famous dungeon in the world, where there's only rebar-like wire frame to guide you, this is among the most difficult and dangerous places.

So if you've got your adventuring sheet and your pen and dice and you're ready to go, then turn the page.

By the way, if you haven't eaten anything yet by this point, you should go ahead and have something—I can wait.

Heh. I wonder how many people will get that?

Those who read the main *Goblin Slayer* series (thank you!) will know that the world does eventually get saved. So this is a story of an adventure to save the world that you read knowing how it ends. My hope is that it will inspire you to fondly remember adventures of your own.

After all, this is a book where you, dear reader, are the hero.

Just as one lone adventurer could never save the world on their own, this story couldn't exist without a great deal of help. That includes everyone in editorial, sales, and distribution. Also: lack, who does the illustrations for these novels, and Aoki, who's handling the manga version. The admins of the aggregator blogs who aggregate the web version. Everyone who's been cheering me on since those early days. All my friends who game with me. And above all, you, for picking up this book.

Dai Katana is here thanks to every one of you. Thank you all so much.

Now, in the next volume, "you" will have to challenge the lowest levels of this deepest of all dungeons. But there's no need to fear. You've made it this far, after all.

And the heroes of the demon palace who have defeated people possessed by demons shall destroy the demonic plane, right?

Having said that, it might take me a while to get that last volume out. But I'll be putting my heart and soul into it, so I hope you'll read it when it arrives.

See you next time!